# A Long Lonely Road

## Volume Three

## Books Seven through Nine

## By TJ Reeder

## All Rights Reserved by Author July 2013

## __Acknowledgments and Thanks__

To the following people who have helped me
clean up and improve my writing and
otherwise made the books more enjoyable-

Editing- Vanessa McCutcheon

Cover designs and formatting - Sheri Dixon

# High Lonesome
## John and the Girls

Book Seven in the Long Lonely Road
series

By

# TJ Reeder

April 08, 2013

Ever been trying to sleep and some troublesome bug just won't leave you be? And it's too big to ignore and too small to shoot? Well my nap is again being spoiled by the insistent sound that goes kinda like, THWOK - THWOK- THWOK, followed by "I beat you!" "Did not!!" "Yes I did!!" "No you didn't!" "BULLSHIT!!" "Stop cussing! It sound like shit!"

Got the picture? It's like this every damn day when we ain't moving. I will never forgive myself for following the smell of wood smoke and the sound of an axe splitting wood.

I swear these two can always find something to spend time trying to outdo each other at and it usually involves something that will ruin my nap. Now here they come wanting me to declare a winner, right, like deciding which rattler to pet. I'm the loser regardless.
"John".. "No".. "John!" "NO!" "If you don't you will be sorry." "If I do I will be sorry longer then if I don't." "Don't bet on it buddy!" Now both are pulling my arms. So like the manly man I am I rise to face my end. It's like being allowed to pick out the rifles the firing squad will use to shoot you.

We walk, arm and arm (only because I'll try to escape) to the target they were shooting at, in the middle was four cedar arrow shafts, two with white and black fletching and two with Black and White fletching. Don't ask, I didn't have a thing to do with it but they know whose is whose. I don't, they look the same to me.

I call it a draw, didn't work. So I resort to whining, not working. So I squatted down which I can do now days thanks to Charley and his happy weed as I call it.

I look closer and I just can't see any difference, none, nada. I finally said "Do as you will with me but I call a draw now stop playing and feed me." I walk away while they squint at the shafts and finally decide they are tied so what do I know and why did they want my opinion, by the time I got back to my nap pad I was at fault for everything. "Shit." "Stop cussing!"

It's like living in a pillow case with a pair of cute darling rabid squirrels. No matter what I'm so screwed, which thought brings the comment that "Don't count on it buster." I don't know what Charlie's Mother teaches them but…I hear "Don't go there" "Shit." "Stop cussing."

I lay down and pretend to sleep. And get dog piled which includes Walker who loves this game, he don't care where he steps. Life in the nut house. But I love it and them and Walker if he will stop standing on my jewels. They got that message loud and clear and dragged the big bastard off me.

They put away their bows and quivers and set about fixing dinner which was always a riot. After dinner we cleaned up camp and after the meal settled we piled into the hot pool we had located in this new area. I keep thinking why leave here but the nights are getting a chill to them and we all know what's coming.

I guess the bows need explaining so I'll back track a month or two. We spent two weeks at the last camp before we decided to move on. We looked at the maps and decided to head due east because we hadn't been there. We spent several days just loafing along not in a hurry and when possible we rode side by side and talked about everything under the sun.

There is something magical about riding a good mount up high, the clink of a shoe on stone, the squeak of the saddle leather, the roller on the bits that the riding stock had in their mouths, never was real sure what it was for but they love rolling it so maybe that's what it's for, keeps 'em from getting bored.

Anyway we were just poking along when we all heard a sound from a ways off. It was the sound of an axe splitting wood, so figuring this far up and back in there wouldn't be a gang for sure. Maybe! We headed that way.

We rode till we smelled smoke and then a bit further until we were really close to the sound, then The Horse with no name let out a "HEY!! Here we are" sound and the axe stopped so with nothing else for it I told the girls to lay back and I'd ease on in, which got me a "Fat chance bud." They mind real well.

We soon rode out on a well-used trail and headed on toward where the sound came from. After a bit we saw a log cabin ahead of us in a clearing with a log barn and a corral with a horse and two mules who right away started talking to our bunch. Then we heard a voice from the side that said "Well a man with two women and a pack train of good looking mules can't be too bad!" And out of the trees stepped a Mountain Man, Not a man who lives in the mountains, I mean a real Mountain Man, like 1825 fur trapping, Blackfoot fighting by god Mountain Man holding a rifle that looked like it came out here with Jed Smith or John Johnston. He also looked old enough to have bought the rifle new before heading to Beaver country.

I looked at him for a moment and said "Well if you ain't gonna shoot one of us I guess we should introduce ourselves. Before I could he said "John Long Walker and his wives Sandy and May also known as Wyatt and Doc."

Well I could only laugh and say "Guilty." He walked over and offered his hand and said "I'm Longbow Daniels but my friends just call me Seth."

He said "Follow me on in" and walked away with a loose gait that belied his years. We followed him right to his corral where he said "Ok boys come on out" and two young lads about fifteen stepped out of the barn and they weren't holding Hawkins rifles, they had lever guns that had pretty big holes in the ends. They both had long black hair and high cheek bones and were a darker tan then their dad.

We stepped down and he said "Follow me, the boys will water your stock and slip the bits so they can eat a bite." In the cabin we met his wife who looked to be from one of the local tribes and was very pretty, we introduced ourselves to her, her name was Clare and she spoke like a school teacher which we found out she was before moving to the mountains with Seth. She poured coffee and offered some lunch which got the girls chattering and off they went with her.

I said "Ok Seth how did you know who we are?" He laughed and said "Well hell everybody in these mountains has heard about you and them two hellions but also we ride down to where our old truck is hidden and drive into places where we can get some supplies, such as they are. But some stuff is starting to move coming in from the west coast."

Now that surprised the hell outta me! And I said so, he just nodded and said "Well it ain't been going on too long and it's a bit spotty but it's coming. Coffee, sugar and such, seems somebody got a small ship working and they load up whatever they can buy or trade for then sell it or trade it to folks along the coast who bring it in to the area. They are partial to gold and silver but will take furs."

I was really blown away at this news but happy to hear it. We stopped talking to have big bowls of Elk stew made with home grown veggies. It was awesome.

Clare and the girls were getting along like old friends and the boys just listened and smiled at their mom, who was very happy to have female company.

The cabin and barn were USFS built to house trail crews and rangers who rode the back country before the event that is. Seth said he knew about it because he worked out of here building trails and when the SHTF he simply loaded up his family in their old truck and headed for the high lonesome and didn't move for a year. But after scouting things out they took a trip out to a small local town where they were known and welcome. After that they went in when they had too, but not often. That was where they heard the stories about us and while some sounded a bit tall he was willing to believe it.

May asked him about his handle of "Longbow" so he sent one of the boys to fetch something and he brought back a buckskin covered bundle out of which Seth pulled a beautiful long bow which he strung and handed to May who stood and tried to draw it. She got about two inches and gave up and Seth said she done good for a smallish person. He placed a shaft onto the shelf and nocked and drew it fully back to the broad head which made his wife shake a spoon at him and declare if he shot one more arrow in the house she was gonna hammer his head with a skillet.

He eased the bow down and winked at

me and nodded at a shaft buried into a log near the ceiling, he said "I slip one time and she never gets over it." She smacked him with the spoon while the boys smiled at their folks.

May said "Where did you get that?" He smiled and said "Well darlin I made it." May lit up like a light bulb and said "Do you make them for other people?" He said "Well yeah, but most folks want them rattle contraptions that pass for a bow these days." May said "I don't, I want one like this! Will you make me one?" By now the other one was there trying to pull the bow and gave up saying "I want one!" May said "I asked first!" I said "Ladies!" That got a glare.

Seth laughed real big and said "Y'all step in here" and headed for the door the lad had got the bow from. Inside was a very nice workshop and the walls were full of bows in all stages of finish. He looked at May and Sandy then reached up to the top of a rack and got down two bows and wiped the dust off them. He found strings and strung both with ease then found leather arm and finger guards and a dozen shafts and said "Let's go!"

Out the back door of the shop was his archery range with targets at ranges from 10 yards to 45 yards. They were full size 3D targets. After helping them get the leather protection on he guided them while they knocked their first shaft and with May going first shooting at the 10 yard deer target she let fly and made a chest shot! Seth looked at her and said "You been here before huh." She smiled and said "Yep, I shot in college on the school team but it was with compound bows and I never liked them."

She stepped aside and Sandy followed Seth's directions and let fly missing the deer, well I saw her jaw bulge and she grabbed another arrow and missed, finally Seth said "Ok little lady you ready to listen?" She nodded so he walked her thru the whole process of smooth draw, look down the shaft and let go. He explained that stick bow shooting was referred to as Primitive because there was no sights or other whizbang gadgets on the bow. It is a learned thing, instinctive shooting that only comes from a lot of practice. And also that as a rule if a person could shoot a more powerful compound bow then they could shoot a stick bow, generally speaking. He also said that every archer had their own limit which they would learn thru practice. He said his limit was 45 yards, beyond that and he relayed on stalking skills that also had to be learned.

He pointed out that the bows they were shooting now were lighter pull weight then they could handle in say a couple of weeks and that the lighter the bow the less killing power it had which would result in wounded game getting away and that was something a real bow hunter would avoid like death.

We left them working at it which they didn't stop until their fingers were so sore they couldn't pull the string back anymore. Seth said that would change over time too.

We settled back and worked out a deal with him for two bows and a huge batch of shafts and a lot of practice points and a few dozen broad heads. He told them to take the two bows and arrows and work at it and to come back in two weeks, he told us where the nearest hot springs were and with thanks we headed for them.

So now for 13 days I've lived with the "THWOK" sound, I hear it in my sleep, that or the arguing over who is getting best fastest. The next day is the 14th day so we left camp and with the pack string headed to Seths place which was only a mile or so. When we got there his wife came out and grabbed the girls right away and off they went to the kitchen to do whatever they do in there, but it smelled good! I went into the work shop just as Seth was wiping down the two new bows and they were beautiful! On the top of each were tied small feathers which I knew was a form of wind gauge.

The bows were the same size and weight and only different due to the wood used. He strung them and laid them on his work bench and we joined the girls for lunch. The boys had hiked down the trail to visit a ranch family a few miles away who had daughters, ahh love thy name is "Youth." I got a look for that one.

After lunch we all trooped into the shop and he pointed to the bows which they both ohhed and ahhed over then slowly each picked up one and held it then pulled it back with some effort. Then they switched bows and did it again, and smiled, they had the one that wanted them, or as they most likely believed, the one the bow wanted to be with. Horse pucky I say and got glared at.

Out the door and after they had their leathers on each nocked a shaft and let fly at the 30 yard target and both hit right where it should be hit! Well I had been watching them like 23 hours a day for two weeks so I wasn't surprised but Seth was, big time. He said he never seen anybody improve like Sandy had since May had a big head start more or less.

When they bent over to pull their shafts May's bear claw necklace fell out of her shirt causing Seth to say "WOW!!" May went over so he could get a better look so Sandy took hers out and that led to having to tell the story right there. Seth said he was filled with envy because he had never had a chance with a big mountain Grizzly. I told him he could have my next encounter.

He explained that the bows were a heavier draw then the practice bows they had worked with and either would put a shaft thru an Elk if it didn't hit a big bone. He was really into their dedication and dragged out a trunk from under the work bench and opened it and took out several quivers, handmade from stiff Elk hide and covered with beautiful bead work. It was obvious Clare had done the bead work from the look of pride on her face.

Seth told them to pick the one they wanted which took a while but in the end they each had the one they wanted. He then placed a dozen shafts in them one set with two black feathers and the nock feather was white, the other set was two white and one black. Now I got it.

Well they were bouncing and both hugged Seth then me then Clare who was laughing at their antics like they were kids and if anything they were the same age as she was. But they were just like puppies. I had to admit Sandy was more so now that May was with us, both turned and smiled at me. I'm lost, and I'll give them whatever they want. When it was all settled they had their bows and quivers and a hundred cedar shafts each. Seth showed them how to mount the target heads as well as the broad heads.

I paid Seth in junk silver coins which the folks he was dealing with took willingly. Gold was too hard to break down value wise. We took leave of Seth and his wife and headed back out on the road to wherever.

It's been about two or three weeks since we left Seth's place and they are still spending time each day training with the bows and it finally dawned on me this was taking the place of training with their pistols because they could shoot the bows and not tell the world we were around. I'm slow at times, like between day break and dark.

Now I made sure we stopped early enough for them to get in an hour or so of practice or maybe play depending on how you looked at it. I will admit they have gotten damn good with these things and I'm waiting for them to decide to get a deer with their "new" weapons.

I knew we were going to need to be dropping lower then we were simply because of the coming cold and snow, not this month but the nights are getting cold. I had been studying the maps and located a hot spring, if I was right, so we drifted that way for a couple of days and sure enough found it after a search and it wasn't developed so we spent a day digging and hauling rocks and mud mixed with grass and finally had a pool big enough to hold us in comfort. And all that digging and rock hauling made me really need it. I was sore.

The third day we were there the girls wanted to go hunting with their new toy's so I said "Cool, wake me when you return so we can dig out some dinner." They jeered at me as a non-believer and off they went. Being in camp alone with the wind in the trees I just laid down for a nap and woke up to Walker growling like he really meant it. I laid there listening and finally heard a squeak of leather and rolled to my feet cussing the fact my rifle was thirty feet away and I was looking at three men who looked like they thought I was a sheep and they was wolves. I was pissed, first at getting caught sleeping like a fool, pissed at Walker for not picking them up sooner and even more pissed that I left my rifle out of reach. They just sat looking at me so I said "Well what can I do for y'all?"

The youngest one laughed a nasty laugh and said "Well I'd say the real question is what are we gonna do to you?" Well I had an idea I could take two of them but one had a rifle laying across his thighs pointing right at me. I'm pretty good but not that good.

I repeated myself and asked what they wanted and the smart mouthed one said "Well mostly everything you have plus where are them women we saw with you four days ago?" I smiled and said "Well I'd say they are looking right at you this minute." I had decided that I was gonna go for it and the rifle guy was first.

I guess something in my eyes gave me away because before I could move he said "Screw this talking shit" and raised the rifle and grew a feathered shaft in his chest, right thru the heart. The mouthy kid was clawing for a pistol when he got a shaft too. The third one spun his horse and was heading out fast when he got hit by two arrows but kept riding. I never heard a "THWOK," must be the difference in the target.

The girls came out of the brush and checked the two and pulled out their shafts from behind as both had gone thru. I was still standing there looking stupid and feeling old. Sandy came to me and said "John they had you cold and you were gonna take it to them, and you would have done a damn good job of it, we just happened to be close to camp and heard them talking so stop feeling down on yourself." May came over and hugged me and said "Yeah what she said." Then she said "Ain't it just the way it goes, we go to get meat with our new toys and the first thing we kill is skunks!" I swear these two are like the black plague. But they are right. And thank god for it because my ass was cooked.

While they used a mule to drag the two well away from camp I saddled Buck and headed after the third one who just had to be laying down the trail a ways, but all I found was some blood and an arrow. I took it back with me and let them figure out whose it was. Now we had a dilemma, stay or go? The girls voted to go and inside of an hour we were riding out of there. They had removed the weapons from the two dead men but other then that left them lay.

We rode all day and stopped to fix dinner then headed out and made more time. By dark we had found a place to double back and set up a camp away from the trail in a gully with a bit of water trickling down it. I headed out and closed in on our trail but it was full dark so I headed back. We spent a fireless night and were awake and loaded before there was even a gray place to the east. I headed back towards the trail and watched it for a good while before returning to camp where we studied the map.

I wasn't sure why we were running but it seemed like the smart thing to do. We made a lot of miles that day and the next three before we stopped to rest after doubling back and doing every trick I ever read in the westerns I used to read. But a pack string like ours leaves a big trail and if we were being followed we would be found.

The last day we crossed a shallow but wide creek and rode down it a ways then headed back up then we left the creek in several places only to return to it in a different place. Then following the advice of every old Marine I served with "Head for the high ground."

We lucked out by hitting a small trail and heading up it we came to a large clearing where the trail crossed right thru the middle and thru a gap in a rock wall. Behind the wall the trail dropped down into a deep canyon with heavy timber. We stopped right there on the canyon side of the gap and set up our camp.

The girls headed down the trail while I watched the back trail and asked myself why we were running; we had seen nobody, not even a ribbon of smoke anyplace. But I just knew we were being trailed so right here we would wait and let them bring it. If they were even out there.

One thing for sure anybody coming at us across that big meadow was in a big hurt.

And we had the best fighting positions a body could ask for. And we needed to rest the stock and ourselves. So here we stand.

The girls returned and said the trail was a good one and went thru places that we could roll rocks down and block it for a good while. I explained the plan and they got to fixing dinner over as smokeless a fire as possible. I wasn't worried about dealing with whoever came at us because we had things with us that would make a huge difference in any fight. I was most worried about being headed off by people who knew this area whereas we don't but we have topographic maps so we can pick our way thru rough country where they will be forced to follow.

We stayed in this camp for three days and got plenty of rest, we rotated the night watch but with Walker there the watcher could cat nap. Walker had picked up our moods and stress and was hyper vigilant. I think he feels guilty that they rode right in on us. I sure as hell do.

On the third night Walker let out a low rumble that even I heard from the bedroll and I was up in a flash along with May who had just come to bed. We joined Sandy who was watching the clearing with the night vision gear we had picked up in the air base which was much better then the one I had way back when.

She whispered that three riders were sitting on horses in the clearing but didn't seem to know about the gap in the rock wall. One thing I had done was fill it with brush that I cut and replaced daily making it look like a big bush growing out of the rock wall. Now at night they couldn't see even the bush. I looked thru the glass as did May who said they were heading back out of the clearing. Right then I took the night glass and eased out thru the gap and around the edge of the clearing and followed them, I could hear them ahead of me and knew they were heading back to a small brook about a half mile away, and sure enough there was their camp with about a dozen men sitting around a small fire.

One of the three walked to a man sitting alone and said something to him, most likely that our trail went into the meadow.

I couldn't get closer and really didn't need to so I headed back and told the girls to saddle up awhile I packed the mules, in an hour with their help we were loaded up, they took the mules down the trail to a clearing with water and using a picket line tied them. May stayed there while Sandy came back to join me.

My idea was to face them right here to

hear what they had to say and hopefully stop this crazy shit but I knew it wasn't gonna work. One person could hold here for a long time but would eventually get flanked. I told Sandy what was going to happen and what I wanted her to do and she nodded with no arguments. I love these women, they are better at this Marine shit then some of the clowns I served with.

At last daylight came and with it a pair of scouts looking to follow the trail which would be all over the entire meadow since we had allowed the stock to graze there. Then after a bit a few more men rode out into the clearing followed shortly by a man on a beautiful horse who I figured just had to be the boss man. When they were all in the clearing there was a dozen of them. The scouts were riding all over the meadow and slowly working toward the brush filled gap. And finally one of them looked closer and then pulled a limb and the gap was exposed. The man who pulled the bush out got a real sick look on his face so I said quietly "Just sit real still and you might see tomorrows sun up." And he froze. I asked why we were being chased and he said we had murdered his boss's son and another man and wounded a third. Talking to him wasn't going to cut it so I told him to call his boss over to where he was.

He yelled out and asked the man to come see this and of course he brought the entire bunch. When he was as close as I wanted him to get I said "That's far enough." He jerked his head up and all his men reached for weapons. I let the bolt slam shut on the AR10 and said "Let's talk, we can fight later."

The boss man looked up at the rocks and said "Mister there is nothing to talk about, you murdered my son and you're gonna hang." I could only shake my head and say "Well your son and his two friends rode into my camp, and made it plain that not only were they gonna kill me but were planning to take all my gear plus the two ladies traveling with me. So murder, armed robbery and kidnapping plus I would assume rape is ok with you as long as it's your kid doing it?" He was glaring up at the rocks trying to locate me and said "You murdered my son!! Why makes no difference, he's dead and your gonna die too."

I could see no sense in talking further so I said "Fine, get on out of here before one of these fools following you decides to play hero for the boss." The man next to him who had to be his forman said "Boss, we are in a bad spot, we can't go forward and we are fish in a bowl."

The old man glared at him and said
"Brad if you're gonna punk out on me then
get on out of here, your fired." The man
named Brad just looked sadly at the old man
and then up at where I was and shook his
head and said "You're making a mistake boss
this ain't some pilgrim we been chasing and
we know there are at least three of them
looking at us over gun barrels right now."

The old man looked at him and said
"Brad I fired you and you're still here talking
like a coward now go before I shoot you
myself." Brad turned his horse and rode away
across and out of the meadow. I saw a couple
of others look at each other and turn and ride
away too. Well we were down to nine and
hadn't fired a shot. Talking does work but it
wasn't over yet, and wasn't gonna be it
looked like, so I tried talking some more. I
told him the entire story of what happened
and why it had ended the way it had, He
actually looked up at the area where I was and
said "Mister, I don't care if my son raped
your women, killed your dog, stole everything
you have in this world, he was still worth
more then you ever will be and you will pay. I
gave up, and said "So the murdering little
loudmouthed bastard could do as he wished
and his stupid self-centered old man would let
him do it simply because of who you are?"

Well he almost blew a vein. While he

was trying to get the breath to yell I told his men that they could all die right here or head out and leave the crazy old son of a bitch to die like the fool he was.

He at last freed up his pistol and started firing at the rocks but had no chance to hit us. I figured about one more shot and Sandy would lose her hold on her temper and simply shoot the fool.

His men turned and rode away as quick as they could, leaving him alone fumbling to get a new magazine in his gun, but he dropped the gun and then threw the magazine at the rocks. I felt almost sorry for him but not much. He sat there for a bit then turned away and said as he went, "It ain't over, I know who you are and I'll send people to hunt you down and kill you, I'll put a bounty on your head so big every gun thug in the country will come for you."

I was tempted to just shoot him and put him out of his misery. I had a feeling I'd regret not doing it. We mounted up and headed out but Sandy said "Wait" and bailed off her horse and went thru the gap and was back in a second smiling. We met up with May and lit a shuck out of there.

Later that evening I remembered to ask Sandy why she went back thru the gap before we rode away, she smiled real big and from her saddle bag pulled a cloth wrapped object. I knew without looking it was a gun, it was the pistol dropped by the old man. I knew without looking it had to be another 1911 and it was. And not just any 1911, this one was a big hand cannon made by STI. It was called "The Perfect 10", a 10 mm, long slide 6" barrel, holding 14 rounds of hard shooting ass kickers. It was done up with hard chrome and every bell and whistle one can hang on the frame, new retail had to have been close to $3000.00 and the old bastard had just ridden off and left it. She even found the magazine for it which was of course empty. I asked her what she was going to do with it because it was big, hell even in my hand it was a hand full. She just smiled that "I got bling smile" she gets when she scores a new toy. Her answer was of course that she didn't have one so therefore, needed one! She also had a evil little smile when she said "Yanno, this thing would fit Bear Jackson's huge cookie crushers!" And there in lay the truth. Bear had something she wanted and this was the prize to pry it out of his paws. Poor bear. She did say she needed a box of ammo so she could shoot it and of course May chimed in with WE need to shoot it. I know one thing for sure, neither will like it. If they kept it the damn thing would end up on the cabin wall alongside Old man Jones 45-70.

Two weeks later with more miles and switch back behind us then we could count we headed to a small town listed on the map as Rocky Point with a pre event population of 450 people. We rode into the town shortly after mid-morning and headed for the general store that every town seemed to have cropping up lately. Inside we found an older couple who smiled and asked what they could do for us. Sandy and May had a list they had worked up and they got what there was of it. After paying with junk silver we headed for the local café.

Inside we found a clean place with good smells and settled in to eat; the waitress told us what was on the menu for the day which was stew and fresh hot bread and butter. We ordered and ate then ordered again then had pie with it. We were just finishing up when three men walked in with badges on who came right to our table and asked if the mules were ours. I said "Yep they are, why?" He said there was a flier going around describing us and our livestock as wanted for murder and a reward for 'Dead.'"

Well I knew I should have shot that old bastard but hind sight is always 20-20 vision. I asked them if they were there to collect on the reward and the speaker laughed and said "Hell no, we knew the little bastard y'all rid the country of and nobody will miss the twerp, but his old man has a lot of gold and some folks just ain't picky about minor details like right and wrong." I thanked him and said we were heading out right away, I paid the girl and tipped her and leave we did.

We headed back up into the higher country and made camp to talk about it. May was all for tracking the old asshole down and just shooting him. I said "Hold that thought." We were faced with being forced to avoid places we would like to rest up in and being on the run wasn't my idea of how our vacation should go. We had some coffee and batted ideas around until Sandy said "Fuck it, let's just head right to that old bastards roost and say here it is come get it!" Between her and Doc I swear they would charge hell for the fun of rubbing it in Lucifer's face.

We camped out in a nice little nook in a valley with a great stream running thru it and feasted on Brookies till I had to make them stop fishing. They don't do anything half way. But the longer we sat there the madder I was getting so finally I said "What do y'all want to do about this bounty stuff?" They were packing up the camp before I got done asking. We headed out and made a bee line for the town nearest to where we thought this asshole had his place.

After a week of moving right along I

figured it was a town named Pineville so that's where we headed. When we got near the place I had to force the issue about them laying back while I went in on my own. It was a nice clean little town, it had some lookouts posted and other then waving me in they never said a word. I headed right for the local office of the town government such as it was; the sign said "Saloon, town hall, Church and any other thing we need it for." I liked it! So tying Buck up I walked in and saw it was a clean quiet place with a few bottles of bar whisky as it was called. The bartender was friendly but could only smile when I ask for JW, so I went out and got a bottle from the saddle bags and took it in and poured both of us a drink, he did have some cold beer so that made a good chaser.

His name was Tome Lane and he had been here all his life. After another drink I asked him what the story was on the bounty I was hearing about. He made a face and said it was some outsider who had built a big stone house more like a fort up in the hills to the east and had moved in just before the EMP. He seemed to have prepared very well since it seemed like he had everything a person could want.

I said "Well hell maybe he knew something ahead of time." That got his attention and a thoughtful look. He said the man's son had got his ass killed trying to rob the wrong people and the old man was bound and determined to get revenge.

I asked who it was he was after but he didn't know except there was an Indian involved because the two dead ones were killed with arrows and the one who got away had one thru his back that just missed a lung. I did ask where he got the information and was told the old man's foreman had refused to get involved in murder so the old man fired him and he passed the word on his way out of the area.

I said it sounded like nobody had much sympathy for the man and he said nope but the kind of folks who would kill folks for a bounty don't care about right or wrong. I heard the sound of several horses walking in the street and heard them stop, and sure as God made little green apples here come the troublesome twins.

Well the bartender took a double take and busted out laughing and said "Well you got me!" He offered the girls whatever they wanted but they said water was fine. I capped the bottle and gave it to him and took another cold beer then headed for a table in the corner close to a window where I told them the news. They said "Well let's just wait right here in town and see what happens."

The bartender said the motel had rooms as did the old town hotel which also served meals so that's where we headed. The stock went into the hotel corral and barn where an old colored man ran things; he looked the stock over and said "Fine animals, very fine!" And he promised to take good care of them, I handed him a 20 dollar gold cartwheel and said "Let me know when this runs out." He said "You know half the trash in the country is looking for y'all, right?" I said "Yeah, but thanks." He promised he would let us know if anybody came around.

Walker listened to Sandy telling him to stay and guard the stock and told him the old black man was ok, His name was Charles and Walker seemed to agree he was ok.

We got two rooms right across the hall from each other, one looking at the barn and corral and the other out at Main Street and the saloon. I figured when it came it would be from two fronts and we held the high ground and both sides.

We hauled the packs with the hardware upstairs and set out our main weapons as well as body armor. We had just about anybody out gunned but shit happens. All we could do was wait and watch and hope none of the locals got hurt when it happened.

Well after a few days I was starting to wonder if we was wasting our time when old Charles came up and said a couple of strangers was snooping around the barn and Walker warned them off, but they looked like they would shoot a dog as fast as anything else.

I decided right then that I was moving down to the barn at night and see what I could catch. Well of course that didn't work because they were going where I went so back to the barn with our gear we went. Well we could clean up in the rooms and even nap so we kept them.

That night went well as did the next; we spent time visiting folks in town and spending money and in general being nice folks. Everybody knew who we were and what was going on and seemed to see it as entertainment like a soap opera.

I guess I could understand that. But I hope they stayed low when it started. The only "lawman" in town was a night watchman who wandered around with a shotgun, we asked him to avoid the hotel area at night and he laughed and said "My mama didn't raise a fool."

The third day after we moved to the

stable we were having breakfast in the hotel restaurant when a pickup rolled into town with a bunch of men in it who were obviously strangers since they were looking around like they hadn't been here before. I counted seven, fair odds, all were armed with a typical collection of weapons. After looking around they headed for the hotel and as planned the girls split up and one went behind the counter and one went into the woman's rest room.

I hadn't wanted to have the ball open here but there it was, several of them split off heading in opposite directions while three headed into the hotel. One walked to the counter and started demanding information on who was staying here, Sandy was behind the desk and said "I'm sorry but that kind of information is not passed out."

The man grabbed for the directory but was too slow as Sandy removed it from the counter. The fool tried to slap her of all things. But she was faster then him and made him miss. The two by the door were dividing their attention between me and the fool at the counter. When he started around the counter I said "Don't" that stopped him, he glared at me and asked me to say it again so I did. Jeeze this was sounding like a grade D Saturday afternoon movie of my youth, shit I could have written the dialogue. He headed right for me and asked why I was butting into his business so I told him the lady was my wife and that was it.

While he tried to understand that May walked out of the bathroom and headed for the table, he said "Who's this?" I said "My wife." His eyes got big and he said "Shit!" as he tried to make it but he wasn't in the same league with us. My 45 was in my left hand so I left him for May and took his buddies at the door who had woke up and were reaching too.

May got hers with her little 380 that he never saw, Sandy got one with her 1911 and I think I may have hit one left handed by the door but Sandy just hosed both of them. I couldn't hear again, I swear this shit is gonna deafen me. "Don't cuss."

Sandy went back behind the counter while May and I headed for better cover, I headed for the back door and May got behind the bar off the lobby.

It didn't take long for the other four to head for the hotel, two by the front and two by the back. I had a shotgun sitting by the door so I was set when they charged around the corner and ran right into it. They never got off a shot, I felt bad for maybe half a nano second. They came to murder us for money and died with empty pockets, tough shit.

I had heard the boom of May's shotgun and the bark of Sandy's 45 and when I got there it was over, seven people dead and gone in three minutes.

This was crazy and it was just starting. We piled their weapons in back of the lobby desk and found the truck keys on the one May got first. I went to the truck and pulled it up to the front door and between us we started dragging them out. Then Charles showed up and several of the other towns folks who helped pile them in the truck. I said "Whoever hauls them out and dumps them in a gully way out of town can have the truck. Charles grabbed the keys and jumped in the truck laughing and was gone! Guess he wanted wheels.

I went in to see the lady who owns the hotel and to offer payment for any damage; she was behind the counter and waved off any offer of pay but asked if she could pick out a gun or two. I gave her all of them. She said I was good for business! It's good to be considered an asset.

Charles was back in an hour and tried to hand me a small bag of coins, silver and gold, he had taken off the bodies. I said "Keep it." He said I was good for business, I laughed.

Later that night the doubts hit again, I

was so tired of this shit, yet we seemed to attract trouble like a magnet attracts filings. We were three normal nice people who made friends wherever we went yet we seemed to be killing some asshole or other daily and we weren't hunting trouble.

Knowing me as they do the girls knew where my head was and waited for me to think it out. I finally said, "You know, when we are in the canyon at the lake we don't have trouble but as soon as we try to just travel around we seem to piss off people." The girls had learned to let me get it out before beating me up.

Surprising me they both agreed but neither had any thoughts on how to change things. Trouble always came at us; we never went looking for it. Well sure, we did when we went after the cannibals and maybe another time or two, but that was different then this shit. I was really regretting not finishing this mess when we had the chance. One bitter old man with a spoiled out of control kid was now responsible for how much death before it was over.

The solution might be to just go after him but if nobody knew he was dead the bounty hunters would keep coming. No, we needed to get him into town where it could be ended in public so word would get out. And

there the plan was born. We had just had a
fight and really who knew we won outside the
townies? I went to see Charles for advice and
information on this old man. Charles said
nobody in the town really knew who he was
or where he came from just that his kid had
been a worthless waste of sperm that should
have been buried long ago, like 5 seconds
after he was born. I asked Charles how one
could get word to the old man that we were
dead and the killers wanted the bounty.

He said he would think about it and get
back to me. I rejoined the girls who were
ready to spend the night in our room in the
hotel so we did. I told them what Charles said
and it seemed funny nobody knew the old
guys name.

The next morning Charles joined us for
breakfast and said he would get a message to
the old man's compound and we would see
what happened. He said if the old man
brought all his men it might get nasty but the
townspeople were behind us and we could
expect some help, maybe not a lot but some.
Charles of course said he would be there. I
really liked this old man, he was a good
troop!

Charles sent word that we were dead but
we took all but two of the bounty hunters with
us and they were wounded so he needed to

bring them their loot. Whoever went out there returned and said the old man was coming and wanted to see our dead bodies before he paid a dime.

The next day we were ready, all armored up, girls loaded for bear with their sub guns. I stuck with my AR10 with a shotgun over my back and with my 45's I felt like I weighed 400 pounds. One of the girls giggled and with a stage whisper said "Felt that way last night too" both laughed loudly. I hate 'em! "Do not" came the usual answer.

Just before noon Charles' lookout sent word they were coming, several truck loads. We had decided to stop them in the middle of town and no talking, just hose them. But at the last minute I decided that maybe just taking the boss off the board might stop the game, no pay no work.

I waited till they were right in front of the hotel and I stepped out from behind a pickup, I had left the AR10 behind the truck.

When they stopped I realized they had no idea who I was, they hadn't seen me so the old man got out surrounded with his people. He asked who I was and I said "Well, let me ask your men a question. How many of you liked the old man's kid enough to die right here, right now for him? How many of you really give a shit about this old bastard? You all stay for the pay or the shelter? Is the food that good? From what the townspeople say the punk was a just waste of sperm." Well I had him so confused he was still trying to understand me. I looked each of his men in the eye and said, "I'm the one who killed the kid, and if y'all wanna die for him then let's dance, but if not get in the trucks and head out of here."

I saw them all looking around and knew they were looking at rifle barrels pointed at them, of course most had nobody behind them but they didn't know that. The old man got it at last and started shaking so hard I thought he was gonna fall down, then he started screaming "Kill Him!!!" But nobody moved and then a few headed for the trucks then a few more until he was alone in the street. I saw May walking out of the Hotel with the 300 blackout in her hand; she walked right up to him and looked closer and said "Doctor Raddly? No wonder we never knew what happened to you! You slimy bastard, you helped do all this shit to the world then slipped out to your prepared place to wait it out? My brother died because of you and your friend's plans."

Well I was stunned, Sandy had joined us and looked at me, we both shrugged. He was looking at May and suddenly recognized her and screamed out that she was a traitor and had ruined everything! As he reached inside his coat May raised the 300 and just hosed him, when it went click she looked at him and then spit on him then walked into the hotel with Sandy close behind her.

I needed a drink. I headed for the saloon. Charles joined me as did several others, one handed me my AR10 I had forgotten. What a turn of events. Everybody wanted to know what that was all about so I told them what I knew and what I thought but left it at that. After a while the girls joined us, May had been crying, for her brother no doubt. She even took a drink from my glass and forced it down; mostly the girls weren't drinkers except in private with just the three of us and then usually wine. But the whiskey brought color back to her face.

She looked at me and said "Raddly was in bed with the people behind the events that led up to the weapons being used, but he disappeared two days before they went off. Now I know why, the bastard."

It was over, but surely not in the way I thought it would end. Charles said the word was going out over short wave right now that it was done and the reward was rescinded due to the timely death of the man offering the reward.

Now that this latest mess was settled I was really thinking about going back to the canyon or Texas and retiring. I knew the day I found the EMP had hit and then found the poor man in the ditch only hours after it that shit was gonna roll out of control but I had no idea it would be like this. Had we always been a people willing to do anything but held back by the thin screen called law? Was the world full of Murderers, Rapist, Slavers, Scum of all kinds that we lived with but never saw? One would think by now that they would be pretty well thinned out. Yet it seemed like every other day we were in the middle of a gun fight or heading to one or and I thank our lucky stars "finishing" one.

I can't understand it, the most famous of the old time gun fighters never got involved in crap like this, oh sure some Marshall in a cow town may have had a run in or two, but look at the most famous shoot out of all time, the "OK Corral" what, three dead and a couple wounded. John Wesley Hardin killed 20 or so men but took as many years to do it, hell the girls between them have out done Hardin in two years' time total and make Wyatt Earp look like a limp dick piker. Doc Holliday was a different story so we won't go there.

I'm really beside myself with this. Don't

get me wrong, I believe 100% in defending oneself. I believe a person who tries to take from others by force gets what they deserve but spread a lot of pain and suffering until they get it. But how does this affect our problem with it? And why do we seem to attract trouble? If I knew a shrink I might ask them but I don't. I wish Charley was here, he would have thoughts on it.

We were free to move on and that's what we did, we paid our hotel bill and stable bill, got what we could of supplies and lit a shuck out of there. I had no idea where we would go next but for now we are heading "up." Up is always good, take the high ground. We didn't push it but we didn't stop to smell the wild flowers either. Just before dark we stopped at a small stream in a clearing where the stock could graze, fixed dinner and just collapsed by the fire depending on Walker to stay alert, as I watch him sleeping by the fire.

I never realized how much being hunted takes out of a person, the eternal vigilance and only dozing not sleeping. Even the lay up in town wasn't restful. Maybe I was getting too old for this crap. Sandy and May both snuggled close and Sandy said "John, stop thinking so much, we don't hunt trouble, yes it finds us, but then, think how many people we may have saved by being there. Not everybody has the skills you taught us and not everybody is cut out for this life but for me and May we wouldn't be anyplace else in the world."

May kissed my cheek and said "You know she's right John, look at the good instead of the bad, everywhere we go we have helped people, even if it's just buying supplies we are bringing new money into small communities just surviving like everybody else, we aren't bad people."

My wives are the smartest two people on this old earth, both have an insight that is hard to believe and they are two of the funniest, happy loving people I've ever known. I'm blessed. Both of them said "Yes you are." "Stop it" I said. They laughed and scooted closer if that was possible.

I don't know why or where these thoughts are coming from but I wish they would stop, doubts at the wrong time could cause hurt to one of my ladies and that would tear the heart out of me. So ok, I'll stop doing it, they are right we have never done anything to cause a fight and in fact have run away from it until we couldn't run any longer. So there, glad that's settled, "Us too!" Came the thought, "Stop it!"
"No!" Giggles. Actually I believe most of this stuff playing in my head is of my own doing

and not really them; laughter. Sigh.

We stayed in this camp the next day to decide where we were going next plus to see if anybody was interested in our trail. While relaxing we read the maps like a book, Of course we were all looking for the little mark that indicates hot springs, yes we are addicted to these thing but why not?
We did locate a few within a couple of days ride so come morning we were up early and on the road, we did a loop every few miles to watch our back trail but saw nothing. Yet.

We found the first spring and it wasn't worth bothering with, too much sulfur and stunk so bad we smelled it a mile away. Own to the next one which being on the other side of the ridge might be better. It was and we didn't even have to improve it since it was an old Elk hunting camp. The hunters must have used this camp for many years because it was really improved. Even had fire wood stacked.

We set up camp and after putting the stock out to graze we hit nature's hot tub and it was heaven, over to one side was the outlet where we soaped down and got clean with the soap flowing out right away. Nice. With morning we looked the area over and while it was nice we decided to move on.

Two weeks later we were due west of

Jackson Hole and were turning south, we decided freezing our asses off wasn't the way to go. There are thousands of square miles of beautiful desert country we can explore in more comfort.

And winter was snapping at our heels for sure, we didn't have to urge the stock into stepping it out, they weren't slowing down a bit, days passed into weeks, as we dropped lower and lower the land was opening up letting us make better time, I figured we could make it to Rock Springs and winter there if we had to, or rest up before the push home. Margo and Harry had become friends when we rolled east to look into what was going on there.

We started early and rode late, stopping to camp where we found water at days end. We had water bags we filled in case we had to make a dry camp which we did once or twice. But it worked out because we watered at every trickle we found. It was funny how we suddenly couldn't wait to get back to the low country which really ain't that low. I guess events that happened just made us want to get back to the canyon lands where we had found more peace then any place and right now we were looking forward to just standing down for a change. But this trip was awesome and we had a blast.

We rode into Rock Springs just minutes it seemed ahead of a bad storm; Margo and Harry were blown away when we popped in out of the gloom. The stock was put away in record time and they offered us a bed at their home, we accepted with no arguments. We woke to find a foot of snow on the ground and still falling, we had just made it. We headed to the nearest place to get breakfast dragging a protesting Harry and Margo along.

Before we left the house I opened a pack I had kept closed since we left Harv and the canyon dwellers when they rolled out heading south for the Canyon lands. I called the girls into the bedroom after we had showered and dressed.

They wear their necklaces all the time and when they came into the room both were wearing form fitting black jeans and matching tops. I handed each a rolled up bundle to open which of course excited them just because. They worked thru the knots as fast as they could which was how I made sure they didn't sneak a peek before I was ready to give them their new goodies.

They managed to get them open at the same time and rolled the bundles open and went quiet, for once I had got them! They were just stunned. They looked at me then the gifts then put them on. Harv's family member who did the bear skin and the necklaces had made two beautiful winter coats from his wolf skins, he had lined them with Hudson bay wool trade blankets and when the hood was pulled up the wolfs head was the crown of the hood. They were beautiful, both hoods were trimmed with Ermine fur and they reached almost to the girls knees.

The buttons were made from Elk horn and polished to a high shine. The hugs that followed were well worth the cost which was to be paid when we meet up again. I've seldom managed to surprise the girls but the bear skin rug and the coats did for sure. When we met Harry and Margo in their living room they were blown away at the coats, they hadn't seen the necklaces yet so the entire display was awesome!

I looked at them and thought "I done good!" and heard "Oh yes you did!" in my inner ear I guess. We made quite an entrance at the local café and the girls, who always attract attention, really over did it this time. They had every eye in the place on them. Harry made the introductions and reminded the folks that we were the ones who dropped off all the supplies that helped them out plus the weapons that brought a round of smiles and a lot of handshakes.

While we were eating the girls hung their coats on their chairs allowing everybody to see the bear claw necklaces which drew a lot of attention plus too much from a table next to us. I was watching the looks and could see something was sticking in their craw, but I wasn't gonna worry about it. We had a good breakfast with Harry and Margo who wanted to know all about our trip, the bear story really got them going.

That was when one of the women at the next table spoke up and said "So, you intrude in the bear's area and just have to kill it. How crude!!

I looked at her for a moment before saying "Well I guess I could have let the bear kill us, would that make it all better for you?" Her reply made me laugh out loud; she said "Well if you had stayed out of the bear's home it wouldn't have tried to defend itself." Margo, seeing the looks the woman was getting from the girls stepped in and said that if the whole bear wolf thing offended her to leave. But she wasn't having it, she said "Oh so if the mighty man is intruding in my home he will kill me and make a rug out of me?"

I was doing my best to avoid this when one of the men with her said I would play hell doing that while he was around. Well shit, here we go again; I'm really ready for the canyon lands. Of course Sandy and May weren't gonna keep quiet. Sandy said "Well what if I make you go away would that be better for us all? The woman was the main issue here; the man was just trying to fill a role he felt he needed to play. May spoke up and said "Look we have spent the last several months riding all over the mountains and are heading home now and we really don't need any more shit out of a bunch of bark munching tree huggers!"

I stood up and said "lets go guys, we don't need this crap from a bunch of dip shits who never had to kill the meat they eat thinking it comes in a package." I was turning away when the other man at the table said "Well old man don't run away yet, I'm just getting started" and jumped to his feet and found himself looking down a really big hole. He never saw Sandy move she just grew the gun in her hand

As he was back peddling he fell over his chair which brought loud laughter from the other folks in the place. From the floor he was yelling he was gonna sue us causing even more laughter. The other people at the table were frozen in place. I stepped over and offered him a hand up and got him seated in his chair, then I told him that was the only time I ever saw Sandy pull that gun and not kill the reason for pulling it and it would be smart to not say anything more.

May said "Y'all ain't from around here are you?" Margo said "nope they dragged ass in here a week ago from California or some such place and have been a pain in the ass ever since, this is just their latest thing to bitch about." I asked how they managed to get this far alive. Harry said they were part of a convoy of people who came thru and plainly left them behind, I could see why. I asked where they thought they were going and the man in the chair said they had friends in Chicago who would help them. I was tempted to tell them about Chicago but decided Rock Springs would be better off if they kept going. At that moment Harry told them that as soon as the storm was over they were leaving. They had not a clue that the world had changed. I wondered how they could not know.

I was proud of Sandy for not shooting the loud mouth because it would have ruined breakfast. I can respect the fact somebody may not want to kill animals for food or whatever but to sit in a café bitching about those who do while filling your face with meat others killed, dressed out and cooked is plain stupid, but nobody ever accused such people of being rational. I was just surprised to see it still lingering around. And I saw it as a sign that as things settled down and became safer these kinds of fools would crawl out of the woodwork. I could see a very rough road ahead of them. It's a new world out here and their old ways just won't cut it.

We headed to the stable to check on Buck and the gang. They were warm and dry and fed, life was good from their point of view. We spent a couple of hours brushing them down, checking hooves, looking for rub spots from the pack saddles or cuts from rocks, all were in good shape but all needed new shoes bad. The stable guy said he would get the local Farrier to take care of it. I told him to let us know as I wanted to be there, anybody can say they can shoe a mule or horse but I want to see it not hear it.

After we returned to Harry and Margo's home we told them we really appreciated the bed but we were going to
move into the local hotel where we could get a king sized bed, but also we felt that the scene this morning might put them in a bad spot with some folks so it would be best to just be folks moving thru. They understood the need for more sleeping room but said they weren't worried about what the few fools might think.

Harry drove us and our personal packs to the hotel and introduced us to the owners who were happy to have us and they had a nice room with a king sized bed and never blinked that there was three of us.

The storm blew itself out in two days and took three more to melt the snow as early storms do. The stock was in good shape and all had new shoes so it was time to go. We made our manners to Harry and Margo and the few folks we had gotten to know and on a chilly morning we rode out heading south.

We left Rock Springs and made a beeline for Moab Utah, about 330 miles or around 6 hours driving, cross country on horseback it's shorter but a lot longer. We have had 10 mile days and 20 mile days depending on the lay of the land. We stayed low where it was flatter and made good time, not loitering along and twenty days later we hit highway 70 and felt the weather changing, still cold but not like the high country although it's still high here.

Several days later we hit the great little town where had stayed a week or so. We rode right to the stable behind the motel and sure 'nuff there was Jack and Jill cleaning stalls. Those two kids were workers and were thrilled to see us again. After unloading the critters and storing the stuff in the locked tack room the girls left to get us a room while I rubbed down the stock. The kids offered to do it but I needed some relaxing time, before I was done they were back so I took Jacks offer to finish the job while we headed to Ma's café.

Again we were greeted like long lost old friends. Ma bulled out of the kitchen and got swarmed by the troublesome two, when he got free he shook my hand and said how good it was to see us. He winked and said he had a new price on his menu, it went by the pound, food pounds that is. I laughed right out while the girls started pushing him around all the while calling him cheap and a slim ball. Ma was laughing and gave up and said "fine, no food by the pound!" Having won a great victory they plopped down while Ma headed for the stove. The young lady who worked for him brought us coffee smiling all the way. She said the girls made Ma smile for the first time since his wife died of the flu that hit while we were far to the north. We were shocked to say the least, we had never met her but still we really liked Ma.

He returned with a big serving tray that sagged as he walked to the table. He had learned the last time and put a huge stack of hot cakes between "them" with a smaller one for me. I swear the ham slice was an inch thick and as big as a cars steering wheel. I waited while they whipped out their switch blades and had their way with the ham. I took the bite around the bone and just shook my head, Ma headed right back to the kitchen and returned with a whole slice of ham for me and put a dozen eggs on the table. Hot biscuits and honey rounded it out. Ma sat down and watched while "they" wreaked havoc on the table full of food. I filled my plate and put my arm around it leaving them the rest. I was pretty sure they wouldn't cut my arm to get to my plate but then again…

After it was gone down to I think they licked the plates, they sat back and May asked what was for lunch!
Ma just leaned forward and banged his head on the table. The other folks in the place were looking at the girls like they might attack any minute for their food; I assured them they were safe but to not make sudden moves. That got a good laugh.

Sheriff Ben came in and joined us, said he heard there was some wild critters trying to eat Ma's place out of business and had he known who or maybe what it was he woulda brought his wife coz she didn't believe him when he told her about them.

They laughed at him then Sandy reminded Ma he hadn't answered May's question about lunch. He just shook his head and said he was gonna kill a cow and cook the whole thing! May said "good but you don't have to cook it." Now everybody was laughing.

Ma left for a minute and returned with
Ben's breakfast which got their attention but
Ben was not to be messed with, he wrapped
an arm around his plate and said he would
bite the first one to reach. Both said "Oh!!"
"Promise?" Ben turned red, and gave each a
biscuit. They asked him to dip them in his egg
yolk, he just pushed them the platter. Ma went
back to the kitchen.

I told Ben I'd pay for his breakfast if he
would wait till I got them out of there before
he got it…again. I should be embarrassed at
their antics but I'm not, they are cute, fun, and
if they didn't get enough to eat they may start
looking at the small kids or dogs or cats. That
got a nasty sound and threats for later.

When I got up the next morning I was
alone, no shower buddy, no hair brushing,
nada I felt abandoned, not a nice feeling, so
after a quick shower I headed out to the barn
first and was only half way there when I heard
"THWOK.""THWOK.""THWOK." I could
only shake my head but there they were with
Jack and Jill showing them their new toys. I
was hoping they didn't tell the kids about the
first use they put to the gear. Well they were
busy so I figured I'd head over to Ma's for
coffee and made it two whole steps when I
heard Sandy say "Freeze Bud!" May followed

with "Unless you wanna explain an arrow in the butt to the local Doc!" Well the twins were laughing while they put away the gear with promises to teach them to shoot when we got back.

Ma's was fairly empty so we got our favorite table and the young girl brought our coffee and pointed to the menu on the wall, it read " Breakfast" that was it. I said "Well I'll try the breakfast," she smiled and said "good choice" the walking food pits ordered the same but I asked her to tell Ma it was for them. I figured he would have to run a wheelbarrow out which I thought was funny but others didn't it seems. I was both hugged and kissed and elbowed. It was worth it. I was feeling left out with the whole bow thing, I should have gotten one for myself. Oh well, months late and four mountain ranges short, maybe someday. Sandy said "See." May said "When will you ever listen to us?" I ignored them.

Ma came thru the door with a big tray, and I swear he was staggering with it. His young helper followed with another tray. I said "this is getting to be ridiculous!" Then Ben walked in with a smirk and sat down and said "I figured if I got here right at serving time I might get to keep my food. They smiled at him and May said "Careful buddy boy, you might catch a fork in the wrist."

Well it worked, Ben got to eat a full plate, I got most of mine, and several locals just watched in awe. Ma joined us for a cup since he was caught up, Sandy asked the young lady if there was any pie left from yesterday and she ran to the kitchen and brought back a whole apple pie! Ma said he was learning and had made extra. Sad I say, so very sad, these tiny women should weigh 200 pounds each but I swear they never gain an ounce. I will say this for them, they settled for cutting the pie into four pieces and giving Ben and me one. I ate mine fast. I got a look but I got to keep the pie too. Taking the hint Ben did the same, Sandy said "Yawls sorry." May offered "Yep, just plain sorry." We smiled. Ben was catching on alright and after another cup of coffee he looked at me and said "I need to walk this off." I got the hint and headed out with him, the girls decided to help clean up with the young lady. I looked at them with a thought of "Run Jack!!" Both turned and smiled at me. Poor Jack.

We walked up toward the stable and after a bit Ben said there was some short wave traffic about a reward for me and the girls, dead. I told him about the events that caused that and that it had been rescinded because the old man was dead. Ben thought about that a bit and said "Well I'll put that out from here and maybe that will help but yawl keep an eye on yer back trail."

I told him we had been doing that ever since the crap started. He asked if the girls really took out three would be killers with arrows? I could only say "yep." We talked a while longer and I could see he was not done so I asked him what was going on, he said there was rumors of a pretty large, for lack of a better word "Army" of scum bags rolling across the country raiding and in general just killing people. He said all he had heard was they looked like former military mixed with biker trash and it was all "White" but that didn't matter since they were raiding everybody regardless of race.

I asked him where they were as of the latest reports, he said headed this way but were in the Vegas area where pickings seemed to have been pretty good. But they were rolling right down the main highways and picking off the small towns along the way. I looked off toward the mountains we had been in and wondered where we could go to escape this shit. The answer was no place, we couldn't turn our back on this anymore then we did the other times we helped people out.

We sat in the shade of the barn and worked thru it until I had all he had but he promised to start probing for more information right away. I was faced with should we head for the canyon to get ready or stay and have the troops come to us, that made way more sense plus we could find some wheels and do some scouting although they were a long ways from us. I needed to talk to the girls so Ben headed off to start getting info and I gathered the girls up.

We held a war council in the room where I explained it to them. Now most women would say something like "Why is this our responsibility?" My women asked when we were leaving to scout them out. First we needed wheels, reliable wheels. Plus something was bothering me and I couldn't put a finger on it. May leaned over and said "I think the people in that last town, the ones from California, were advanced scouts for this outfit." Sandy jumped right in with, "Yeah, that would explain why somebody looking for refuge would be so obnoxious as to be sent packing after a week! Just think how much could be learned in a week! And if the group they belonged to left some people at every place they wanted to raid, it would make sense! Leave them then go on dropping spies off at every town then head back picking them up along the way."

My ladies were spooky sharp and I was glad they were on my side. They smiled and hugged me. Ok we had it figured out. Maybe.

But I was sure they had nailed it. Now the way to find out would be to head out on the highway and stop in every place and ask if they had some people who just didn't fit in and were sent packing.
Next stop was Bens to see about some good wheels that would get us there and back.

Ben took us to see a man who owned a pickup that ran and was very reliable being as usual a diesel. He agreed to loan it to use after hearing the story. Back at the motel we put together out bug out bags and our assault gear, we were hauling a lot of ammo and body armor plus our freeze dried food and one tent, by the next morning we rolled out after breakfast, Ben was there and pissed that he wasn't going but he understood. Ma had fixed us some road food that might get us a good ways down the road, or not. We were just rolling and stopping to talk to people. The truck had a 100 gallon tank in the back plus two 55 gallon drums filled and with a hand pump so we had about 250 gallons counting the stock fuel tank. We told Ben we'd shoot for a four day trip, but he would see us when he saw us. I also gave him the radio freq.'s for the Fort and Canyon and asked him to tell them to stand by for action.

We rolled out about two hours after sun up and headed back to I 70 then due west at a good pace. But I slowed down and finally pulled over and asked a question we all should have asked. "If" the people at Rock Springs were scouts, why were they so far north of our location? There was no way they were going to try anything in or around Salt Lake City, or even close to it. So the only thing I could think was "If" the ones we met were really scouts and not a figment of our imagination, and if they weren't going near SLC, then they had to be coming North to I-70 then East then North again to I-80 and that brings the question of "Why? Why not just take 70 East if that was their plan?"

We were basing a lot on the "thought" that the Rock Springs people were in fact actually scouts, now I was confused and the girls were burning brain cells working it thru. We needed some solid intel so we decided to just follow thru with our plan and if we were right we would know pretty soon or so I hoped. We stopped at several small towns and talked to the local people in charge and found out nothing so we kept on moving. May brought up the fact that the places we stopped were so small as to not have enough ability to stop a large force but also they had nothing much to attract a raid. But maybe anything beat nothing.

We spent the first two days stopping and talking to anybody who would talk to us, a lot of the smaller places had road blocks and let nobody in but we were able to find that nobody had stopped off and stayed. But a couple of them had seen a small convoy of vehicles with a lot of people passing thru and asking to buy supplies and in one case wanting to leave a young couple for a few days while the wife got over some female issues. They were turned away. This sounded like our bunch.

We made it to St. George Utah before hitting the jackpot, they were set up to allow some commerce but restricted visitors to one area where they could stay over at a motel and shop in the few stores there, We headed for the cafes where we talked to the wait staff and bingo, found what we were looking for, A couple who stayed a week asking to be allowed to move into the city, when that didn't work they spent every day just walking around looking at everything.

The guy we got the most out of was the deputy Sheriff for this small area, he was an older gent named William Potter who after a while asked me if I had spent time in "The Land of Bad Things?" I said "Yeah." He asked if I ever heard of the locals who worked on a fire base or outpost being spotted walking funny, I say "Yep" to that also, he nodded and said, "Step counters, measuring the area by paces. "I knew exactly what he meant, Victor Charles used to use threats to kill a whole village to get several people who worked on a base to map out the area, they would pace off the areas they were allowed into and later it would be fitted together like a puzzle. It then allowed the commander of the coming attack to lay out a damn near perfect map of where each bunker was, where the ammo dumps were from a certain point, usually the observation tower. They could then rain down mortar fire damn precise!

The deputy said what he observed was the couple doing the same kind of walking and looking. And one day they just loaded up and left. He said they turned toward Vegas.

I could not believe that there was a force out there with the ability to attack and overrun St. George; it wasn't some small settlement just making it. The LDS folks being prepared for damn near anything had clamped a lid on the whole damn state from the minute the lights went out. To them prepared meant "Prepared" it was a way of life not a hobby. Now for sure the area that allowed visitors in could be overrun but the main city had to be damn well covered and protected. But if they could bust thru in one place and had the fire power to hammer the defenses they could cause a great deal of damage and harm a lot of good people. St George was only a couple of hours away from Vegas.

The Deputy also said there had been a complete stop in traffic out of Vegas for over two weeks and now that we were here asking questions he was noticing it as suspicious

Well we now knew something was gonna happen and I believed it was gonna be soon. He said SLC had resources but it would be too hard for them to come to help with any speed.

I asked if they had any decent communications set up, he said for sure and we followed him to his office where we found a man sitting at a radio of some kind and that was the extent of my knowledge on radios.

I took a few minutes to think and then asked if there were any Navajo peoples living here. He said sure because a lot of them joined the LDS church, He said he could have one there real fast that spoke the language. I asked if he was sure the man could talk the talk. He smiled and said well "she" can and I know that for a fact. He walked to a door and went thru it only to return in a moment with a middle aged Navajo woman who was introduced as the wife of the deputy, we all laughed at that one.

Sandy and May spoke a greeting to her which made her eyes widen and for her to start rattling off at high speed, Sandy slowly explained the limits on her speech abilities. I heard her say Charlie's name and the lady became very excited, then thankfully switched to English and said she knew of Charley and his mother who she called "Old Woman" as if it were her name. It's a damn small world for sure. After explaining why we needed her she was all for it and happy to help out because her grandfather had been a code talker in WW2, smaller world even more!

I sat down and took my time writing out what I needed transmitted to The Fort using the frequency used by all our main outposts. I kept it simple and as short as possible; by the time I was done the comm man had made contact with the Fort. The lady took over and rattled off something, then there was a longer comment and one returned. The deputy said she was giving her pedigree so to speak, meaning who she was born to, which clan, and the person on the other end did the same. Sort of "Hi my name is Bill Smith, I was born to the Oklahoma clan and the Texas clan, meaning if a wedding was to be planed everybody knew the blood lines were far apart. That made sense to me of a people living close in an attempt to avoid close blood ties that could cause health issues in the kids. Or so I thought.

Anyway she got to the reason for the contact and as they talked she would translate to us. Although her husband was able to understand a good bit of it, Sandy just shrugged meaning she was lost as it was too fast and complex for her. I can't even say hello although I think it sounds something like "Yatahea" but I'm not sure.

The upshot was that the Fort with their much better comm equipment had been monitoring radio traffic that had a distinct military flavor to it but they were speaking in some kind of code that meant nothing to anybody at the fort.

Both sides signed off with the call back time set for one hour. We went to the café for lunch with the deputy whose name was Wilfred and his wife whose name was Marylyn.

At lunch she and the girls talked slowly on her part and they were laughing at the misq's. I think Marylyn had really missed having her own people to talk to. Well that was gonna change damn soon if the plan could be brought together.

We got back just in time to hear the call coming in. After all the radio talk was done Marylyn took the mike over and went to talking to the other end but it sounded like a different person to my ear. He asked if I was there and was told "yes," he then asked something and Marylyn translated for me, the upshot was that they had made contact with Charley and the canyon and passed the word. Charley said his group would be rolling by sundown; same for the canyon, the Fort would wait for them to get close then join up. I told them to bring the kitchen sink, Marylyn looked at me real funny then smiled as she got it but she had trouble translating it so she just used that one word out loud. It was funny to hear.

It's so funny to look at a map and see it's only about eight hours from Shiprock to St George, yet with all the stalled vehicles and trees down who knows how long it might take but I figured three days tops so we had a lot to get done before the troops arrived. It was going to involve heading almost into the lion's den but I figured we had as much experience as most anybody we might encounter.

So off we went right down the I-25 South just like a Sunday drive. And we saw....nothing, nada, no signs of a army nor even a Boy Scout troop.

So on we went seeing no traffic heading north, none going south, we were alone on the planet. We followed the road thru curving canyons and at last broke out onto flat country and scattered houses and finally the town of Littlefield. We turned off to check it out and approached it slowly, nothing was moving

except dust in the wind, some dogs running
around but no people. No signs of a reason
why they weren't there. We had seen this
before but usually with remains of people
laying amid expended ammo cases and shot
up buildings. This place looked like it had
been sucked dry in a flash.

Now I was getting worried and Walker was
acting funny so I stopped by a building and
leaving the girls I went to the door and
opened it. It looked like a tornado went thru it
with desks overturned, papers everywhere,
and on the carpet what had to be dried blood
stains. There was a lot of blood in several
places but the place wasn't shot to bits, it was
like somebody walked in and simply shot
people where they sat!

I walked outside and closed the door
then told the girls what I saw, there was
nothing for it but to move on but I really
wasn't up for it. I was really spooked and then
to make it worse Walker let out the worst low
gut growl I ever heard him make, that had
both girls falling out of the truck and behind
the doors with guns up. I let Walker out and
he tore around the building at a run barking
and raising hell so I took off around the other
way, and found him standing on a man's chest
all teeth showing and that growl rolling. The
man was shaking so hard I thought he was
gonna pass out. I called Walker to back off

but he ignored me then Sandy spoke from behind me and he did back up very reluctantly. I looked at the man who was very dirty and gaunt looking and looked to be on his last legs. I asked May to bring some water and a couple of candy bars which she did, I told the man to stand up and got him to the shade beside the building where I handed him the bottle of water, he fooled me by not trying to gulp it down in one go, he sipped it slowly and held it before swallowing it. I opened a candy bar and he took small bites washing it down with sips of water. Sandy asked if I remembered when I found her. I did, she had gulped the water and several candy bars and tossed them almost immediately. This man was smart about it.

At last he said "I know you're not with them or I'd be dead." I motioned him to keep talking and he told a tale of the small town being hit one day by Army people who just rounded them up and killed any who resisted. They loaded everybody into trucks and rolled out heading south towards Vegas, this he had seen from a distant hill. He had been taking his morning walk with his dog in the desert country and returned to an empty town, he searched but found nothing but the same blood stains I found except he found them fresh. He raced for his home and found the door open and the place empty, his gun safe was gone, the whole damn safe, the gun he kept under the mattress was gone too, he said he was scared to death and ran from house to house finding food on the tables from breakfast, people just gone, he searched for weapons and found nothing, not even a sharp knife. He went to a friend's house where he found blood stains in several places and bullet holes in the walls.

His friend had put up a fight; all his guns were gone too along with the safe they were in. These people were under some control for sure, somebody was in charge and it showed. I had no doubt we could find a body dump if we looked but that wasn't on our agenda.

The man, Jason Robbinson said he would like to come with us but I asked him to remain in the area and out of sight and we would pick him up on the way back. He didn't like it but that was the way it was, I wasn't going into a bad situation with a stranger behind us.

We rolled out and moved along a fair pace and stopped frequently to scan the area ahead and it was good we did. We were stopped when we saw a dark spot coming at us from a ways off, when they dropped into a dip we left the road and got out of sight in a low spot then we bailed out and laid down on the crest with our rifles ready.

They came tooling along like they had nothing to worry about; it looked like four men in a crew cab truck. We watched them roll on down the road and we scrambled to the top of the next rise and plopped down in time to see them suddenly brake to a stop and get out, they moved off the road; they were flanking us! They had to have seen the tracks where we turned off. They weren't real good at their job so I assumed they had been dealing with just ordinary people trying to get to some place better then where they were.

In fact two were carrying cut down shotguns, great if you were in a fire fight in a phone booth. One carried a bolt gun and one had a AR type weapon, those two were first. I dropped back below the hill and quickly screwed the can on the 308, the girls both had their suppressed sub guns so we needed to let them get close. The way they were closing in pretty well cinched it, the AR guy was further out looking to gain some high ground and he was my first shot. When they were within 45 yards of us I took the AR man out with a head shot at about 100 yards, they heard the sound of the supersonic round and were standing looking around when the girls cut their legs out from under them.

While they were flopping around we rushed in and disarmed them. They were a sorry looking lot for sure and I was hoping we hadn't ambushed some poor folks just trying to sneak up on somebody to maybe offer them something to eat or maybe a few cold beers. I wasn't inclined to think the latter. After we had their hardware and patted them down we used plastic ties to restrain them. The girls kinda got the bleeding stopped so I asked them why they were attacking us, only one answered but said "Fuck you" so I shot him in the head with the suppressed 22 ruger.

It may seem harsh but these assholes were going to do it to us plus god knows how much misery they had already spread. I asked again and one said they were part of a big army in Las Vegas and they were looking for prisoners that they could collect a bounty on. Younger females being worth the most but anybody who could work was worth something.

I asked why and was told slave labor and the women had other uses. I was wondering why he was talking so easy when I heard Walker do his low growl. In a second we were on the ground and out of sight, Sandy got Walker into a low spot with her while I made it to a small rise. May had gone completely out of sight. We waited and shortly I saw movement off to my right. It was a man low crawling from bush to bush; I waited and shortly saw three more moving in on us from different directions.

I had clear shots at all of them but wanted to wait a bit so the girls could spot them, I also knew the girls would wait for me to open the ball unless one stepped on top of one of them, and think of the devil etc etc. I heard the 300 blackout quietly pop off to my left and saw one of the people drop, the one I saw first heard nothing, the guy closest to the dead one did but wasn't sure what he heard, it was really the action working more then the round going off, I figured screw it and dropped the one I was watching. Sandy opened up and stitched the one nearest her spot and May got the forth one. We stayed in place just in case and waited for thirty minutes, when nobody else showed up May eased up onto the high spot we had first used and after a bit made a hand sign that it was all clear.

But to be sure Sandy let Walker go and May got him to come up to her, when he saw the vehicle the others had left a quarter mile away he was off to check it out and was back shortly and flopped in the shade of a bush, I guess that was his all clear.

All the newest gunnies were dead as was one of the two we left alive, the one who was talking had died and the other one wasn't gonna talk since he was in shock.

Shit, all this crap and all we knew was a bunch of slavers were in Vegas. And I guess we knew that already anyway. Eight more dead and for what? We loaded their weapons and stripped anything they had on them for later inspection and got our ride back on the road, we decided to take their wheels just to confuse the issue.

We headed back to pick up Jason who was shocked to actually see that we had come back for him; he also identified one of the trucks as having belonged to his friend and the AR as belonging to the same man. We put the extra truck in an empty garage, loaded all the guns in the second one and told Jason to follow us. We headed back to St. George where we told it like it was and said we needed to mount a blocking force in a place to keep the enemy penned in until my people could get here.

One place to set it up was in a winding canyon we had driven thru but I had another idea for that and wanted to avoid attracting attention to it. We finally just really beefed up the off ramps and hauled a lot of junk cars down the ramps and formed a solid block that would be hard to breach. I wanted them to see that and think that was it.

I suggested they mount a lookout someplace a couple of miles out and up high and a good ways away from the highway to spy on the spy's. I figured it would be a while before they made a move depending if anybody actually missed the dirt bags we took out. Hell maybe they were the people who were supposed to watch the city.

I didn't have a plan outside hopefully finishing this latest problem once and for all, even if we had to chase them right into Vegas itself. And that made me head for the maps again. I wanted to have a blocking force south of Vegas to stop the rats when they ran if they did but it was just not logistically possible in the time we had. Also I didn't know the exact extent of the enemy's control of Vegas since it was a really sprawled out place and I couldn't see a bunch of raiders having that kind of manpower.

After I thought about it a bit I decided we would be the over watch outside the city. I trust us more then others and because we really weren't comfortable with so many people and we like the privacy and open country.

We found the perfect place after following a dirt road a couple of miles then cut across country and up a steep hill and into a pocket where we would be out of sight and could have a small fire at night to make our coffee.

Once we were settled in we took a sand

colored tarp and put it on low poles with plenty of tie downs then sprinkled sand over it and some local bush on it, with the bushes in front of the thing we could lay under it or sit up and see the road in comfort. The girls brought our bed roll and put it under the cover and we were home! With a nice pair of binoculars and a spotting scope we could see the road very well so I figured it was maybe no more then half a mile away. The girls and Walker would hear any vehicle traffic, I never would of course.

We spent the first day just relaxing and talking while keeping an eye on the road. We talked a lot about the fact we had been in so much shit and had escaped without a scratch so far (yeah, I got shot in the ass so bite me.) All we could believe was we were lucky, we would have maybe been toast if Walker hadn't reminded us of security. I will admit we have some good skill sets, and we work together very well and that counts also, but over all we were well ahead of the game I think because we are observant, we are aware of who is around us. But I think the main thing is that people under estimate us. They see two "cute chicks" and an old man and they never seem to notice that watching me isn't in their best interest. Most people will watch the male figuring he will be the one to deal with, "Wrong!" Like the dipshit Higgins who tried to sneak shoot me, he in his mode of "male superiority" dismissed the woman as not a problem, bad mistakes, man!

So I guess the answer is we work as a team, we watch everybody, everything, we don't disregard anything as unimportant until we know for a fact it is. We watch each other's six and we never sit with our backs to doors or windows. One of us always is in position to see anybody coming thru a door, and the other two are watching the door watcher. I think we read each other's eyes and subtle body movements like they are open books.

The upshot is so far we have won, one day we may not, I hate to think about losing either one of them. They snuggled closer and Sandy said "You won't" and May said, "You're stuck with us for a long time."…Witches. But lovely witches. That got smiles and cheek kisses. Finally we left one watching and two napping and Walker on guard.

The day passed slowly, the night was beautiful with a gazillion stars for us to watch after we moved the bed out from under the cover. We slept like logs knowing Walker was on duty, yeah right, sleeping on our feet. But an ant couldn't walk past without him knowing.

Just before day break Sandy woke me

saying Walker had alerted and was looking at the highway, we crawled under the tarp and watched a vehicle dropping off several people wearing camo BDU's that was just like ours, after the vehicle left they headed out in our direction but more toward the city.

They set up an observation post on a hill north of us and closer to town. We spent the day watching the watchers who had set up a camp behind their hill. There was four of them and after watching them move to their OP and how they set up I came to the conclusion they were either former military or had been well trained by somebody who was military.

They pulled back to their camp at dark and didn't build a fire, nor did we. We spent another night like the one before and at first light watched them getting back into their OP nest. Watching them was as boring as watching paint dry but had to be done.

Finally just at dusk they packed up and headed back toward the highway where the same truck met them and headed south. What they saw was a good barricade with several men manning it. I could only assume the attack was coming soon.

We headed back to town and found that Joe and Willy had arrived and left their equipment a few miles back in the mountains and Charley and his people were moving with the Fort Navajo group which had the lowboys with the tracks. They should be in during the night.

I was feeling the push for time. At daybreak I took the girls and Joe and Willy on a recon so I could look the canyon over with them. It had several really good choke points where we could bottle them up and finish them off.

We drove all the way thru to Littlefield and stopped. After looking the area over I felt we could leave a heavy blocking force in the town with vehicles in garages and when the enemy passed by our people could pull out and follow them into the canyon and road block them in.

We have a couple of six-by's that we put sand bags in the back and mounted in several MG's. One of them along with a few HV's with guns should be able to hold them, that and some grenade launchers. Willy wanted the blocking job so it was his, we needed to get moving so we could get the vehicles in place and wipe out signs of their passing, all in the dark.

We found the right place on a tight curve in the canyon. With tracks at each end and a couple in the middle I figured we could chop them to bits, Joe and Willy also had a surprise, they had taken a couple of six-by's and made them into rolling mortar carriers. I know nothing about mortars except they are heavy to carry and are great if you are on the outgoing side but suck if you're on the incoming side, anyway, these were awesome because they could park at each end of the ambush and just blow the shit out of the whole area. I liked it! It would also give Willy extra help on the back end.

We got back in time to greet Charley who smiled and slowly shook his head and said "When will you leave me alone to sit in the shade and think?" I laughed and said "Never! You eat this shit up!" He asked what we had going so I held a meeting and explained the whole thing, I admitted I knew little about these folks except they seemed to be a mix of trash and former military and were involved in the same old shit of slavery and selling girls.

I explained the ambush point and said if we worked it right these shitheads wouldn't be able to do us much damage if any at all because we held the high ground and would have them bottled up. I wanted all our people dug in and nobody closer then a couple hundred yards. With the fire power we have and the experience I hoped we would do it

with no losses. We moved out with a couple
of hours or so of good light left and rolled
into our ambush point.

We rolled on in with Willy and helped
them get set up out of sight. The girls and I
helped them clean up any traces of our arrival.
We then headed back to the main site. As we
drove into the kill zone things were looking
great, the tracks were hull down behind small
humps that left just the main gun and the co-
axle gun exposed but between the turret armor
and the sand bags being piled on I figured
they were as safe as could be. The riflemen
were further back from the road where they
could give excellent cover for the tracks. It
would be like shooting fish in a barrel,
between the 25 mil guns and the m-60 pigs
we had the whole area covered. Joe had put
people up above on the other side of the road
where the ground was very steep; they were
there to toss hand grenades down on people
hiding behind vehicles. A very good idea!

By midnight we were set and the work
on removing traces of our activities was done.
Everybody used heat tabs to heat some chow
and settled in for a wait, maybe a long wait. I
really had no way of knowing when they
would come. We had a comm unit on the top
of the hill with a direct line to Willy and his
bunch. They would be our early warning. All
in all we spent three days laying there in that

damn canyon waiting to the point I was ready to just roll into Vegas with all guns blazing. Then Willy called to say several scout vehicles were coming and we had time for last minute checking to see that nobody had left something exposed, nobody had. This was as good a unit as any commander could ever ask for.

We heard them coming before we saw them and every one of the people in the two trucks were covered, if one had made any move to alert the others they were all dead. But they kept rolling; I counted about 10 people jammed into each truck all armed to the teeth but no supplies we could see. They rolled on while the comm man notified the city about their coming. I had no idea what they were there for since it was way too many for a scouting party then Joe said they were probably going to infiltrate in close to the road block and take it under fire when the time came. It might have worked but now it wouldn't. We had people waiting for them and I doubted anybody would get away.

Night came and we waited because we all felt this was the night they would come in preparation for a dawn attack only they weren't gonna make it.

My fighting place was in a nice deep hole the girls had worked on while I was running back and forth like a hound crapping peach seeds. They put a cover over it and camoed it, all the bennies of home, well maybe not but it kept the sun off. We all took cat naps while waiting, the comm unit on the hill would give us plenty of warning. I will admit I was worried about Willy and his unit, they were heavy on fire power but low on personnel but Willy and his gang knew what they were doing and anybody trying to take them was dead, they just hadn't found it out yet.

Just around 0200 the comm outpost called in to say there was a long string of lights coming at us, ETA approx. one hour. We got everybody awake and reminded everybody to stay low and use single aimed fire.

Tension grew with each minute while I ripped myself for all the things I hadn't thought of, Sandy put her arm around me and said "Chill slick, you done good." May scooted over and said "John you have done everything possible and giving over some control to Willy and Joe was smart, they are good at this stuff too. Charley and his troops will handle any who get thru this phase of the fight. It's fine."

One smart thing we did was roll a large boulder down onto the roadway to make the lead unit have to stop which would cause the rest to close up more then they should.

And then with a roar of engines they were here. The first truck thru was a six-by full of people, followed by several more, the first truck came to the boulder and stopped and a voice was heard ordering the troops to dismount and move the fkn rock. In the meantime the whole convoy closed up bumper to bumper just as advertised.

But we had trouble! Right in front of us was three trucks with tracks mounted on them just as we haul ours, and the turrets allowed the crew to fight from the trailer just fine. It also changed the point of contact because they had to be dealt with first "If" they were manned. I made contact with our track gunners and told them to be locked on them when the shooting started and if one even moved an inch to hose it. If we could take them without shooting them up I'd be a happy camper.

The radio clicked and Charley said the ones who went thru first were laid up and ready to hit the people at the road block so it was a free fore zone as far as he was concerned. I told him the dance was starting and I sighted in on the man who was yelling up at the boulder but not helping. I dropped him and that opened the ballgame. I kept my eyes on the tracks and at first nothing happened, then the middle one fired up and the turret was moving toward us, I said "Light it up" and our 25's did just that. It stopped running and sat there smoking.

Meantime the enemy troops were piling out and hitting the ditch on the cliff side of the road. It turned into a sniper match and we had them there because of our cover and because we used aimed, controlled fire power right out of the US Marine training manuals. They were dropping as fast as they put their heads up. I waved at the people above them and that was the killer, grenades were dropped from above and they never stood a chance.

Several stood up to surrender but we weren't taking prisoners today. But it's easier to deal with that when they are a couple hundred yards away and not standing right in front of you. We didn't know who they were but we knew what they were. So it was no quarter, they were laying down a high rate of fire but they weren't hitting anything simply because we were above them and to even aim up at us they had to almost kneel to shoot, and they had a short life span.

I could hear heavy gun fire back toward Willy's people but couldn't see how many had not made the curve before it started. I had all the faith in the world in Willy but that didn't stop the worry. All I could do was wait and not bother him with radio chatter like some bird sitting in a chopper at 10 K ft. trying to guide each and every man on the ground, seen it, been there, didn't participate, radios kept breaking.

An hour after the last shot was fired some of the troops started cleaning up, nobody was gonna get killed by a wounded actor. It was a nasty job but it had to be done. They used 10-22 rifles with 25 round mags. One round did the trick but two really nailed it.

I know it seems like we killed a lot of people on very flimsy evidence but I never for a second felt we were wrong.

At last Willy's voice came over the radio saying all clear and no runners made it. He also said he thought he got the "Head Rat." I told him when the cleanup crew called all clear I'd head back that way. Thirty minutes later the all clear was given and the real cleanup started. All weapons were gathered, and loaded in any trucks that would run; these were moved out to the city. Charley called and said his scouts had taken a couple of the enemy alive and they were babbling as fast as they could. He was coming to meet me.

After the weapons were collected, the trucks with the tracks were driven out. The two people in the track that got fired up were tossed out for the cleanup crew, and washed out with cans of water and bleach right there. All vehicles that would run were driven and were towing the ones that wouldn't run. When the area was clear we started phase two. Charley arrived leading to a command meeting with every hand there. Charley spoke about what the two prisoners were telling. He said the main Dog wasn't here, that he waited until later to come in.

So we were going into his den and drag him out kicking and screaming, but he also had as many as five hundred shooters in there with him. We also learned he had been held back from taking anything outside the strip due to the people refusing to give up. His tracks didn't scare them and he lost three to homemade road side bombs. But the people weren't pushing him to move on. I guess they figured he would when he ran thru the supplies he got there.

The two prisoners were brought to me and after looking them over I told them they had one chance to live and that was to get us into the area where their boss hid out. But I wanted every tiny bit of info they had.

Charley had his lads take them away and dig thru their heads, then somebody else did it again and again, when the data was all correlated it showed they were both telling the truth with some small differences probably because they weren't privy to the same intel.

With no further delays we rolled out, HV's in front with the big six-by gun truck in the lead. The track haulers were spaced out thru the convoy; never would we make the same mistake they had.

Willy and his bunch fell in line as we passed them; the girls and I were in a HV three behind the gun truck. That was as close as I was allowed to get. Friends? Bah!! The girls were looking smug but I was driving and I was in charge of this HV and I would drive it wherever I wanted to. May leaned over the seat behind me and wrapped her arms around me and said "Try it bubba." Sandy laughed, the other passenger, Mister Charley himself just shook his head and sighed. I ignored them all.

With the information we had from the two prisoners we stopped just outside the area we were going to hit and unloaded the tracks, we had thought to bring the captured tracks but I wasn't willing to risk people in equipment we hadn't maintained ourselves. We started forward with the tracks leading. The big gun truck was following with HV's spread out behind it, six-by personnel haulers were back a good ways and the mortar trucks were in front of them.

We started taking fire within a half hour, scattered at first but getting heavier. The middle track opened fire and lit up a track hidden in an alley, when it started rolling out it rolled right in front of the gun and the alert gunner hosed him. The track started burning then blew up. People were running everywhere and the gun truck started doing its thing. People were falling by the dozen.

We started taking heavy fire from a pair of MA deuces so we stopped while the tracks dealt with them. Then several explosions hit right where they were, the nortar trucks were dead on! I have no idea where they got the guys manning the tubes but they were damn good! Among the best I ever saw. The 82 MM mortar is an awesome weapon and mounted and mobile made it even better, shoot and boogie.

My comm man called me and said he was getting some strange contacts, I told him to answer them. He called back with the news it was the people surrounding the other side of the strip asking us to watch the mortar rounds when we started getting thru the center of the strip. I laughed and said tell them to pull back further because we intend to finish this shit head since they wouldn't.

He said they replied 10-4; he laughed when he told me that. Maybe I was being hard on them but so far I had seen nothing from these people other then they had some armor that impressed me. I think the locals had settled into a leave us alone and we leave you alone. Not a good attitude! Because sooner or later that snake will whip back and sink its fangs in you.

We kept pushing forward and had taken a few causalities, mostly minor wounds from bullets fragments, then one of our HV's got hit by a track 25 and it was trashed in a second. Our tracks lit it up big time, the medics rushed forward with a track blocking incoming fire so they could work but it was soon obvious they could do nothing.

That really hit home after so much fighting to take four KIA's in a heartbeat. The medics got back in their ambulance and back behind the trucks. Our tracks really lit it up, they were hauling ass shooting into anything that might hold a track, the enemy ground pounder's had hauled ass and weren't slowing down.

I called our people to a halt and when I had everybody on the comm I told them to torch the whole place, I figured there was nothing here worth saving since gambling was done these days by just getting out of bed. Soon it was a raging inferno, we backed up and split around the strip and simply shot the rats running from the fire. I was pissed I hadn't done this sooner; the HV team might still be alive. Both girls laid a hand on me and soon I felt better…. "Witches." I heard a laugh and "Are not" more giggling.

Comm called and said the locals wanted to know why we were burning the strip. I told him to tell them we were exterminating the rats. He came back and said they were very unhappy; I had him patch them thru to me. I said "This is John Walker who am I talking to?" A woman answered me and without answering my question said, "Oh great, we've heard of you and your crew of killers!" I laughed and said "conversation over" and told the comm man to break it down and to not talk to them again.

The fire raged unchecked, and it would burn for days, the shooters inside had quit trying to leave where we could see them meaning they would soon run right into the folks on the other side. I hope they were ready. But there couldn't be many left. I knew they had lost two tracks and assumed they had more, if so they were hauling ass in the other direction. Comm called me back and said there was another call from a different person, a man. I told him to patch it thru while the girls called me a chauvinist pig, I laughed. I might pay later but I laughed now.

The man said his name was Clint Flint. I laughed out loud and he answered laughing and said "Yeah Johnny Walker is pretty cool too!" I already liked this man. He said his group wasn't involved with the woman we spoke to and he asked what his people could do to help. I told him the enemy was on the run and anybody coming at them was a target. He asked about prisoners and I said "You can feed 'em and house 'em" if you want to keep 'em." He said "Got it."

We simply followed the flames and met no more resistance, now I was really sick over the HV team. Charley placed his hand on my shoulder and said something in his language and I swear almost instantly I felt the weight leave my chest. I just sat there and didn't move, when he removed his hand I felt at peace. I knew the men had died but I also knew they went into this with eyes wide open and they didn't blame me.

With night fall we went to 100 percent alert with every gun up. Thru the night there were explosions inside the fire, I figured there must be thousands of cars with fuel in them and god knows what else. We did move back a good bit and were able to a degree use the night vision gear. With morning we went to 25 percent alert. People crashed where they were. The rest of use moved in close and looked for targets. None appeared.

Around midday Clint called to say they were getting runners and none were making it, I warned him about the tracks, if any remained, we took three and killed two. He said he thought that was all they had. I asked him if he had ever seen the leader of this bunch of rats, he said he had from a distance and he was a big black man who carried himself with military bearing.

I had to wonder how somebody with military training and back ground could be reduced to doing the things they were doing. I guess it takes all kinds. Clint said he had somebody waving a white cloth and he was going to let them come out, shortly he called back to say it was a large group of women and girls mixed with a few young boys, they had been prisoners and the guards on the building they were held in had let them go and led them out to where Flints people were. He said the ones who freed them never came out.

Charley suddenly laughed and said "Johnny Long Walker, the man who burned Las Vegas to the ground."

The girls burst out laughing and WTF I smiled, it was a nice title! I had never cared for the place. I'd been here maybe eight times in 50 years and had spent maybe $50.00 playing the machines, the last time I was there I think I won $75.00 so I quit while I was ahead. I did shoot in a couple of matches there back in the 90's the old SOF match and had a great time. But that had nada to do with the Strip. I was amazed watching the place just falling down. It was turning into a pile of rubble that IMHO looked better then it had before.

So far nobody had seen the leader of this bunch of trash, and I was thinking he made his escape alone by preplanning as most rats do, always having several ways out. I didn't know if it was worth trying to hunt him down but figured it was out of the question.

We watched the place burn for days but saw no more people trying to escape, Flint said there were a few runners on their side but he didn't think any made it but he also had no night vision gear so I'd say a lot of them made it out, hell if I could they could and I knew I could. The snakes back was broken but the head could still bite so I really would like to have finished this guy.

I finally had the sense to ask Charley if the

two POW's who were talking before were still able to talk, he said "Of course! Why hadn't I thought of them? I must be getting forgetful hanging around you old people" the girls liked that one, I flipped him off. He was on the radio the next second rattling off something, got a reply then signed off. He said the two were on their way.

When they arrived they wore blindfolds and gags and had not been together since capture, I took one away in my HV and asked him to tell me everything he knew about their leader. He said all he knew was that he was a black man, tall and well-built and a former military officer or so the word was. I asked when he had joined the bunch; he said about a month before they came here. He said he had no excuses for being with them but it was better then being alone in the new world. I asked why he didn't join some community. He said he did but got bored with working gardens and standing guard duty.

I asked where the bossman was from, he said he had heard the LA area but really didn't know because he kept to himself with his few trusted officers. He said those had all been black too.

After I was done with him I had the same conversation with the other one who was able to provide the man's name but it was some Moslem sounding street name which can be changed like ones shirt.

He also knew from overheard conversations that the man had a special place where nobody but his trusted staff was allowed. He said he had heard it was a big house with a wall around it and a guard force of very loyal troops and was located near Barstow California. That was where the US Marine Supply Depot was located. If he had taken that place he had access to about everything one could want to wage war with but I had doubts he had done that. Regardless I wasn't gonna chase this asshole all over the Mojave Desert. If he could he would pop up again someplace and we would get another chance at him.

It was time to go home, the girls were making jokes about the great time I showed them in LV, and how everything that happened there stayed there "In ashes!" laugh laugh…Or how I showed them a "hot time in LV" more laughs, they were working overtime. I think Charley was even quietly chuckling. I told them they were as funny as a dose of clap which set them to clapping their hands in time with each other and saying "clap, clap, clap… Charley told me to just shut up and they would get bored and maybe go to sleep. Funny thing is he was right, in five minutes they were sound asleep. I looked at him and asked what he slipped into their water. He smiled. I wondered.

Driving back thru the canyon reminded me we had the sad duty of burying our people who died. We had lost a total of six people, four in the HV and two who were hit by rifle fire from a sniper who was taken out by a HV mg gunner, too late for them. The good folks of St George offered their cemetery but so far we had always buried our friends on high ground so that's what we did. We picked a hill out a ways from the city and there we laid them to rest.

As had become out way, everybody took part in the grave digging. We laid them together in one grave, comrades thru time. The mechanics used their equipment to make a marker out of polished stainless steel with the names in raised weld and the words "Freedom is never free" We then took turns burying them, with rocks on the top and the steel rod of the cross pounded deep into the earth.

We stood silent for several minutes saying our private goodbyes and slowly in ones and twos we left them there with our love and we would hold them in our memory.

I was saddened that I really hadn't known them personally but that was just not an option. It was enough that they were a part of us and would remain so until the last of us were gone in our own time. It makes me sad to think in a hundred years somebody will say "Wonder who these people were" and nobody will know.

But surprise! When we returned to the city the local deputy Wilfred and his wife Marylyn said the locals had asked if they could build a monument at the grave site detailing who and why they were buried there and they would build a stone wall around it. We thought that was a wonderful thing and said so.

Marylyn and Charley were in deep conversation and I could see she was enjoying talking to him. Wilfred looked at me and suddenly said "John, you think there is anything in your settlement an old busted down lawman could do to survive." I told him we would make a place for them and the canyon would be an ideal place because a lot of the Navajo lived there in the area and it was close to Shiprock.

He walked over to his wife and greeted Charley in Navajo and told his wife to start packing because they were moving to the Canyon near Shiprock. She threw her arms around him and started crying with joy.

Charley was smiling as big as I had ever

seen him do, was a good end to a sad day. Marylyn was going home to the red rock canyons of her birth. Wilfred was going into a whole new part of his life and both were happy. And if they could garden and he could fish and maybe hunt a bit they would find a happiness they had never known. He said they had that part down pat!

A few days later we were ready to head home. Wilfred and Marylyn were packed in short order with all the help we had and trucks to haul their things. These folks were prepared! I think it took one truck just to haul all their canning stuff and canned foods and a ton of empty jars. I love these folks; they are what we all should have been "Prepared!"

Wilfred had a truck of his own that he was driving and I could see a few sour faces of people who resented them not so much for leaving but taking all of their stores, even among good people there are always a lot that resent others for almost nothing.

Then it was head slapping time! I said "Shit!!" they said "Stop cussing!" I said "We forgot Buck and the gang plus the guy's truck we borrowed," they said "SHIT!" With a big smile I said "Stop cussing"! They said "Shut up! How could you forget our family?" I think I was gonna say "Hey WE forgot them"

but they both said "Shut up" before I could
get a word out. I really hate them! "Do Not!"
Stop it! "NO" (giggling). I told Charley what
was going on and he looked at me so sad and
said "How could you forget your family?"

They piped up with "Yeah! Heartless!" I
simply tucked my tail and slinked away. I had
the thought of how peaceful it would be if I
just took off in the truck and returned it by
myself and then enjoyed a quiet ride back to
the canyon.

When I got to the truck they were
leaning on it with disgusted looks and glaring
at the same time. "What now?" I asked. Both
just climbed into the truck so I did too. It was
a chilly ride thru the desert. Even Walker was
glaring at me. Finally I said "So, where yawl
wanna stop for dinner?" That worked, food is
one thing that will break thru their pouts. "We
don't pout" I heard "Fine, whatever." We
decided to just drop the hammer and get back
to the family. We really miss them even if
"we" forgot them in all the excitement; after
all it's not every day you get to burn down
Las Vegas! That made them laugh and the
freeze was over and the fun started. They are
like puppies, puppies with really sharp teeth!

We pulled into the motel tired and starving,
but showers came first then food, or so I
thought, we showered ...pause...showered

again then went to dinner where we found Ben and half the town waiting for us, Ma brought out our dinner before we could sit down, everybody was polite and let us eat before telling the story.

The first question was from Ma, he asked if the girls really burned Las Vegas to the ground. I let them answer. Sandy spoke of the loss of our track crew and the decision to just burn them out but that we only burned the strip and maybe a few blocks around it. Ma said "Good! I always hated that place." Ben asked for us to just tell it as it happened and for everybody to hold their questions. I let the girls tell it because folks like them better then me and they have a way of telling a story that I can't compete with.

I mean how many ways is there to tell the story about my getting shot? Yet Sandy has told a dozen different versions of it and all of them leave the listeners with tears' rolling down their faces, and not tears of sympathy for yours truly, that's for sure.

They took turns telling it and made the canyon ambush sound like Custers Last Stand, and the burning of the strip sounded like the burning of Rome. They do have a way of telling stories. The entire place was so quiet you coulda heard the proverbial pin drop. When they were done there was even applause. I think for them not the story.

After the folks drifted off I looked for Ma's helper for some more coffee, seeing it he went for the pot, I asked where his helper was. Glaring at the troublesome twins he said she seemed to have found some reason to hang out at the motel stables a lot. "They" started laughing and high fiving, Ma asked if I had ever thought about selling them but he retracted it pretty quick. The girls took off for the stables to check on the stock, yeah right.

Ma sat with me and asked about the lake settlement project and the plans for it, I told him I had not a clue what or how it was gonna go but that May's people who were all one kind of an engineer or another seemed to think it was mostly just a job of diverting some power lines or stringing new ones using available resources and that from there on it was adlib as we go. I asked if he was interested in moving. He said he might because the place just wasn't the same without his wife Jane. I told him all about the canyon home and that while it was getting full up there was almost 2000 miles of shore line with canyons everywhere and open areas that looked over the lake.

I left him thinking and went looking for the match makers who were once again shooting their bows with an audience made up of the twins and each had a friend with them. I could see the seeds the girls planted with Ma's helper had taken! When she saw me she said "OH!! I gotta get to work! Ma will be angry" which caused us all to laugh, like Ma could ever be angry at her. I had the thought that if Ma decided to up root the café just might have a new owner, not a bad gig, motel, stables and café! These kids were all workers and I could see the future right here.

Leaving the girls I went off to do what I do best, I took a nap and woke up to the usual tangle of arms and legs, but for once they weren't buttering me up for something I would say no to. Naps are gifts from a higher power; they are made so wonderful that you almost have to feel guilty over taking them. Almost.

When we woke up it was late afternoon and the first thing I heard was their tummies growling, I said "you ate half a cow this morning how in the hell could you be hungry, they just laid there limp, "from hunger" they said. I said fine lets go eat.

Not now they said "we have other plans," I reminded them we had already made love earlier, they reminded me so what, I reminded them I was old, they proved I'm not so old. Tired? Yes. Shaky? Yep! But old? Not so much!!

We made it to Ma's just in time to still get breakfast, Ma having gotten smart filled the table for them then brought me mine. Ben came in and just sat and watched, he asked if I'd had them on short rations, they said I starved them the whole time we were gone plus watching cities burn down made them hungry. He was impressed. Ma joined us while his helper removed the dishes as they were emptied figuring they wouldn't bite the girl.

I was surprised when Ma mentioned maybe moving to Ben, Ben wasn't surprised at all. He said he had always liked the Lake area himself and had planned to retire there and spend his days fishing. I asked him why he wasn't doing that, he said well the world ended and he just settled in and forgot about it. He started asking a lot of questions about the lake settlement, I told him what I could, he looked at Ma and said he was gonna talk to his wife and see what she thought.

I was kind of blown away at how acceptable a lot of folks were to the idea of just up and moving on but I guess in unsettled times people wanted to be with others who think along the same lines. Speaking for myself I had to admit I loved the desert more then most any place I ever spent time and it was awesome riding country, so much to see if you could get away from the roads.

After the girls were done eating Ma out of house and home, again, and asking what was for supper they helped the young lady with the dishes then the three of them went to the stable, Ma said you know I feel like I'm losing the daughter I never had, We had never asked about the girl even her name, at least I hadn't, I'm sure the girls knew all about her. Ma said her name was Alma and she lived with her grandparents, her folks had been on an anniversary cruise when the EMP hit and never made it back, he was her uncle a couple times removed and had been best man at her folks wedding, so he helped take care of her and her grandparents who were getting on a bit.

He also said he was glad the girls had gotten her interested in as he put it "The stable" and laughed. I told him that if the town wasn't careful it would wake up and find it was owned by the twins and Alma and the hard working unpaid stable hand who was courting Jill. He laughed and said yeah, everybody in town was talking about that.

I was conflicted on hanging around here or heading out for the canyon. I decided I'd let the girls be my barometer on that one, when they got bored they would let me know. I really enjoyed the place and figured we would be hated by all if we took Ma and Ben away, but oh well, been hated before.

Being bored myself I decided to saddle Buck and take a ride before he got so fat he waddled, while I was saddling him the girls showed up asking what I was doing and why I didn't say anything to them, I asked why they showed up when they did, they said to find out why I was going riding without them. "Ta-da! There's your answer" I said, "You knew what I was doing and why I was doing it and you came, what's to tell you?" You already knew. Well for once I had them, they just looked at me. May said "He's getting smart huh?" Sandy said "Yeah, maybe too smart for his own good. We need to do something about this!" So off they went to saddle their horses, both came back ready to go and I wasn't surprised to see both had their rifles in the scabbards.

Now I will admit I wondered fleetingly about why they had bed rolls tied on the saddle, but I really didn't think it over, I found out why later in a nice little bowl of a meadow while the stock grazed. I'm old, but getting younger every day. Maybe.

When we returned to the stable all the young folks were there, the boys asking about the ride and the girls looking at the bed rolls and smiling real big. I hoped the girls were

having motherly talks with them. Hay lofts
have a reputation well deserved!

We stayed for a total of 10 days and rode
every day, there was even some rain that blew
thru for part of the time and turned the area
green and the wild flowers did their thing,
they usually only last a day or so but for a
while the mountains look like a colored
carpet, mother nature at her best. At last we
knew it was time to head out so we loaded up
one morning and had a last breakfast with Ma
and Ben who had decided to take a ride up to
the canyon area and look it over. We were
looking forward to hosting them.

The girls spent some time with Jill and
Alma, I assumed a birds and bees talk but I
had a feeling these kids were smart enough to
keep their priorities in line. And with that we
rode out heading home to the canyon, more or
less. We weren't looking at a time clock or
any clock cos time really didn't mean much, it
was either be up time or be in bed time and
well I forget feeding time! I laughed, they
glared.

We had Charlie's map with water holes
marked and decided to take a different route
back. I know I needed time to decompress,
things happened too fast, one minute we were
just minding our own business and the next
we were burning down part of a city and

burying six of our friends. Life had changed so much in the last few years that nothing was simple anymore if it ever was. Regardless I needed down time away from the world.

We found one of Charlie's water holes with a good flow into and out of a deep clear hole with graze all around since the rain came. In dry country you never camp right on the water simply because it deprives the wild life of water, but in this case there was plenty of places for animals to drink both above and below us so we camped right at the deep hole. And it was cold!! But we got clean and felt much better, a good hot dinner and early to bed.

If you have never spent the night in the desert with no man made light anywhere around then you haven't seen stars, one can spend an hour just looking at the equivalent of a six inch square and be amazed at the number of stars.
It's one of life's truly beautiful things. And it's free! No dish needed, no monthly bill to pay and the stars didn't go out when the lights did.

The next beautiful thing is watching the sun come up in the desert. If you just sit still it will astound you at the life all around you where it looks like nothing can live. I guess I'm a hopeless romantic but I see beauty everywhere I look, right now I'm watching God's most beautiful work of art standing knee deep in the pool trying to keep from screaming at the cold!! They are so cute but I best get up and build the fire or I'll pay later. Nice view anyway.

We wandered all over the place for three weeks, just riding and looking but even here in the desert it was getting pretty cold so we decided to head for home. It's always warmer in the canyon, why I don't know since cold air settles in the low spots, may have something to do with the red rock absorbing the suns warmth, same in the summer when you can fry an egg on it or so it seems.

Do you ever have voices in your head? I do, lots. Here's a sample.
"You know what would be so cool?"
"What"
Silence………
"Well?!"
"Well what?"
"What would be so cool?"
"What?"
"Yes, what?"
"What what?"
"Shit"
"Stop cussing it sounds like shit"
"Yeah right miss potty mouth"
"So?"
"So what"?

"So what would be So Cool"?
"Oh"
"Oh what"
"Oh, right, I forgot"
"Forgot what?"
"Would be so cool"
"Shit"! I hate you!"
"Do not"
"I could"
"Not!"

Get the point? Ever have that problem? No?
Wanna know why you never have that
problem? Because you don't live in a pillow
case with two rabid baby Badgers. Nope, I
have the lock down on that.

"John?"
"What?"
"Who you thinking at?"
"I'm asleep, stop getting into my dreams."
"John?"
"WHAT?!"
"You were talking out loud."
"Shit."
"Stop cussing."
"John?"
"What?"
"We're hungry."
"So? Go chase some small creature down and
kill it and eat it."………'
"OUCH!!!"
"John?"

"What?"

"Where you going?"

"I'm gonna get up and feed you two before you hurt me, or kill me and eat me."

"Giggling…Who say's we would kill you first?"

See, voices in my head, all the time, day and night. But I wouldn't trade them for anything.

"John?"

"What?"

"Where you going?"

"To feed you, you said you were hungry"

"Giggling again, Poor John, who said we wanted food?"

"Oh"

Sometimes the voices are pretty nice mostly, kinda, sometimes not so but always entertaining.

We were riding side by side with the pack string loose behind us munching pretty much everything that didn't have sharp pointy stuff on it. We love our mules, they really are family and each has its own personality, just like people, they respond well to kindness but will remember a harsh word or deed for twenty years while they wait for you to forget for just a second. Then watch out.

May suddenly sat up straighter in the saddle and said "Hey! Know what would be cool?" I seemed to remember this conversation but kept my mouth shut, earning me a beautiful smile and a kiss even tho she had to climb damn near all the way up on Buck. Sandy on the other hand wasn't about to be quiet and said "Hey we went thru this crap before day light and you forgot what it was."

May flashed a bright smile at Sandy and said "Well I remember now!"
"So speak up" say's Sandy.
"No I think I won't because you were snotty at me."
"Was not!"
"Was too!"
"Enough!" says I. Which surprising me all to hell and back worked, both looked at me in something akin to shock for maybe 2.2 nano seconds before they started poking my ribs and telling me I could be in big trouble if I wasn't careful. I said "I'll be in trouble regardless of being careful." Which both agreed with.

It took another hour to get to the bottom of what would be so cool. May says with a straight face that we should go to the Canyon, spend a while then take a HV with loads of fire power and a trailer full of ammo and spare parts and go have some excitement. Now I shit you not, this was what her cool idea was. Sandy was all for it and already planning what hardware she could pack along.

I finally got a chance to say "We spent the entire summer riding to Montana, we got involved in a war up there and had to shoot up half the countryside, then we headed home and had to detour to burn Vegas to the ground and wipe out a army of bad guys. And you're bored? Really?" I mean "REALLY! REALLY!?"

May looked at me like I spoke in tongues and continued the big cool plan with her sister in destruction.
Most women would be talking about nails and hair and dresses. My two ladies were talking about how many guns they could pack in a trailer and ammo of course and maybe we needed to find a bigger trailer! I think you can see where this is going right?

Finally I was asked my opinion, I wondered why they wanted my opinion because it wouldn't matter right? Well "Yes" they both agreed it wouldn't but it made them feel better asking me. Now if you can unravel their logic please explain it to me.

I have no idea what it is that drives them, maybe it's some latent gene from so many eons of suppression so now that they have more guns then God and are both faster then chain lighting and never have a second

of remorse when they drop some shit head.
So…. maybe it's just payback time. I'm glad
they are on my side. "Smiles and hugs"

Sandy "See I knew he would come around."
May "There was never any doubt silly! He
was never gonna let us just take off without
him."
Me "Let you?" I laugh HA-HA - FKN- HA, I
never had a choice, never for a second. If I
had balked I would have woke up three days
out of the canyon and cuffed to the roll bar in
the HV, so who are they shitting?

I did try one more time and finally May
turned to me with tears in her eyes and said
"John that son of a bitch in Vegas killed god
knows how many people and got away with it
but he screwed the pooch when he killed our
people. And we know he's in the Barstow
area and I'm going to get his black or green or
white or spotted ass. Makes no never mind
what color he is, he will look good all grayed
out and laying out to be converted into
buzzard shit!

So I hauled her over into my lap and
wondered if I was getting played as is normal
with them but Sandy was wiping her eyes and
I knew she felt the same way.

So I said "Well fine, lets go kill the
bastard," now it's all hugs and kisses and

promises of good things to come! I asked if that meant a full nights sleep. I never know when to shut up.

So now we had a plan more or less, a destination, sorta, and a purpose. That was for sure. The rest of it would fall into place when the time was right.

And someplace to the West of us some asshole didn't have a clue what was coming his way. He would know when we got there but he would not know when we left because he was gonna be dead, not because I say it but because "They" say it and I know that makes it so.

I asked them if they were ready to head home and put the plan into action, they were so we are.

I was thinking it would be about five days to the canyon but that strung out to ten. One of the mules threw a shoe which hung up in a rock and snapped off a part of the hoof, he was ok but wouldn't be able to be shod for a good while until the hoof grew out. Mules have hard hooves and as a rule can get along just fine without shoes so I removed the other three and let him run barefooted. We split his load up with the others which wasn't a burden since our supplies were getting low. We put the stuff like the tents and bed rolls on him and he was fine but we took it slower for a day or two.

Then Walker came in on three feet and looking for sympathy which he got way too much of in my opinion, which was grounds to discuss current sleeping arrangements all while the big sissy smiled. I hate him. "Do not!" I now shut up. "Smart man"

I will give the mutt his due he had cut the hell out of his right front foot. I had some of that stinky black crap that's good for cuts and after washing the cut and looking close for anything that might be in it I put the stinky stuff on and wrapped the foot real good. While he was playing it for all the sympathy he could I found some leather and in about an hour had a bootie for him which would be on in the morning when we pulled out. By evening the leather was almost worn out so I fell back on an old Marine trick, I used duct tape. That lasted most of the next day so I just put another layer over it, I figured by the time we got home his foot would be as big as the roll of tape, I laughed and they glared.

All this did slow us down but they used the time to work up their idea of a supply list for the coming invasion of California.

I would describe it like this. "One HV with Pig, extra pig in trailer, 50,00 rounds of belted ammo. Fifty extra assorted weapons with another 50 K ammo for them. Then our American Express weapons we never leave home without. A few cans of fuel, a few cans of beans and we were ready to go.

I'm glad I'm the adult in this cluster fk coz somebody best be! I believe we might trade some ammo space for more food and fuel. But I'll do it quietly. "Just try it buddy boy!" "Why do I bother?" "We ask that a lot too." "Shit." "Stop cussing." You see? Life in a pillow case with cute rabid baby badgers.

We had a surprise today. We were riding along enjoying the sun as it washed the cold of the high desert away when we heard a sound not heard anymore, it took a moment to recognize the sound of an airplane off in the distance, I moved us close to a overhang and into shadows, careful is not a waste of time.

It became obvious the plane was flying a search pattern and shortly it was in sight. Sandy had the glasses out and after a long look said "It's our plane!!" I took a long look and said "Well yeah it looks like it! It has 2 wings and a spinnie thingie on the front." She didn't laugh. As it came closer on every pass it did become obvious it was our plane, our "Air Force." We rode out into the open and were spotted right away; it banked toward us and flew overhead. I could see somebody looking down at us and a hand waving.

When it flew back over as slow as it could go a message tube with a high glow yellow streamer flew out the window. Sandy took off to recover it and returned with it. Inside was a note that said. "Chopper coming soon stay here." It was signed by Willy Bean. When the bird flew back over we all waved, the wings waggled and it flew away.

We looked around a bit and found a wash with graze in it and turned the stock out to eat while we sat in the shade of the overhang. Walker stayed with the stock; he was turning into a wonderful addition to the family. I mean he always was but he was so smart he picked out jobs for himself to do that relieved one of us.

We spent several minutes talking about what it could be but gave that up and just settled into a restful silence. It was three hours later that we heard the chopper coming. As soon as we heard the chopper May went to the livestock to keep them settled, not that we expected any problems but best to be safe.

As soon as the bird was down and the rotors slowed a bit the door opened and Willy and Joe jumped out and were running stooped over headed for us. After the howdy's and hand shaking and hugs from the girls we retreated to the shade and sat down to hear the news. Ralph finished walking around the bird like he was looking for bullet holes then joined us.

Willy made a 'you first' motion to Joe who said "Guess what!" I hate this game so I refused to play, but Sandy and May started off with wide eyed wild assed guesses that went from not likely to fkn never gonna happen and after a while Joe waved his hands and said "Shut up and let me tell you." He's better at the game then me. He said "You ain't never gonna guess what anyway!!" Sandy slugged him on the shoulder and he got back on track.

The news was Ta-Da!! The Asshole from Vegas had surfaced and our radio geeks snared him like a fish and knew right where he was!! I turned and looked at May and then Sandy and asked "How did ya'll know?" They both just looked smug and then I had to explain to the guys what was going on.

Willy said "You three were planning on heading out with one HV to find this guy?" I shrugged and pointed at "them." Joe just nodded in understanding. Willy said "Have you ever just once said not only no but HELL NO!!??" I laughed out loud along with Ralph; Joe kept quiet while they stared at Willy. He finally held his hands up and said "Pardon the hell out of me!! What was I thinking?" Now we all laughed, Willy is such a coward!

I just sat back and made a come on

motion so they got back on track and told the story.

"The comm geeks had set up a tower on a high hill with a damn near straight shot to the west, then they started monitoring a scanner that grabbed every signal that popped up and after a week they hit the jackpot. They were getting clear transmissions from a powerful base station and from conversations in the clear soon knew they had located the leader of the gang in Vegas. That was the up side, the down side was he was recruiting as fast as he could and was openly saying he was coming for us!"

I sat there for a bit and decided that this was good news, we knew he was coming, we knew where he was and we knew this area, he on the other hand was out of his element, even if he had fought in the Middle East his experience there wasn't gonna do a lot of good here in this desert, this would become a rifleman's war and one thing we had was riflemen, everybody in our "army" was first and foremost a rifleman and all were well versed at long range shooting and even if you have armor sooner or later those men in the armor have to come out and when they do a single rifle shot from 300 yards out will put the fear in them. No, this piece of garbage wasn't gonna do well here.

But we did have a problem in that as he rolled along he would be adding other trash to his gang and causing a lot of trouble to innocents just trying to survive. We would have to find a way to deal with this problem because we couldn't just sit back and let him roll over people while looking for us.

We spent a couple of hours brainstorming it and decided we had time to figure it out and get it right before he got here.

We were only two days riding time out of the canyon area and if we pushed it we could make it sooner. Walker was doing ok with his foot and the mule was fine with the light load so we told them to head back and start working up an inventory of supplies on hand including the vast pile of stuff at Fort Navajo. They were going to fly to the Fort and do just that.

We headed out on as much of a direct course as we could and pushed till just before dark.
We had water at this camp and had a hurried meal, and sacked out, the girls chattering about the coming battle, me just counting stars; I think I was asleep by two hundred.

Morning came and by first real light we were on the road again and moving at a good clip. I kept an eye on Walker but he was doing ok as was the mule so we kept pushing and by dark we were only hours out from home Camp was the same as the night before but no water so we used the water bags and everybody got a good drink.

Morning found us moving with just some dried trail mix and coffee in us but we were almost home so that wasn't an issue. Just before mid-day we rode into the canyon and were surrounded by everybody. It felt good to step down off of Buck who was just as happy to have me off of him.

The older boys took the stock away and unloaded the packs at our cave door then took them to water then into the deep blind canyon that had graze.

I stood there for a minute and then headed for the lake where I pulled off my boots, emptied my pockets and removed anything water might damage and fell over backward into the cool water, close to shore it was warm and a dozen yards out it was cool, I just hung there floating while the girls hurried to catch up. Being smarter then me they took time to pull clean cloths and soap and towels from the pack and then joined me. In the water they peeled off their clothes and turned it into a skinny dip. I joined them.

Everybody stayed away and let us have

some privacy and we really scrubbed the road dust off. May swam back to shore and walked out in her beautiful birthday suit and returned with a bottle of JW!! God I love these women.

Walker did come down and wade around but he was not gonna ever be a water dog. We soaked and just relaxed for an hour then got out and dried off and put on the sweats the girls brought. We wrung out the wet clothing and carried it to some bushes near the cave as I insist on calling it.

We went in and fell into bed and never moved till early evening, then we went out front and sat down in the deck chairs salvaged from a hardware store.
After a few minutes the girls went off and returned with a lot of food. In the canyon you could get a platter and wander from fire to fire and fill up on whatever was being served. Everybody was welcome at anybody's fire and it made for some great conversation and fellowship. People would leave their fire and go eat some at a different fire. We have a good life here and I intend to see we keep it.

Willy drifted over and was followed shortly by Joe then Ralph. All that was missing was Charley whom I missed a lot when we were off on some trip. Sandy leaned over and smiling gave me a kiss and said "It's ok baby." And there come a pickup that pulled up and Charley got out. I should have been surprised but I really wasn't, this is the canyon, this is Navajo land, nothing surprises me anymore, in fact I would have been very surprised if Charley hadn't arrived right after Sandy said that.

I stood to meet him and told him I was happy he was here. He smiled and said "I'm happy to be here my brother." I've never had such a bond with another human with the exception of the girls. It's a wonderful thing; a gift to be cherished.

We sat in the cooling evening and drank some new kind of tea made from some weed the women of the canyon had found that hadn't killed anybody yet and it was good and pretty cold too, since it was pulled from the depths of the lake. As I said, we have a wonderful life here and we will keep it.

Charley said the comm geeks had called his people and since we used only Charley's people as our talkers nobody knew what was what unless they had somebody who was able to translate it. Doubtful. Anyway, he headed this way as soon as we arrived so it worked out very well

We talked late into the night about how to save the folks in this turds line of march and all we could come up with was to have people moving along his route a day or two ahead of him spreading the word to get out of the way, and hope they would. We also thought about offering a new home here on the lake, but only to the ones who looked like they were workers and who had built a decent community, anybody else was on their own. The one way to really screw up what we were building was to invite in trashy elements and that was out of the question. Picky? You bet, non PC? Fkn A.

Everybody here was a worker, a grower or a builder or a shooter who guarded the area. In other words doers welcome takers not so. Hard yes for sure, but we here in this place were not going to make the same mistakes that were made just a few years back. We were no longer an entitlement society.

Here everybody was entitled to get up with the sun, entitled to work and build and be a productive member of the community or they were entitled to pack their ass on down the road. Minus any small kids, teens fine, they could choose, under that and they couldn't, they would have a nice home here with people who cared for them and would show them a better way. Of course that was just talk; it had never been an issue, not once. I couldn't even think of anybody who shirked any job, people would just show up to help

with anything being done and when it was
done they would wander off looking for
something else to do.
We have a good life here. Did I mention that?

After a couple of days talking about
how to deal with the guy who was coming to
fuck with us Charley headed home but not
before making me promise to bring the girls
to see the Old Woman and of course I did,
like I have a choice.

Now it's time to get the plans we made
going and then work out our battle plan. War
sucks but damn it we sure seem to spend a lot
of time doing it.

For now it's days end, the nights
are cold here in the high desert but the cave is
warm with a couple of sticks burning in the
fireplace, more to look at then anything else.
The girls are reading, I'm just staring at the
fire and Walker is trying to weasel up onto the
bed but that ain't happening.

The girls just had the idea of getting the
bearskin out and putting it on the bed.

"I wonder why?"

Until next time.
TJ

Thank you all, I hope this book pleased you all as much as it did me. I was stuck for a week trying to come up with an ending and one came up. I like how that happens.

Book eight will be starting soon..

Thank you for enjoying my efforts and if you didn't then thank you for trying and I'm sorry it didn't work out for you.

TJ

# The Long Lonely Road

## Desert Winds

### Book eight

### By
### TJ Reeder

We had spent the last couple of weeks in the Canyon we called home, peaceful, quiet, Silent.

Well most of the time it is quiet, I'm up in my secret place, it's a ridge splitting our canyon from the main lake. If I want I can sit on the edge of the cliff and look down on the entire settlement, or I can walk about fifty or so yards and look out at the lake. It's fairly flat up here and I've packed up a rubber sleeping mat and love just watching the clouds drift over.

The sounds of laughter can be heard like a distant bird calling. I can see sail boats out on the lake where folks are running fishing lines. The lake is our bread basket so to speak, Water, food, and it keeps us cool in the heat of the summer. The canyon shelters us in it's heart of stone thru the cold. I love it here.

I love dozing in the warm winter sun, I can

sleep and hear the birds. They call my name.

"John"
  Silence
"JOHN!"
"Go away, I'm not here."
"Yes you are"
"No I'm not"
  John If you don't open your eyes we will throw you off the cliff!
"I laugh"…..wrong thing to do.
 One sits on my chest, one on my belly and that fkn mutt trying to step on my balls, I hate them!
" Do not"

Finally after not breathing for five minutes I asked what they wanted now. They didn't move, I asked them to pout off of me. Nothing. Shit, I groveled and said please tell me what I can do to make you happy.

I hate myself for being weak, but with no air in my lungs it's hard to be a walking talking bad ass.

At last they slid off on each side, now they were bringing the other weapons to the fight, they must really want something big. I may as well give in now.

   After I could breath and they buttered me up a bit we got down to it. And they surprised me, A lot!

May said, John you love it up here in your "secret" spot. We love it up here in your "not so secret spot"
( snickering) and we love our Hobbit home but we like being able to look out over long distances.

I looked at Sandy who said 'Yea what May said" then added that they wanted a place they could look out and see the world, not the other wall of the canyon, plus after being with me they had learned the value of taking the high ground and would rather be up here.

I said why not just tell me this instead of crushing my ribs in? They both gave me their killer smile and May said " cause it's more fun to torture you into giving in"? then they both laughed, shit so did I.

I love them. Dangerous pets, but loveable.

So we took a walk and I looked it over with a different eye and soon I could see what they meant. The view is awesome, and it's for sure the high ground! Hell we could see the settlement across the lake, well we could see the smoke and smoke from several smaller places along the shore line.

We walked out onto the very point of the ridge where it dropped off what looked like a mile but was probably three or four hundred feet. A long way!

I did point out that if we were ever over run and had our backs to the edge we were fked!

May said well then don't ever let that happen ok? Sigh. Then I asked what and how we were going to build up here when getting stuff up here was damn near impossible.

That's when I learned they had been working on this all the time I was laying up here soaking up the quiet.

First of all I have failed to mention that when we got here we found that Harvey and his family of miners had arrived and fell in love with the place, but they needed more room then we had so they started looking for a home canyon of their own, and found it about a half mile away, it was as big as ours and it too had a creek of fresh water running into it, as hard as it is for people to believe there is a lot of water in the desert country. Their creek was smaller then ours but was plenty for them.

They had also found a great place for digging cave ( Hobbit) homes into the red rock of the canyon walls. I call it sand stone, hell it could be granite for all I know, rock is rock. Anyway they had found a good place with soil above the high water mark in any low spot, the run off builds up soil pockets and makes for great gardening.

Harv and his clan had brought everything including the kitchen sinks and among their goods was air driven rock drills and a pretty good supply of blasting powder and the knowledge to use it right. By the time we had got home from burning Vegas and all the other stuff they were settled in and still working deeper into the cliffs, our places were small but comfy theirs were large and very comfy!

It was great seeing them again and of course I caught a lot of shit for burning Vegas. The girls got to use all their comments like
" What burns in Vegas stays in Vegas ." I won't go into all of them, some get pretty raunchy and there were kids present.

Anyway, they had been working with Harv and his Moles and had cut a deal for them to bring their rock working experience up here and build our home, which they had already drawn out! While I snoozed.

I looked at their plan and could find no fault with it, oh sure there was minor details like getting water up here but they had talked to others and they had a plan. It was looking like the whole damn group was involved.

I was kind of ashamed of myself for crapping out while others planned the work.

Sandy patted me on the head and said it was ok, building big fires was hard work. (Laugh - laugh) They never let up.

May snuggled me and said "It's ok John, it was a really nice fire" ( laugh-laugh) Actually it was a really cool fire, I didn't know concrete and glass could burn so well, but those many tens of thousands of cars parked in the city with fuel in them were an added bonus!

They had laid out the new house with a decided Spanish influence, open rooms, plenty of windows to let light in and a couple of fire places. A large master bedroom and a pair of smaller guest rooms. And of course a large gun room, very large, May was just starting to get into collecting but Sandy really had a big collection, I will say that they were all unusual or real collectors items she had found or bartered for, plus the troops went out of their way to bring them both goodies. I left it to them. It was their baby I was just gonna live in it, the living room was huge by hobbit hole standards, the dividing wall between the living room and our bedroom had the bigger fire place which was open into both rooms. They had really worked on this and I was proud of them.

The whole place was going to be made from big blocks of stone quarried from the ridge. The walls looked to be two feet thick. I had to ask just how we were paying for this? Of course they smiled that smile and said " Don't worry John, you'll think of something." (sigh)

I left that to them and the Moles, I had bigger fish to fry, mainly the asshat in Barstow who seems to be pissed off about something. Dude either don't have a sense of humor or don't drink enough!

I could send him a slap in the mouth and challenge him to a shoot out but 'they' would drug me and one of them would shoot the bastard and I'd be snoozing. I know them too well!

I did have boots on the ground out there close to his rats nest, thanks to Charley and his people who seem to be everywhere. Somebody's brothers first cuz's aunt's uncle knew somebody who lived near the area and so Charley sent a radio team out there so we knew he was there and not sneaking up our ass from the East.

They didn't have eyeballs on the dude but they did know where he lived and it was a big place with a wall and guard.

My first thought was to cobble together an air strike with Ralph and his air wing, but we couldn't get anything off the ground big enough to do the job . But he was working on some other stuff and I knew from the smile from "them" that it had to do with the chopper and some kind of guns. I really thought I raised them proper but someplace they went wrong. Or maybe I did? Naaa, can't be that. Whatever, I plan to keep them both grounded where the chopper is concerned. (" keep thinking that buddy boy") Get out of my head!

May looked at me all funny and said John? Are you ok? Are you have daymares? While awake? I told them both no way were they gonna lay this shit off on me! They do something, whatever it is, it ain't me! I hear them in my head when nobody around us hears them. Now they are laughing so I tell them I'm gonna have a talk with Charles's mom! They really laugh and say his mom don't even talk to him about anything so good luck with that. I file that one away.

Back to the asshat, my plan is to wait until he makes a move and then plan a counter but I think I have it lined out so I'm gonna start the first phase of the plan today. I ask them if they wanna be included in the plan but they say no, they already have a plan, I know better but I have to ask what that might be? Sandy said "well we decided to kill him". May said "yep, that's our plan. Simple." So I left them there and went in search of my troops. Actually I had told them to meet me in the blind canyon we used for a range. When I got there I had about 30 people, both sexes, all had rifles with them which is as it is, always.

I explained what I had in mind and said anybody who wanted to opt out of this phase was free to go. One of the ladies said she had a cake in her earth oven and took off. We sat around for a while talking about what I wanted to do and what the idea was and everybody liked it a lot, coz nobody wants to play Marine (" Hey diddle diddle, straight up the middle") nope we were going to fight the careful war and if my plan worked we just might win and not lose anybody. I like that.

We had the ability to shoot out to five hundred yards here and I had steel targets made out of good steel cut in the shape of a human torso. First thing was to sight in the rifles at 100 yards then get to work. I should add that all the rifles were bolt guns we had picked up as we went. I guess I had a plan like this in mind all along because all of them were whatever the shooter wanted and could handle, nothing smaller then 308 up to a few 300 magnums.
My plan was simple, when we knew the Asshats route we would pick the place for the fight and it was gonna be a long range sniper battle between us and his ground troops, Our armor would deal with his, but the shooters would be in secure bunkers built to hold up to three people, I wanted help in case somebody got hit, one shooting and one doing first aid, I had this plan all laid out in my head and I believed it would work. I wanted no more

funerals if we could possibly avoid it. The when wasn't important, the where was critical.

We had 10 shooters on line and the rest acting as spotters, the 100 yards sight in was just a formality because everybody here was a damn good shooter, so the 100 yard stuff was done pretty fast. I wanted them sighted in dead on at 300 yards and to know just what to do to make 500 yard shots.

The first relay started slow firing and the steel was clanging, I saw a couple working on their scope adjustments and when everybody was happy I called out one at a time, the object was to hit the 300 yard steel with the five shots in the bolt gun. But also with speed. The first shooter had five shots off in under ten seconds with one miss, the rest took a bit longer but nobody missed a shot.
        The first shooter ask for a reshoot and was hooted loudly while smiling and flipping everybody off. At the buzz of the timer he opened fire and did it in under the 10 seconds with no misses, amid more teasing and some clapping he bowed. We got everybody thru the three hundred in good order with only two people having trouble, I was willing to believe it might be a scope problem or maybe a tight spot in the stock warped and pressing the barrel a bit, we would work on that.

At the four hundred the firing slowed a bit but the hits were very good, a few misses but that's to be expected. At the five hundred I told them to slow it down and work at a hit every shot. By now they all knew where their rifle shot and they delivered. Nobody rushed it and other then the same two with the rifle issues it was a clean sweep.

I saw everybody look past me and turned around in time to face two very pissed off ladies, who marched up and started finger poking me in the chest while taking turns talking. The gist of it was " How can you just go off shooting and not tell us? How can you treat us this way? What did we do to deserve this?" On and on until I felt terrible which was their goal.

Finally I just gave up and told them that tomorrow we would do it again just for them. Smiles, I hate that I get played like a cheap piano in a whore house, but that's my fate so I take it like a man, after I gave in and gave them what they wanted the others applauded the performance and got bows and curtseys out of the two...

Of course everybody had seen them work me before and everybody loved the show, sometimes when I try to be strong and fight back the audience boos me and if "they" start pushing me around they get cheers and shouts of " Hit him, kick his ass!!" well you get the picture? I'm abused. Now why did I say that out loud? I'm being booed. I give up and take a bow myself which gets cheered.

We really don't have much to do so we make fun when we can. Why am I always the bad guy? Now they are each holding an arm and we head home. Life took a twist and a lot of turns but I swear that outside the deaths and the hardship at the beginning it's turned out damn well.

I asked what was for supper and they had no idea but grabbed their bowls and tossed me mine, so I guess we were going bumming tonight.

First we had rabbit stew with wild greens of some kind and garden veggies.

The next fire had thin sliced deer with a garlic sauce and new potatoes creamed with new green peas. And so it goes, hot bread and fresh butter at the next fire where we sit to eat, then on to the cake that Beth, the lady shooter took off to save! It was awesome! She told the girls about having to leave early so they told her they were shooting the next day and she was welcome. Everybody was happy, I was stuffed and as the sun started hiding behind the edge of the canyons rim we thanked everybody for the great meal and headed for the hobbit home and early night to bed, not sleep, just to bed. I'm too full of dinner, that didn't work.

Morning is my favorite time of the day, the

canyon is still kind of warm from the day
before, there is a wisp of foggy vapor curling
off the water and I head for my stump outside
the door, cup of coffee in hand and followed
by two quiet, sleepy snuggle bunnies who
drag a blanket with them so my stump ( log,
flattened ) gets crowded in a nice way, one
under each arm. It's hard to drink my coffee
this way but it's how our day starts and I love
it.


I get a lot of thinking done this time of the
day, but soon it will get to be a normal day in
the abnormal life we now live. Well our new
normal.

Without giving it any thought I got up and
ambled over to another of my sitting spots on
a rock point that jutted out over the canyon
back water, during the heat of the day the kids
played here using it as a diving cliff all of
four feet to water about six foot deep. I liked
the spot because you could see down into the
water and watch the fish. I stood there just
looking at my shadow jutting out over the
water and soon I heard "them" coming, still
grumping at the early day.
We stood there me in the middle and them
on each side just admiring the day. Until I
dropped my hands down to their butts and
with just a little push off they went!! It was
beautiful!!

Well it would have been but each of them grabbing frantically managed to get a bit of my shirt and we all three went off the rock!

They screamed! Loud! I would have but my nads were trying to climb up into my throat. Then they were sitting on my head on the bottom. I think, which they later denied, they were trying to drown me. Just as I got loose and stood up that fkn mutt hearing his mommies screaming launched himself right into my chest and back to the bottom. And he hates water!

With Walker working his feet to get someplace else I was getting scratched all to hell and gone so I launched away from it all and surfaced twenty feet from shore where they were still trying to make shore and cussing a blue streak! I started laughing and couldn't stop. Most of the community was now standing on the ledge looking at us, most were holding weapons. I love my extended family.

I saw Joe look at Willy and nod and their wives were launched into the water and it turned into a free for all with people falling in as they lost out in the battle to remain dry. I was still laughing when "They" came for me. Both had stripped to their gym shorts and tank tops and were hell bent on drowning me.

The water war as it came to be called lasted for a half hour with the kids getting in to it which kinda tamed down the action since we

are after responsible adults ( yea right ) I
grinned at them and caught them both up
since I was standing on the bottom and they
were a foot away from touching, a kiss and a
big hug got them to laughing and we all
realized we were freezing so I walked out
with one on each arm.

Great way to start the day! Next, Breakfast!
Community breakfast, decided by the women
while they were peeling off the soaked cloths
and wringing them out. While nudity isn't a
practice here in the canyon, working on ones
all over tan is accepted and everybody has
seen everybody else in their skin suit so it's
not a big deal. Plus from all the changes in
our life style we all looked pretty good so!
Just saying.

    Now that that little note is settled the ladies
trooped off to find dry cloths and started
getting breakfast ready.

    After they were gone us guys sat down on
the rocks and were soon talking about the
coming battle, I went over my plan again to
air it out and get input to fill the blank places.
If everybody is involved in the decision
making it makes it better.

    One very valid question was why I was
restricting the snipers to bolt guns? It being
pointed out that we have enough very good
auto loaders to do the job just as well and
have much better fire power. Good point!

    I get stuck in my old Marine head on the

subject because I was trained to believe the bolt guns our snipers used were the cats ass, but in truth my AR 10 was just as good as my bolt gun. So we changed that right there, everybody could use what they wanted.

One of the guys pointed out that his lady was a damn good shot with her AR 15 because it didn't beat the shit out of her. And 300 yards wasn't much of a shot at a human size target.

So I was getting good feed back and all valid points leading to a change in the tactics I was planning. One of the men asked why we were doing it this way and I reminded them how well the canyon ambush went and that this guy wasn't going to get caught again so what better plan then to hit him in the open, the last way and place he would expect?

All this gave me more ideas and were going to involve a road trip to recon for the right place to meet the dude. Breakfast was calling so we trooped off for that. My ladies were helping by doing the pan cakes which with eggs is their idea of heaven only made better with bacon which we have. It's canned which is fine but we will need to be thinking about that in the future since we can't live off a dead country forever. One of the really good things was some jelly made from a cactus by one of the ladies and when heated it turned kinda back to like thick syrup! Awesome! Have I mentioned life is good here in the canyon?

After breakfast we headed to the hobbit hole to clean up after the "swim", Then I took the girls and Beth to the range for some rifle work.

The girls needed rifle practice like a duck needs to practice swimming but it was their chance to have fun and of course compete against each other, Beth the other lady like most of the ladies in our bunch had been involved in our little wars and showed her stuff real fast. After punching the five hundred target eight out of ten I told her to go make a cake or something, she laughed but said she was gonna get involved in the on going match between "them" when she got into the equation they settled down and quit screwing off. I'd have to say they were all about even so that was settled, Beth asked to the 1911's. so I wondered off to tell the loading crew to step up production of 45 acp since I could see a new rising star.

The funny thing about hand guns is that most people seem to think the "plastic" guns like Glock and the Springfield XD series are the cats ass, now I've owned several of both in 9mm, 40mm and 45 ACP and I like them , they are very good weapons.

But I believe if your out of ammo you should be able to beat the bastards to death with a solid chunk of steel. But that's just me. The girls just followed along with me I guess. I never really asked.

I know Sandy grabs every 1911 she see's unless it's some off breed type. She does love them, May, I think just went with Sandy because. Beth I don't know really, I think she's about the same age as the girls with long light brown hair and green eyes, she's really good looking and I wonder why she lives alone, but it's her business, She may be one we rescued from the slavers and don't want anything to do with a man. That's fine, can't blame her a bit.

I wondered over to the loading trailer and put in my order for more 45's and the two old boys laughed and said they had already started because they could hear the bark of the 45's going pretty steady, These two ol boys had loaded every round of ammo ever fired by man kind I believe, if it used powder and a primer they had loaded it and they were a couple of interesting old coots. One asked me if we needed some 45-70 rounds for Wyatts 1886 she got from old man Jones, I laughed and said nope, they each fired it 5 shots and cleaned it and hung in on the cabin wall by my hundred year old Swedish Mauser, both laughed and said they would load some rounds the girls could handle just so they could shoot the rifle with out breaking a shoulder. And a light bulb went off!, I asked them if they had any 10mm's? they laughed and said shit John we got ammo for stuff that ain't seen the light of day for a hundred years.

I took a couple of boxs and headed for the cave where I found that STI and hauled it to the range where they were taking a break, I laid it and the boxes of ammo down and they were both up grabbing.

Sandy said I'm first coz I went back for it! May said big deal I killed the fucker!! Beth asked to see it and asked if she could shoot it?

Both of the girls said sure with smiles, then went to fighting over who was next, I sat in the shade and waited for the fun. I felt sorry for Beth but she would soon know.

I watched Beth load the mag and call out 'fire in the hole" which stopped the cat fight since they had to put ear plugs in as did I. Beth took a good stance and in one move brought the gun up and dumped 10 rounds into the 25 yard steel target that could be covered with my hand, now I was interested, the girls were busy both trying to loading the mag and I settled it by flipping a coin, May won, she took a good grip and fired a shot and looked a bit surprised then another, after a total of five she handed it to Sandy without a word, Sandy let fly and almost lost it! She looked at me then May who was smiling a " Gotcha" smile, so Sandy fired four more and laid it down and kind of shook her hand. I loaded it and fired 10 rounds off fast and when I looked I had to admit Beth's target had a bit tighter group then mine! I took another look at her and saw her eyes kind of sparkling a bit so I reloaded the mag with 10 more and handed her the gun and mag, she loaded it and took her time aiming and I noticed she was aiming high, she fired and the 100 yard steel rang out then she did it nine more times. Doc and Wyatt were kind of stunned and I was pretty impressed myself.

She laid the gun one the bench and smiled a big smile and said did I pass the test? I said what test? but she was looking at the girls, both smiled real big and said OH Hell yes!!! Sandy picked the gun up and handed it to Beth and said welcome to the club babe!! And they all three laughed out loud. I was slow I'll admit. But I had to ask how in the hell she learned to shoot like that. She said her Husband had one and she used to shoot it a lot with him, He was killed in the raid that took her as a slave.
    I told her I was impressed and that I'd work on finding extra mags for the gun if she wanted, she did, so I put that on my list,

looked like Old Bear wasn't getting this one.

I told the girls we were leaving in the morning to see Charley and we might be gone a few days on a scout to the west, I headed back leaving them collecting brass and chattering away like old friends, they could become best friends with somebody in a heart beat, or kill them in the same time span, I'm afraid I somehow raised them wrong.

I went by the vehicle storage area and was checking the dodge out and the mechanics wondered over and after hearing what I had in mind said they would look it over for me, well I was feeling pretty useless so I went off to the ridge and took a nap.

Morning came and I started hauling our gear to the truck and found it all cleaned up and looking new, the guys said they were bored. I thanked them and headed back for more gear, I passed the girls who said they had it and I should look around to make sure I hadn't missed anything. I hadn't and joined them and found Walker sitting on top of the canvas covered load like he owned the damn truck.

I just mumbled and climbed in, fired it up and was rolling before I noticed somebody sitting right behind me. I turned the mirror and saw Beth sitting there. Sandy and May had small smiles on their faces and I had a

funny feeling something was going on that I
didn't know about (Voice in head " no shit
Sherlock!) I refused to bite I just took off and
we were on the road again, Sandy turned on
the radio and there was Willy singing it! What
a crew, I figured I'd be informed in time what
was going on but I think I already knew, I
think I just got another orphan. How they
work this out is beyond me but I'm not gonna
ask, maybe it's just taking Beth under their
wings as a friend ( Laughter in my head) Shit!
( Stop cussing!)

We rolled into Shiprock and there stood
Charley waiting with a smile, I love this man
like the brother I never had. He makes my life
complete family wise. We unloaded and the
girls headed right to him with Beth in tow and
Sandy did the introductions. He greeted Beth
with a smile and offered his hand which she
took, he didn't shake it he just held it then
nodded and said something to Sandy who
smiled real big and they were off to see Old
Woman who was waiting on the front porch.
They disappeared inside and it was quiet
again

We sat in the shade and time passed and
finally Charley did the little polite cough that
was his notice he was about to speak.
He looked at me and said " How do you get
into this much trouble"? What trouble I asked
? "Beth" he said, Oh she's a friend of the girls

and they brought her along because she's lonely. He just shook his head and sighed and after a bit said " You are without doubt the dumbest white man I ever met!

Well I was a bit shocked at that so I had to ask why he said that. He shook his head again and said remember when Sandy brought May into your family? I said you were gonna do well in Utah? I just looked at him and then started stuttering and said oh no!! no way! He sat a while and I pondered what was going on, He sighed again which he does a lot around me and said are your eyes open yet?

I just sighed back and said maybe your wrong? he almost smiled at that and shook his head slowly. I could feel a door closing behind me and didn't know why.

At last I had to set this aside and asked him about his thoughts on a scouting trip along the likely route of march of our enemy. He said it was a good idea and he wanted to show me something so we went inside to find the ladies ready to serve lunch so we sat and ate, Beth was paying way more attention to the girls talk then was needed with quick glances at me, Finely I took the reins in my hand and said" Welcome to the family Beth, if you want to be" The sneaky pair jumped up and took turns hugging me and then Beth and the Old Woman was actually laughing out loud, kinda.

Beth had tears in her eyes and I stood up and offered my hand which she took and I hugged her for a long time while she cried quietly. When she was back under control we finished lunch, I asked the girls how they felt about waiting here while Charley and I took a trip to look at something, they surprised me by saying fine.

Charley took a black hat off the pegs by the door and handed it to me saying with my dark tan and the hat and riding in his old truck I would look like one of the people, several more men were already in the back of the truck along with a couple of women.

We looked like any one of the trucks you see in this area full of people heading someplace where it seems there ain't a place.

We were all armed which was normal so off we went, the old truck was old on the outside but whatever was under the hood wasn't old!

But we just poked along like all the people do, never in a rush, that's reserved for the white man.

We drove for a good ways on highway 64 until it turned into the junction of 160 and 91, from there we headed West on 160 and then it was off the pavement and over back dirt roads and goat paths and no paths and eventually we slowed down and stopped, where we all got out, the women stayed by the truck and

the men and I headed up a small hill, near the
top they dropped down on their belly's so I
did too, when in Rome and all that jazz!
When I saw Charley ease up behind a bush
and take his hat off I did the same and
crawled up beside him. We were looking
down on the small town of Kayenta which
was on state road 163 and below us about half
a mile from the road was a small camp, with
binoculars I could count four men in the camp
and one up on a hill doing just what we were
doing except we were higher and could see
the small town over the hill they were on.

Now I will admit I was a bit puzzled and
after looking at Charley he eased back down
the hill leaving a couple of the others
watching, back at the truck he said he had all
along figured this junction was the one the
Enemy would use instead of the big interstate
40 to come at us because the Interstate had a
lot of people around it and word would leak
out ahead of him.

Charley said he figured the man was going
to come at us with hit teams leading the way
quietly killing everybody in their path. While
I know it's cold and not something I would
ever be a part of I knew where he was coming
from.

He wanted us dead, Me dead and he wanted
to take no chances. But this wise Warrior was
leagues ahead of him and had people in the
hills just waiting to see who might show up
and they did. Now we were forewarned, and

could prepare for the fight.

I told Charley about the idea of using long range firepower to chew them up and with the mortar units and the tracks we could rule the battlefield from a distance reducing our chances of losses. He nodded and said he just might know of a place that would work perfectly but we also needed to wave some bait under his nose, something to make him come when we wanted him to. That was something to work on.

We headed back and arrived at dusk to find the ladies chewing their nails, they thought we were going away for an hour or so.

I credit the presents of Old Woman and several of the other women in calming them down so I didn't get beat to death. We all sat and ate a nice rabbit stew and what's called fry bread, filling and tasty.

Afterwards we sat outside and watched the night gather and the stars. listening to the night birds. We didn't talk about the day or the coming battle, that was for the daylight, now was the quiet time to just breath and feel mother earth. While we were gone the girls had set up the big tent. I had no idea what was on the evening agenda but I was tired, Charles's old truck may have a wild assed motor but the suspension was rough on my ass. I told Charley I was heading to bed and got a chuckle in return, he headed inside where the girls and Old Woman were doing whatever, maybe stirring a caldron full of bat wings, I smiled at that thought and went to the tent where I found the bed all made up and looking bigger then usual, also I found a glass of JW sitting there so I tossed that back, undressed and slid into my usual spot. I don't even remember my head hitting the pillow, I remember waking up rested and alone then not alone, left side? May, so I gently pulled her over and curled up like spoons and went back to sleep.

At some point my mind woke up to the fact that May felt different some how, I checked and all the parts were where they belonged but different, And her hair was tickling my nose so I blew it away like always and opened one eye and found that over night her hair had changed color! I did another inventory and realized I had been ambushed…again.

I gave up without a fight, weak sorry example of a man that I am. Later, I'd like to say much later but maybe not that much later, Beth and I made our way to the café and found the girls helping make lunch and they grabbed Beth and away they went.

I went looking for Charley and said ok, what did they put in the booze? He looked at me and said
" Beats the shit out of me! They don't talk to me either" Now this was so out of character for Charley I just busted out laughing, then he

joined in. After a bit he said he really didn't know what I was talking about but asked if I woke up refreshed and feeling good? I said oh yea, he nodded and said don't ask, you really don't want to know. Now I was really worried but WTF, I was alive and felt good even if I did feel like I had been put out to stud. But somehow I figured this was more then that and I would be informed when it was time. Ours wasn't the only "extended" family in the settlement. One lady had two husbands and another was three women and two men, all were happy as could be and nobody thought anything about it. Several of the ladies we rescued lived together and nobody asked or cared what was what. It just wasn't our business

I know some might say how about the kids? Well a lot of the kids here with us are orphans and were saved by us and had a sad lesson in growing up fast and we as a whole were raising them with all the love we could give, they were happy, safe, warm and fed and cared for, they didn't care who slept with who, just being here and with us was all they cared about and every person in our family, clan, group, tribe whatever would fight thru hell for these kids and in most cases had in fact done so. Nuff said.

The kids pretty well lived where they wanted, here one night there another, they were with family no matter where they laid their head down.

I love our clan and life is good in the canyon, have I mentioned that?

I should wonder about how it looks to the others but I don't care nor will they.
After so much death we have learned to live for the day and to love the same way.

The important part of the whole trip had shown that whatever was coming was coming soon, the advance scouts being watched by Charles's people wouldn't be here now if the attack wasn't coming soon. But we had to assume that the leader if he was in fact a former military officer would have had some training in the art of war altho the ambush in the canyon showed he didn't have much or just didn't care if his troops got wiped out.

After we were all fed we loaded up in the Dodge and followed Charley in his truck to see the area he was thinking of as our battle zone.

The main advantage of making him come to us lies in the fact that a long road march of military hardware always results in break downs, also the troops get exhausted with the constant movement, even just sitting a truck for hours and hours followed by days and weeks will beat down anybody and that's how we wanted them, tired, wore down and with their equipment in rough shape, And of course it's always best to fight on ground you've had your boots and eyes on.

The plan was actually very simple, the troops riding in open trucks were sitting ducks for good long range shooters. They would have armor of some type for sure but so do we. If they bring tanks then we will need to deal with them but we have tracks with anti tank weapons, we just never used them before. But the crews were trained very well by the people who had used them in combat.

All I could ask for was a nice place where the road passed thru a low spot where my people on the high ground would have a turkey shoot, the tracks would be once again dug in, hull down as it's called or was a long time ago when I was young. I wanted all our people shooting from strong cover and nobody exposed more then they had to be to use a weapon.

There is nothing that says there have to be big charges over open ground right into the face of heavy fire, this wasn't Iwo Jima or Gettysburg and I damn sure ain't General Pickett. No ride of the 600 here and no Custers last stand, nope this was gonna be an ambush leaving the enemy exposed and our side under good cover.

The canyon ambush worked like a dream but that wasn't gonna work this time, everybody learns over time and this dude wasn't gonna roll right into a narrow canyon again, but open empty country? Yes I think so. I planned some false radio traffic, seemingly not aware of his advance we would be sitting ducks. Not even. Never fight fair! I used to shoot with a guy whose motto was " If you're not willing to cheat you don't want to win bad enough" I always just shook my head when he said that, but this time I would cheat and lie my ass off to lure this guy into the net.


When we returned to Shiprock Charles's scouts had reported the enemy scouts had packed up and moved out of the area to avoid any chance of contact now that they knew the area, they had headed back the way they came. The way was now open for us to start deciding just what to do and where to do it.

I had given thought to not just where to ambush the man but also how to get him there. I knew where the fight would be or so I hoped as to the bait, well it was me he wanted so I was going to be the Judas goat, except this goat was gonna be armed and ready for the tiger.

We had returned to the canyon to find that Harv and his people were having a grand time making big flat thick rocks from a solid rock area of the ridge and the area was right where anybody attacking the house would have to come meaning a deep hole to get across and since it was possible to drive up onto the ridge if one was very careful, they left a narrow area wide enough to drive across but no more then one vehicle, I don't know or understand the ways and means of working stone but these men had it down for sure. But they had worked in mines all their lives and knew it inside and out.


Bill and Bob Bremmer and families had shown up when we returned, it was good to see them, they had settled a few canyons further down the lake from us and were busy building a home with the help of some of Harv's clan.

The brothers had it in mind to gather some of the wild cattle gather the calves to start a small beef herd since they were happiest on a horse and meat is always welcome, really it was all about doing what they wanted so if herding cows worked for them fine. Their wives were already planting their gardens and their kids were boating to our place to attend the school such as it was, an open air affair with plenty of books that allowed the kids to find something that interested them and several of the people were there to help them in whatever they wanted to study. we really were a diverse group,  so many people with different areas of knowledge that "school' as such was more fun for the kids and the adults enjoyed it as well.

May's group being mostly higher educated
people were awesome at teaching things most
of us had no idea of but kids are sponges and
soaked it up.

We spent a few days on the ridge trying to
help with the house but really getting in the
way, the knowledge and skill of moving huge
slabs of rock where you want them is just as
intensive as building rocket to the moon, just
different skill sets.

After damn near getting my toes flattened I
said to Harv. Fine! I'll stay out of the way! He
laughed and said thanks John, hate to lose you
now that the girls got you house broke (
laughter...right)

They had done some leveling for the
foundation stones and drilled then thru and
deep into the rock floor and used real big
rebar to pin them, when they had the entire
outer wall laid out they floated the floor
inside level using concrete mixed with some
coloring stuff the same as the stone and when
that was dried it was nice and flat, then they
went at it with raising the walls, set a stone
and drill it thru and into the one below and
hammer in the big rebar, they put a layer of
the colored mud between each stone just like
a brick layer would and dressed it as they
went. I was amazed at how fast these guys
worked and it was easy to see they had really
missed working in the sun with good stone,

how they had stood working underground was beyond me.

They had it in hand and knew just what the girls wanted and with Beth now a member of the family they had three people adding their personalities to the mesh and it was working like a well tunes motor.
I wasn't needed so I went about my business. I had people working on getting our battle gear in order, weapons checked and everybody at the range working on improving their skills at long range shooting. The machine gunners spent some time getting laid out to support the riflemen in the unlikely event they enemy attempted to make a full out frontal attack to break our lines. And even the MG gunners would be using long range rifles until needed on the guns.

All the armor was ready and loaded, as were the gun trucks, I started sending the ready units to Charley to take to the ambush area where he was getting them set into place.

We still hadn't had any word that the enemy was on the move but it was expected most any day. I knew all about road marching and knew they could only make so many miles a day and doubted they would just switch drivers and keep rolling.

So it was going to take a good while for

them to get where we wanted them. I was worried that this guy was thinking ahead of me so Charley had scouts out all over the country in all directions looking for any signs of large scale movement.

I was pretty convinced that if this guy was in the Barstow area he knew about desert country and would want to get this out of the way while it was still cool, well cooler then it was gonna be down the road. I know I would.

It was another week before the far western scouts reported movement and as they watched over the next few days people were pouring into the area in all forms of dress and then showing up in BDU's the style called Marpat, (Marine Pattern) which had me wondering if he had access to the supply center in Barstow. I expect he had something going even if it was just side deals with supply personnel. Which would not be good from my point of view.

A week after the people started showing up and getting geared up the transport units showed up. When the word came I was really blown away, they were coming without armor, no tracks!, HV's with MG's, lot of them, but it looked like it was going to be an infantry war.

Which was fine with me. I was not understanding this guy at all, unless we had killed or captured all his tracks, now that was an interesting thought. The scouts reports kept coming in as the days moved along.

One surprise was when a report came in that the scouts had finally noticed some odd vehicles in the convoy and after hearing the description there was no doubt they were Marine LAV's aka, light armored vehicles, these were bad boys! Eight wheeled vehicles that can ford rivers or lakes, armed with the usual M242, 25 mm chain gun plus two M240 machineguns, they carried an operating crew of four and four scouts who also acted as security infantry. This was not real good news but we have the tracks and plenty of armor killing goodies, but and a big BUT, I wanted these units! Really wanted them big time. Meaning I didn't want to kill them if I didn't have to so this was something to be worked on.

It was starting to look like this guy really had access to the supply base in Barstow and something needed to be done about that....someday.

I was kinda bothered by the girls push for the
" Big" house on the hill above everybody else and really thought it might seem a bit like I was having elusions of grandeur and that was the last thing I wanted so I had a talk with Willy and Joe and several of the other folks

and learned that generally speaking most
folks were happier in their hobbit holes
simply because after all they had been thru it
made them feel secure, I guess the girls and I
had been out and about more then most
everybody else and didn't have the desire to
"hide" so to speak.

They thought we were doing what we
wanted to do and everybody knew they could
do the same, no rules, no laws against.

Everybody would help anybody who
wanted to do something from tilling a new
garden plot to building a high dive off the
cliffs, well maybe not that because our kids
had no fear of anything and would be doing
crazy shit, or more crazy shit then they
already do.


We had to really watch them, one of them
found an old bike someplace and they were
riding it down a slope and off the edge and
out into space for about a 40 foot drop into
the canyon waters. Then they would dive
down retrieve the bike and use a rope to drag
it back up the rock face, that lasted until one
didn't get loose from the bike and got a nice
deep cut on the head, "she" was back at it still
bleeding when a "mom for a day" throwing a
fit telling her to get down off that cliff. It was
actually funny because here's this cute little
button of a girl maybe seven years old,
wearing cut off jeans and no top ( just one of

the boys) bleeding from the head who smiles
real big and waves and dives off the edge.
And like a cork bobber shot up and flew thru
the water to shore. We were all watching
while she got chewed out with not a sign of
remorse and got doctored up and started to
climb back up the rock wall.

I never knew that lady knew those words!
It was really funny, well us guys were
laughing for a moment but that changed fast,
women have no sense of humor or don't drink
enough, whatever. It stopped that activity for
about a week then they took the bike further
down the canyon and got back at it. I guess
when you've seen the shit these kids have you
don't fear much.


Our enemy was moving slow and raiding as
they went, but they were finding mostly
empty places since our scouts were spreading
the word about them. People just loaded up
and taking everything they could and moved
out of the way, not that there was that many
people out on that route. In the mean time the
girls and I headed out to the site of the forth
coming battle to look it over from the
highway.


Hell I knew where they were dug in but I
couldn't see shit, nada, nothing. We headed
on down the road until we were flagged over
by a scout who guided us back into the area
where the troops were working and gathering,

there was only about fifty people there doing the work at the moment just to hold down on the traffic in the area, we weren't using deep bunkers just shallow shooting trenches with poncho covers with bits of cover just in case the bad guys had some kind of air but nothing had been seen of any.

At their rate of travel we figured a week before any advance scouts might come into the area. In the mean time we started some chatter on the radio, talking about an unmentioned "find" up in the area we wanted them to go, finally a call was sent out to me telling me I needed to come see this because it was big, real big! The hint was some kind of hidden Government facility that had very interesting goodies. I told them I'd be there on a time frame that might make the enemy speed up to catch me away from my base.

Mean time more of our people were filtering into the area from back roads and improving their firing places, no fires and MRE's, sucks to be them ( I laugh) But I was going to be there soon enough and try as I did I couldn't get "them" to stay home and pester the builders.

Harv and his guys were ready to come join the fight but our people had been working together for a good while, plus the home area had to be guarded so they became part of the home guard.

When the bad guys were a day out we

headed in to our spots which we improved, the girls will fight and squat in the mud to pee but they will have the best shelter they can possibly build and they will do it themselves, no wimps in my family.

We were here, loaded for bear, every shooter had their favorite rifle and all were checked out on the ranges involved. We had some heavy weapons on the other side of the road on some higher ground where they could be brought under fire when they tried to take cover behind their vehicles when we started shooting. We had our tracks hull down and well covered and protected, I had given them their orders to do their best to not kill the Lav's, I really want those baby's, shoot out the tires and leave them stranded if possible, unless they had run flat tires, whatever just try. The only track fire would be to take out the first and last vehicles if my first plan didn't work, but also any that try to get away across country. I wanted to salvage every bit of their gear we could because I had a feeling we were going to be going West. The mortars were zeroed for blocking fire. We were set as good as could be, we ended up with 300 snipers with troops held in reserve to back up any part of our line that night get breached. Now we wait. It looked good but the best plan seldom survives the first shot.

We had warned the people of all the settlements in the area to get out and most did, some refused and were rolled over with little effort. Our scouts were reporting the usual, kill the men and older women and keep the young girls and boys, 8 to 30 it looked like, I hated it because we were going to be in an all out war and some of the prisoners would likely get killed or wounded. All we could do was hope.

Morning came with word they were heading right at us and there was a lot of them, no count unless " A shit load" is a true measure of numbers.

We heard them long before we saw them and according to the scouts they were strung out pretty good having learned from the canyon ambush, but we were prepared for that with two tracks set to slam the back door closed hopefully before the front got past and to insure that I had a really good shooter using a suppressed rifle in place to shoot out the front tire of the lead truck, with all the noises they wouldn't hear the shot even tho it was not a sub sonic round, and that's what happened, tire blew out and truck stopped, simple, we didn't move or even breath hard and like a slinky the vehicles contracted before word passed back to the tail. Leaders had troops bailing out and taking cover but when nothing happened they soon relaxed and were smoking and some were heating rations. All in all it was a big picnic. A HV rolled to the front and a large Black man jumped out and began yelling to get the tire fixed.

I thought we had hit the Jackpot but it wasn't to be, he went to a radio and was obviously nodding and saying yes sir, a lot. I contacted the tail gunners and they said they could see nobody on the radio in the commo unit, the way back scouts said they couldn't see any sign of anybody shadowing the convoy, our people finally found the freq they were using and just caught the end of somebody with a deep voice screaming to get moving. But where was he? I was getting a feeling we weren't gonna get him today, like in Vegas, he stayed back and let his men fight for him. He was no leader but he was smart when it came to covering his ass.

One thing that played right into our hands and gave me a thrill ( woody ? giggling) the LAV troops unassed like everybody else. I ordered the people on my team to take out the drivers and don't let anybody lock them down.

I ordered the battle to start by count down, 3-2 1-FIRE, and with one long crash they started dropping in the dozens, the ones around the LAV's were all down in the first blast, I never took my eyes off of the LAV's and when somebody headed for one I took him down, well I was one of several who shot at him.

It was going as planned, they were lost and

leaderless and most died running in circles, no matter which side of their vehicles they moved to they were in the cross hairs. It was even worse then the canyon ambush. I know they shot back but I never heard a round come close, the girls were slowly taking apart anybody that moved, I looked for the man who was on the radio being yelled at and finally spotted him under the HV hiding between the front tires. Him I wanted alive, I didn't have the shot but asked if anybody could see him and got a few yeses , I asked who could shoot him in the foot and Beth's rifle cracked and he like to have killed himself by ramming his head into the under carriage. I looked at her and saw her smile then look at me and wink, damn! I'm glad they like me! ( you should be !!laughter)

I had given the order that we were not taking prisoners and once again being back away from them made it easier to drop them, a part of me felt bad but what was better? A bullet or waiting for space on the gallows? Nobody running with this pack could claim he was a soldier doing his duty, all were murders and rapist to mention only two of their crimes. No it was best to just put them down. And we did.

As with the Canyon the team with the 22 rifles went to work, covering each other they worked their way thru the mess making sure all were dead. It was a nasty job but several of the people who had been held by the slavers were happy to do it. Their motto was " Never Again" They meant never again would these bastards rape and murder.

The good news was that this time we had nobody hurt, not even a scratch, there were a few burns from grabbing hot gun barrels which got them laughed at. I was so relieved, I had been so worried about losing anybody. I looked at the girls just as Sandy yelled " SHIT!!" I jumped up but found her sucking on a broken nail for gods sake. I just shook my head while May and Beth made a fuss over her, if Walker had been here he would have snarled at me for my lack of compassion, He was at the canyon, pissed off no doubt and blaming me. I smile! ( John...don't be petty...) shit ( don't cuss).

It was time to go see just what I had caused, one should never shirk at looking at the bad things one causes, so I did. It's never pretty but to take the edge off was a few trucks with captives in them, people ripped from their lives by the bastards. No mercy, No pity.

I went to look at the LAV's !! awesome! Only some paint knocked off by bullets and nobody had made it back into them, clean and still smelled new, the Mech. Team was drooling over them. Hell they still had training manuals in them. There were eight of them! What a haul !

I heard the sounds of big trucks rolling in from where I was supposed to be and when they arrived the low boys had bull dozers on them which were unloaded and went right to digging a huge pit off the road when it was big enough we started hauling bodies to it and after they were searched for anything useable the were tossed in, nasty but necessary. I was waiting for somebody to bring some shiny toy for the girls for their new vault but nothing was found of interest.

The Commo team said there had been calls from that same person on the radio but shortly they stopped and they never heard anything again.


I figured the big dog had escaped …again, I was getting really tired of this shit. He had to be stopped "dead" and I meant to get it done some how.

Another thing that bothered me was where was he getting all these shooters? And I had a brain flash! I told the commo man to tell the dozers to stop filling the mass grave, I headed that way trailed by my brides, that made me chuckle. And I heard from behind me " we are funny"? I stopped and turned around and said oh hell yes yawls funny!! They stared for a minute and finally Beth said ,well yea that's true, yawlz funny! They tried glaring at her but it didn't work, May said Oh and your not funny? Beth said well yea but not on your level, I'm new here. That got them to laughing so I took off.

At the hole I slid down inside it and started ripping shirts off and found what I thought, every jail house tattoo ever seen was there, some had full sleeves some just different gang tats, the bastard was recruiting from the inner cities !! No wonder the bastards were so bad, they had not a thread of humanity in them. Now we knew about the cities, but what were we gonna do about them? And this asshole?

I needed some quiet time to think. We had just won a major battle but it was so one sided it felt like an execution which is what winning is when you plan the fight and rule the field. Winning beats losing. But how many times can we get away with it?

It was time to head right for him and end it once and for all. Only we have no idea who he is or even where he is really, hell the place in Barstow could be just a cover.

I still can't believe this mess turned out like it did, but the military had long ago left skilled marksmanship behind for massive fire power. We just took out at least two times our numbers with long range sniping. No bloody

charges, no bayonets in the sun, nope, just
simply a mass ambush with no mercy.
General Pickett could have learned something
today.

By days end the grave was packed down
and big rocks pushed over it and no marker to
show where they died. We settled in at our
fighting holes and spent a restless night, but
morning comes as they say and we started
getting read to roll, the LAV's could be
driven and our tracks were on lowboys.

The prisoners were offered rides back to
their former homes but most said they were
the only survivors and chose to come with us.

I took the girls to one side and said no more
wives! No more adopting another lonely
woman, ok? May said well can we adopt
some lonely men? That shut me up, I sighed
and walked away listening to them high
fiving, I hate them ( no you don't!...) was
there three voices there? Naaa couldn't be..
Could it?
( laughter ). Beth came to me and said John, if
you want I can move on, I think they should
have talked to you before dumping me on you
but I was weak and lonely and I love the two
silly girls, they are so full of spirit they pulled
me out of the dark place I was in but I'm
much better now, so ? I looked at her and

finally said Beth if you leave it will be because you wish to, I don't want you to go, I think you filled a vacancy in our family and I for one welcome you with open arms. That got me a wonderful hug and some tears, Beth in her own way was more mature then the other two, close to the same age, maybe, but more quiet, serious and I think she will have a good influence on the girls, I know I found her calming presents to be good for me. I hugged her back and pattered her on the butt and said , damn nice shot on that dick heads foot! She started laughing and then we both remembered him! Shit I had him saved to get information out of and forgot him and hoped nobody had just shot him.

I kissed Beth and headed for the medics. I found him in the medic van, in pain and pissed and scared as well he should be. Somebody remembered me saying I wanted him alive and made sure he stayed that way…for now.

I stood looking down at him saying nothing and finally he just shrugged and said " What do you want to know?" I waited a long moment and then said "why do you think I want to know anything" he laughed a real laugh and said well that was one hell of a shot to pin me under that HV!

I had to smile at that and said maybe I'll introduce you to the shooter, she's quite beautiful but really hates slavers. At that he got pissed and said I'm no slaver! I asked about the people his troops had collected and he replied they weren't his troops, he had little authority in the pecking order. I was getting some vibes off this man and decided real fast I was going to let Charles's Mother visit him, I had a feeling she would get the truth out of him.

I had the commo man call Charley and "she "relayed my request to have him meet me on the road near the LAV's since I was gonna really look them over since I never seen one before. When I was in the Corps we had row boats and muzzle loaders, ( laughter in my ears) stop it I said! the medics and the prisoner looked at me like I was crazy.

I just walked away while the commo man laughed her ass off.

LAV's are really cool things! Bad assed and can have full eight wheel drive to get thru shit. Plus a propeller to drive thru water. I wanted to ride in one, hell I wanted to drive one, Charley found me drooling over them and smiled at me. I told him my plan to have Old Woman check out this dude, he said all we could do was ask, she would or would not. I got that, I think. Charley had two of his lads hop in the medic van and off they went after he told them what to tell the Old Woman, they got a funny look but nodded.

I asked him if he wanted to ride in a LAV with me, he asked who was driving, I said me of course why? He nodded over my shoulder and there "they" were crawling all over it with Beth standing there smiling like a proud mom watching her cubs playing.

Beth turned and smiled at me while the girls both flipped me off while laughing, then both disappeared inside the vehicle and before I could say a word the motor fired up and the hatches closed and with some jerking ( and I swear I heard gears grinding) it rolled forward, all I could do was watch one of my new treasures rolling away and then the main gun opened up on some big boulders up on the high ground where we had no people, watching the boulders reduced to gravel was interesting for sure but I was kind of pissed off then I heard Charley chuckling and felt Beth's arm around my waist and I started laughing.

I heard others and turned to see the whole unit watching them, now they were racing across the rough ground with the machine guns roaring.

They really are like bear cubs, into everything and yet like kittens, full of fire and off to something new every other second ....and ,like rattle snakes, very deadly. God I love them! Beth hugged me closer and said they are fun huh? Yea I said " they are"!

When they brought the LAV back and

popped out the hatches like two gophers the entire troop gave them a loud round of yells and fist pumping which got the usual bows they were known for, they bounded off the big machine like cats and trotted over to me both breathing hard and trying to talk, when they could they said " We want it!" it's gonna be in our collection! I was expecting most anything but that. All I could do was just shake my head and laugh, they are something else. And WTF we needed to park the damn things someplace so I guess having one for a planter or something would work, I could see it all cover with wild flowers.

And they were gone, off to see what other treasures we had gathered up.

Charley said" I don't know if you are showing wisdom or are simply beaten. I wondered about that myself.

But in a way it would be a really cool conversation piece sitting in front of the ridge house. Beth laughed out loud and said come on we can't let them run loose unsupervised. It took almost thirty minutes to find them, they were sitting under a six-by with a couple of our troops, it was easy to see they were in a barter session, when we got there they both came out from under the truck and showed us their new sparkly's, seems the bad guys had raided some place and found a matched pair of 357 magnum Smith and Wesson model 19 revolvers, the old models, both were well used but in great shape and had consecutive serial numbers, With real old yellow ivory grips, they got the guns and the leather that came with them for who knows what.

They each now had one and were off to try them out. Soon we heard the sharp loud crack of the 357's, I could only hope they had their ear plugs in, more hearing was lost to that cartridge IMHO then most any other. Soon they were back and pissed because they were out of ammo and pissed that some asshole would go into a fight with only 12 rounds.

I reminded them we had people who could load all they wanted, they were smiling again.

To slow them down I said I was hungry and that worked, eating was one thing that would win them over shooting at least for a short time.

While we ate I took a look at the guns. They were engraved with the legend " Col. Barry Sweet, USMC. From the troops". Shit!! I knew him! He was a First LT. when I met him in a place one wants to forget.

He was a good man who took care of his people and that was the best praise any Marine Officer would every want. I guess if these asshole had the guns then Sweet must be dead. I told the girls what I knew and it made them happy that they now had the guns instead of a murdering asshole.

They decided they would get the wood

workers in the canyon to make a fitting shadow box case to display them in our home. I could see it now, every inch of the walls covered with guns. May smiled and said is that a bad thing? What? I didn't say anything. Her and Sandy laughed and scooted over for a group hug. Four is a good hugging number! Especially if you are the only guy in it! ( giggles).

We took time to clean up the area before we left even the empty brass was salvaged. I had no idea how much in the way of supplies we had scored but it was a lot and we needed it, especially the 25 mm stuff, of course the girls had wasted a bunch but I have trouble getting on them, they work hard, play hard and fight hard, so if they wanna run thru a few rounds of ammo I don't worry about it.

I spent about an hour driving a LAV before I decided I might leave it to the kids who had younger butts and spines. Plus I wasn't much into sitting in a steel box and not being able to see all around me. So I joined the girls in our HV with Beth driving and slept, which I'm able to do with her driving, the other two? not so.
We made it back to Shiprock in pretty good order and stayed for the night. I wanted to know what was happening with the prisoner, Charley had arrived before us and met us in the front parking area. He took me aside while

the girls made a bee line for Old Woman.

Charley took his time with it and finally said that from what he understood from Old Woman was that the man has a good spirit and is a good man. Charley shrugged and said " But she says the same about you so take it from that. ( HA ha ha..he's so funny) I said well I guess we best have a talk with him, he agreed so we headed to the room he was locked up in with guards on the door and window.

We entered and found him sitting up with his foot elevated but otherwise seemed at ease.

Charley and I pulled over a couple of chairs and took a seat, I just looked at him for a while, waiting for him to blink, he didn't. Interesting to say the least. I wondered if I were in his place if I could be so relaxed. Since somebody had to open the ball I asked his name, he said Harold Harvey but we could call him Harry but please not "Paul" I had to laugh a bit at that and said I bet he caught a lot of shit over that, he said not as a kid because the place he was raised nobody knew who Paul Harvey was.

But in the Corps, different story. I asked him what his rank was when he got out, he smiled and said I'm not out. I told him I understood the old Once a Marine stuff but he said no, I'm still on active duty. Well that was a conversation stopper, so I made the come on motion and he told his story.

He was Captain Harold Harvey, United States Marine Corps. His present duty station was Marine Corps Supply Center, Barstow California.

His story was pretty simple, when the lights went out the Supply center went on total lock down, gates locked, guns up. Nobody in or out. Now this didn't set well with the troops because most had some family outside the base so the General allowed a convoy under heavy guard to go out and gather all they could find. Which while being a lot wasn't all.     The public also wanted inside the base but they were under orders that nobody was allowed in,

The General had violated his orders by allowing the dependants aboard the base. And it got nasty for a while, But the General decided that his job was to take care of the people not guard the stuff they needed to live, so he set up the area as a shelter for any and all who could make it there.

Big diesel generators to run things like hospitals and food centers, meaning the big grocery stores, they took over the entire infrastructure of the area. They couldn't get power to the homes but they could pump water and that was a biggie in the desert!

His troops were patroling the entire area for miles around which stopped almost all raiding.

They got people making gardens and over time things settled out pretty good, people had health care to a point and food and shelter so things were better then most places. Even tho more and more people were coming into the area things were ok, the desert only needs water to grow anything and the season is long compared to many places., so people were working together and while it wasn't an easy life it was better then the alternative. And so it was right up until about six months ago when the General had a stroke and the XO took over, he was another story.

He wanted to be King. And things started changing for the worse, some of the troops liked his new conditions for receiving support from the base, at first it was paying a percentage of their crops to the new King, then it got worse, he demanded women in trade for fuel and other things the people had gotten used to. When they asked where they were supposed to find women because they sure weren't sending theirs in there he said so look around, use your heads.

So the raiding started, good people can be turned bad for sure but it wasn't happening on the scale he wanted, so he put out the word for people who would play ball. And that's where the real problems started.

Soon he had an army of scum that would do as he ordered. He didn't want the system in place to break down so he backed off on the locals and simply said produce or get out, so everybody was farming every acre they could get water to. Now the scum bags were willing to do whatever he wanted so he took his troops who were willing to work with them and started training them enough to almost follow orders and not shoot each other.

I asked what happened to the troops who refused to follow this asshole? Harry said they were smart enough to get out before they could be disarmed and locked up or killed. He said he was going to leave too but the General who was partially crippled from the stroke asked him to stay and pretend to go over.

So he did, and while it killed him to do it he was able to deal with it by reminding himself that sooner or later he would be in place to kill the son of a bitch XO and his pet mad dog who was his second in command, he had been in the military long enough to know his way around a bit and was fairly well educated but he was 100 percent Ghetto gang banger and he was the source for all the trash we had been killing, he was high up in the gangs running the whole of everything from LA to the border. He had access to weapons and food so he had no problems getting new blood.

Now I understood why it seemed so few of
the people we had fought knew shit about
fighting military style. They were more or
less the close your eyes and just hold the
trigger till it went click. A great number of the
dead we searched had rifles with empty
magazines and they were fumbling their
reload when they died.

The last thing I wanted to know was why
he was raiding with them? He said because
the General asked him to and to try to escape
and make contact with somebody he knew
long ago who was here in this area leading an
army and kicking ass.

I raised my eyebrows at that and said who
is this guy? He smiled and said well unless
you're not Johnny Long Walker former
USMC it must be you sir.

I had a sudden thought and asked who the
General was and he said his name was James
Barrymore Sweet. And I smiled real big as
did he.

I nodded and said I should have known
when his pistols showed up here, that got his
attention so I told him about the ones the girls
had bartered for, he said the General was very
angry at having them stolen and at least some
asshole didn't have them. I said yea but
getting them away from the "Doom Dollies"
might be harder then not, I didn't bother to

explain, I figured he would find out soon enough.

Well all that was left was to hear what General Sweet wanted of me and mine, it was simple, he wanted us to come kill the son of a bitch who had dishonored his oath as an officer in the Marine Corps, that alone was enough in Barry's eyes but the scum bag was dealing in slavery and was a pedophile because he only wanted very young girls. In his mind any over 14 were too old! I agreed he was gonna die.

We talked a while longer and just to make sure I asked him what Sweet had to say about me and everything he said had to come from Sweet because nobody could know those things unless they were there and some of it was when nobody was left alive but us and a few of my unit. And I knew they weren't talking. We left him there to get some rest and said come morning we would have breakfast and talk more. I needed to think.

When morning came I headed to look in on Harry and surprising me all to hell he was up and dressed, the Doc was with him and was explaining that the bullet had been a 223 not a 308, plus it was a full metal jacket ( FMJ) and with nothing but pure luck it had passed between all the bones and left two perfect holes, I could not believe his foot wasn't about to be removed! But the Doc said it happens more then we know, just fate or the Gods smiled. Harry was using a pair of crutches but seemed better then I had been when I got shot. ( inner ear * In The ASS!* ) Without thinking I said "stop it!" now the Doc and Harry were looking at me, but Doc had been with us a good while and like most of the troops had an idea something was going on nobody could see or hear.

I said lets go get some chow, Doc said he had people to take care of which stopped me dead in my tracks. Before I could ask he said it was a couple of sprains, a few burned hands with funny markings,
( A really hot flash hider leaves a nice funny burn branded into the skin) even Harry laughed at that.
Doc just shook his head and muttering about "Grunts" walked off. I was starting to like Harry.

We went to the café for breakfast where we joined Charley, my butt wasn't even on the seat when the bat wing doors opened and out came the girls packing big trays full of food. Harry had an interesting look on his face when he saw all that food, then the girls sat down . None of them were wearing the jackets they usually did so Harry was treated to a nice set of shoulder holsters with 1911's plus one in the small of the back except May who wore hers in a cross draw, Beth being more the lady only had that big assed 10 mm in a shoulder holster with two very hard to find extra mags under the right arm. I was watching how Harry was absorbing the sight.

I finally introduced him to my wives and that got his eye brows climbing his forehead! The " girls" looked at him for a moment like a target that got away and Sandy said well shit I guess if we're feeding him we can't shoot him...yet, eh?

Harry smiled until Charley said " They are not joking" that made him really do a double take, Beth asked how his foot was doing more to relieve the moment then any other reason, he responded that it was much better then it could have been, and must have been a lucky shot. The girls laughed out loud and Beth smiled and said hmm, thru the second lace eyelet from the bottom, outside right foot? Now Harry's eyes got real big! I said meet the "man" who shot you. Beth offered her hand and said sorry bout the knock on the head but it was pretty funny! We finished eating listening to the girls babbling about something to do with Old Woman and parts of it were English and other parts in Navajo, it was hard to follow to say the least, Charley interrupted once and said a word, both girls looked at him and repeated it a few times until Charley nodded and they were off again.

Harry kept looking at me so I shrugged and said shit I don't know, they seem to absorb it like a sponge but have trouble with the right pronunciation.

Charley said they are getting better about that, better then any of your people ever have except some real pros the military used to send around but they didn't get "help" from Old Woman.

I don't think Harry still had a grasp of the issue but was trying. The girls bounded to their feet and gathered the plates and headed to the kitchen allowing Harry to say, please tell me I really saw those two eat what I think I saw them eat. I nodded as did Charley who added that they seemed to be off their feed this morning. Harry laughed , I didn't. But I said don't worry about it, if they get hungry they will chase some small critter down and rip it to shreds. From the kitchen was heard " We heard that and you're heading for trouble buddy boy!" I laughed, Charley shook his head and Harry looked confused.

I asked Harry to tell me about Barry Sweet, how was it he was still active duty? Harry said the General had never married and the Corps was his home and family so the HQMC gave him the supply center because he loved the desert and because he had always been in supply, I said " No not always! Once, Barry ran with Tigers and had seen the elephant so to speak.

After the Un-War and remembering how fked up the supply system had gotten he switched fields determined to fix that problem so never again would Marines be fighting in boots held together with commo wire and duct tape, while REMF's sold the new ones to the black market or traded for dope.

And he had made a difference but like all things in the "Great Green Machine" it took time and hard work and sometimes having to fight hard battles to win the smallest of fights. But he seemed to have made a difference.

I was interested in the equipment on the base, Harry said that supply's had been fully stocked but the wars in the sand box had really used up a lot of the armored vehicles so there hadn't been a lot of stuff on line when the lights went out.

I asked about the LAV's, he smiled and said I heard you joy riding in one and saw the gunner on that 25 and he's as good as any I've seen.

Just then the girls returned and Sandy said hear that May? he liked your driving!! May said yea and your shooting was passable as well, now it was on! Passable?? PASSABLE?? And they were off and running, before I could say anything Beth came out of the kitchen and said, hey babes, be cool and they stopped right then, ! The glares didn't but they weren't reaching for guns. Of course a duel with 25's was the challenge until I reminded them we needed every round we could get, so off they went for their rifles to prove who was best.

I looked up and Beth said I'll go along to keep an eye on them but they are just jerking your chain and trying to make Harry think they are crazy! Charley beat me to it by saying " Think" ?? I laughed. Beth kissed me and with a hug was off to capture her " kids?" she was a good example for them but I doubt it would soak in, they were having the time of their lives and loved it.

Harry sat for a minute and at last said " I think I will assume those two are even more dangerous then they appear at first glance" Charley and I only nodded coz Harry had hit that one out of the park!
I said someday I may tell you all about them but I expect the troops will do it for me coz they worship the two hellions and they will of course make them sound wild but nobody really knows just how wild except me coz I was there and saw it.

He went back to telling me about the way things worked in Barstow, the people there were armed and while they had no heavy weapons they could hold their own with the rabble being brought in, at first some of the gang bangers went in expecting the locals to be scared shitless like their old neighbors were. But after a lot of them got their asses killed they decided to stay out of the town proper, so there was an uneasy peace between the few remaining military personnel and none with the bangers who got shot every time they tried to mess with the civilians.

Now this was interesting and I could see there was room to exploit the situation. All in all outside of the bangers brought in by the head rat there wasn't really anything to stop a well armed motivated force from kicking ass. And with our force and Harry's knowledge we could do just that.

And what better time then now since we were already here, we just needed to gather more troops and supply's. Harry said between the LAV's and the Tracks we had all we needed but it wouldn't be a cake walk.

Harry had some good news too, a lot of the Marines who got out before the clamp down with the XO were still in the area and were willing to fight plus there was a still a few on the base who were just marking time waiting for a chance.

Harry also had some very interesting news about a flu or something like it that was slamming the big cities, He thought it was from all the unburied bodies left since day one of the EMP. Plus the general filth left in the rubble. He said so far none of the scum recruited from the LA area had shown up with it but it was only a matter of time.

The word was it was spread from contact not airborne which was good if you could isolate the people in ones area, This was all we needed on top of all the rest of the shit. It was only a matter of time before it spread to other areas where the gangs ruled and traveled.

So besides having to kill off the assholes running the Supply base we needed to find a way to keep this crap pinned up in the cities.

And I have no idea how to do it short of fire bombing the entire city. Harry said it might very well take that to stop the spread in it's tracks. He also mentioned with a big smile that I did have a reputation of burning cities, that pissed me off, but Charley did smile pretty big and said well yea you had to be there but it was a nice fire.

My main worry was how many innocent people were trapped in the cities but Harry said they had long ago either escaped or joined or died. That was a pretty cold analysis but I hadn't been there so I didn't know. I asked how many people they could gather if they really wanted to. His answer scared the shit right out of me! Probably 35 to 50 thousand! And all hard corps killers and rapist just waiting to be called out.

This whole situation just changed fast. It was time to do some real planning, so I set up a meeting right here and sent word to the canyon for Joe and Willy plus the leadership folks at Fort Navajo.

With a brain flash I also sent word to Harry and Bear asking them to attend, it was set for three days later so we had time to get an idea of what we needed and where we needed it and how to get it there, the big issue was all the " It's" we don't have and really need.

They started rolling in a day early which gave us time to have a feed thanks to the girls and Old Woman who really did it up good. We spent the evening just having a few drinks and filling each other in on all the latest goings on. Word from home was all was well, Mom was doing just fine, happy every day to meet "new" people and getting to tell stories of her life.

Bear and Harry had never met Charley and were real happy to do so having heard so much about him, Harry asked about the magic weed I spoke of because his old body was starting to kill him, Charley said he would take care of getting a good supply of it, everybody got a good laugh when I told Bear to hold a gun on Harry when he drank the first few cups or he would lie and say he drank it while pouring it out.

The next day everybody was here so I laid out all that had happened since we last were together. Most of the people here were involved in it all but Harry and Bear so they got to hear the whole thing. After that I brought out Captain Harry and introduced him and we grilled him and picked his brain until lunch time when we took a break.

After lunch I asked for thoughts on the subject, and wasn't surprised when the general opinion was to wipe out the vermin in their city holes.

I mentioned I was troubled by the fact that there had to be a lot of innocent people trapped in that place and asked for thoughts on that.

I was surprised when after a bit with no response it was Charley who spoke up and said that if there was in fact a plague burning thru the place then we had no choice except to wipe it out and if innocent people died then they were to be mourned along side the many millions who had already died.

Beth spoke up and said that if we as a nation were to survive and hoped to rebuild a better place for our children then we were going to have to do things we hated but by us doing it others wouldn't have to later provided there was a later and provided there was others left to do it.

Well that was a show stopper and a curtain dropper if I ever seen one, So it was decided thru the words of the gentlest person among us to wipe out Las Angeles.

I could only hope it wouldn't weigh heavy on her heart, Beth turned and smiled at me then leaned over and whispered into my ear that this was one of the reasons she loved me, I cared about peoples feelings.

I hugged her close and whispered I loved her too. So much mush in the middle of planning to destroy what had once been one of Americas greatest cities.

I asked for ideas that didn't require us shooting our way into the place, Vegas was fresh in my mind as well as the lonely cross on the hill in Utah.

We hashed it around until Sandy said "I wish we had some of those big cannons like the military use" my first word was "NO" you're not getting a damn 105 to hang on the wall! Which got a lot of laughs but I swear I planted a seed, she and May looked at each other and smiled. Charley just looked into my eyes and shook his head.

But Bear bless his heart said well shit why not use our artillery? Sandy pounced on that in a heart beat "We got Cannons"?

I swear she was breathing hard. Bear said well the Republic of Texas does since we held on to all the National Guard units and their equipment and there was a few units that used 105's, before I could say a word Sandy said " is this a big gun" ? Bear laughed and said it sure is lil lady!

That was all it took, she was ready to go get the big guns. I asked Bear if the troops were still there and yes they were, do they have access to ammo? yes they do! How long to get them rolling? Bout a week. Do it!

God being a General is awesome!! Joke!! Anyway, that part was done, now we needed to get a plan ironed out. We spent the next few days looking at maps and talking about the logistics of the road march plus the best strategy to handle two battles at once, taking out the XO in Barstow along with his top flunky and LA.

Harry said in his opinion if we removed the XO and the other dickhead he felt the rest would break and run, so I set him to planning how to get both of them. And called for ideas on LA besides shelling it for the next year.

Willy spoke up and said he had been thinking about something he had read about in a book several years back, Sandy said WOW, it must have had a lot of pictures in it, May said yea, and small words.

God they are fun, I asked them to hold the jokes but of course May said " Who was joking"? poor Willy.

He finally spoke up and told us about the

book, it was funny because I had read that same book! Neither of us could remember the name of it but we both liked it. The plot so to speak was somebody wanted to get the attention of the Government or something so they emptied out a small town in the desert and flew a large plane with a cargo ramp over the town and rolled out a 5000 gallon fuel blivet with a detonator on it and at about 3000 feet or so it went off the air burst flattened the town completely and in the rain of fire burned the scraps, instant no town.

Great idea but where would we get a C-130 and who was gonna fly it?

Again Bear spoke up and turned to Harry and said your turn boss. Harry said well we also acquired a lot of airplanes and pilots and I'm sure we have a C-130, I was rather astounded and had to ask just when they were planning to find a use for them? Harry said when things settled out they figured the planes could really help in rebuilding the country, but he saw no reason to not use them for a good cause. He would just pass the plan up stream.

So we had tools to work with and a plan, now to bring it all together.

While we waited for word on the air craft we studied maps and came to the conclusion that this was going to be a major issue! The sheer size of the city was mind boggling when faced with mounting an attack. Capt. Harry as we took to calling him since we had two Harry's in the loop said his understanding was that the main gang turf was located in the center of the city and they had some power from generators, Big generators, so we might be able to centralize the attack.

Joe offered the idea that if we had some artillery coming we might just shell the outer edges of the area and start driving them south toward the border area and then fire bomb them while they were running. I liked that idea.

We were not going to lose one person if I could help it, We had one big advantage in that they didn't know we were coming. Capt. Harry was going to put together a plan to take the Base from within, I asked Harry 2 if there was any spec-ops troops in Texas? He asked if a Platoon of Rangers would be of use? Well yes I guess, jeeze Harry tell me what there is we can use. He said pretty much whatever we wanted.

Well I sat down and said Harry, why have I been running my ass off trying to stomp snakes when y'all got big boots just sittin in Texas.

He smiled and said John, how many people have you lost since you started burning down cities, blowing them up and in general raising hell all over the heartland?

I was ashamed I couldn't tell him for sure but I thought it was 15, He said well you've done more with almost nothing and very low losses then a regular army command would ever get done and they would lose a ton of people. He said your people mean more to you then the average grunt means to the upper level of command, they aren't evil they just see things in a different light. He also said if the Rangers worked under me he was willing to bet most if not all would get home, that wasn't the case if the high command was running things.

I leaned forward and said Harry I feel either a snow job or a blow job coming and before I could say more I felt a hand on my shoulder and knew it was Beth from the warmth of the feelings going thru me. I shook my head and said "I'm sorry Harry, I was out of line, you don't deserve that shit.

He smiled and said sure I did because that's what you were getting only you never gave me the chance to finish.

Beth sat beside me and leaned against me with her head on my shoulder while Harry finished, it was simple, they would make anything available to me as long as I was in charge of the way the assets were used. No high brass looking over my shoulder. No bird in the sky trying to run fire teams from 5000 ft.

I felt real bad and said "Oh" he laughed and said you're a good man John you just ain't found it out yet, look around you at the quality of the people who follow you, they are the best troops you could find and have very little training beyond that which you taught them, you care for them, you lead from the front when Doc and Wyatt let you, he then smiled at Beth and said I think this lady here is controlling all three of you. I knew she had a way with the girls who I had forgot about and I started to sit up but Beth said they are napping so relax. I was the luckiest man alive.

Other then setting out our line of march and helping Capt. Harry cook up his plan there wasn't much to do for now. We just rested and helped the Mech crews until they ran us off saying if we watched their price went to double. I said hell you work for free so big fkn deal. Beth took me for a walk.

A week to the day after the call went out to the folks in Texas we had the word on the C-130, it was a go and the crew were pretty wild about the idea behind it all.

The Rangers took a bit longer because of a General who said "His Rangers" would work under a crazy son of a bitching Marine only after he was dead!!

Sandy and May were all ready to go see to that but Harry said it was settled, I asked if they killed him he said no, worse, he was put in charge of a small reserve base counting mess tins. I had to laugh at that because I had seen it a time or two myself.

I believe in calling the troops "MY" troops but if they go to a fight I will be in the front rank with them, Generals as a rule don't do that. So we were waiting for the Air Force to work out the pay load and how to set it up while the demo folks were ironing out the ways and means to make it work at the elevation we wanted to go off, plus how many chutes it would take to float it down to that area.

Hell I thought it was just toss it out the fkn door with a grenade up it's ass, Grunts have a more colorful way of looking at problems then logistics types, but I think we have more fun and usually put on a better bang for the buck.

We got some requests about how we wanted to disperse the load, Capt. Harry said the five K load was about max pay load for the 130, they wanted to know if we wanted one 5000 gal unit of avgas or 5 1000 gal units, after thinking it over it seemed that five smaller loads spread over a bigger area would be the way to go.

Also the chutes would handle the loads easier, so we sent that back. The also sent a message that if we could secure a landing field closer to the target with fuel to use they could fly several missions using extra units they could squeeze aboard, Capt. Harry said that could be handled after he took the base so that became the first and main priority.

The Air Force also sent a message that the proper term for the fuel delivery system was called a bladder, I replied that in the Marines a Blivet was a five pound sack with 10 pounds of shit in it so what's yer point. I'm still waiting for a reply.

Harry did say he heard the laughing went on for a good while and the Air Force General made some noises about turning "his" C-130 over to a fucking Marine! But his aide whispered in his ear about the mess tin counting jobs still open so he shut up.

Harry said the Artillery was on it's way and would be here in a few days, they had put command of it under a Captain who was under orders to follow my orders without question.

This was gonna be fun! I just had to figure out how to keep "them" from stealing a 105 for their collection, but then again it would look good sitting by the LAV.

I do have some questions wondering around in my head. But damn few answers are forthcoming.

Such as why has the nations military sat on their thumbs while the country went to hell and millions died? Part of me realizes that there was little they could do simply because the task was too huge, I get that but it sure seems to me some effort could have been made. Like this dick head in Barstow, WTF? Couldn't they have at least sent people in there to waste the fucker?

Capt. Harry said in the long run it would have simply drained the resources the military had and to what gain? But now that things were getting sorted out they would be able to do something.

When I asked why we were going to have to deal with the LA gangs he said if the Military did it there would always be fear of them by the citizens and that wasn't a good thing.

But if some "cowboy" did it people would be cheering loud and long. So now I'm a cowboy? He laughed and said well not really since you do ride a mule which no self respecting cowboy would do.

I was starting to like this guy, he fit right in with the rest of the wise asses around me, Just can't get any respect!

I asked about General Sweet and why he was still alive, Capt Harry said the XO kept him alive as an ace in the hole to control the loyal troops.

The troops loved their General because of the kind of man and leader he was so they won't endanger him by rebelling but that thread was very thin and the XO knew it and made sure the Old Man ( military slang for the unit leader just not to his face) was well cared for.

Also Harry said Sweet wasn't as out of it as he pretended and was marking time before he made a move. So many of the military walked away after the EMP to try to get home to their families that it left damn few to handle security much less anything else.

And this happened all over the country. I could understand that. Home and family were more important to most men then anything else.

I enjoyed these talks with Harry because it brought back my years in the Corps and as they say, Once a Marine…etc. And it's the truth, no matter what ones experience was while there, you never leave it behind and those few who have were never really there. You are either a part of the Green Machine or your not, there is no half way. Guess ya hadda be there.

The Army moves at a slower pace then my

troops do, we just decide to go and do it, thus it was almost two weeks before the Rangers showed up and another few days for the artillery to make it.

The Ranger unit was about platoon size, around fifty men and they looked as you would expect them to, in great shape and very sharp in the brain department.

Spec-ops troops are picked for their brain power as much as muscle power, in fact most of these warriors surprise folks when they see them, as a rule they don't look like body builders, all that kind of muscle gets in the way when creeping thru a jungle, thin wiry strong men move thru the bush like a ghost where a bulked out defensive lineman type moves like a bull in a china shop, what they don't step on and break they shit on. Nope, long, lean and mean works best in Spec-ops and these lads were all of that.

Their commander was a First LT. who started to report as trained but I stopped him before he could by saying "At Ease LT" he kinda froze until I smiled and offered my hand, after shaking hands I said from now on saluting and standing at attention is out, snipers look for those things. If you need something just walk up and say so, we will deal with it, my names John what's yours? He was a fast study and said he was used to just using his last name which was on his BDU

shirt as "Watson" so that was what I would call him. I asked about his second in command who was a Master Sgt. He called him over and his years showed, he had seen the little thing between his LT and me so he just walked over kind of casual and we shook hands, his name  was on his shirt
" Holmes" I said your shitting me ain't ya?

Both laughed and said we get that a lot, I told them right then that their commo call signs were Doc and Shurlock which got a good laugh from everybody in the area.

I heard voices pick up from the Rangers and turned to see the girls heading toward me. Both were dressed to get attention as usual, black tee shirts, black jeans, bloused boots and enough weapons to fight a war which is what we do it seems. I just shook my head and introduced them to Watson and Holmes who were kind of big eyed, I asked if they had never seen women before and the LT said is this "Wyatt and Doc?" The girls swelled up with pride and Sandy said damn skippy bud! So be careful sonny said May. I looked around for Beth who was headed that way dressed like them but only carrying the 10mm instead of looking like a walking ad for a gun show.

I introduced her and in a heart beat she came up with something that got the girls all fired up and off they went, I hugged Beth and said thank you! She smiled that soft sweet smile and said I'll think of something for payment! I think I turned red and off she went to stop the destruction before it got out of hand.

How I survived before she came along I'll never know! She could calm a rabid skunk.

The LT said come on, is that really the ones they call Wyatt and Doc? I said yea, but don't let looks deceive you, they really are a danger to everybody or thing that gets close to me in a way they don't like.

I explained about Beth and how she seemed to have that something that kept them from getting into to much trouble. I could see he was still confused so I said and yes all three are my wives. Watson laughed out loud and said LT, John is a pretty tough man to handle those two not to mention being married to all three of them. The LT was a youngster but he was getting it.

After getting his troops settled I called a meeting with all the unit commanders so to speak, but we needed to lay it out. I explained it from the top for the Rangers troop leaders which included squad leaders. I told them we needed the Barstow Supply center back in good hands before we dropped hell on LA and I needed the Rangers to help with that.

I told LT Holmes that he would lead his people but Capt. Harvey was in command of the opperation. I asked if any of the Rangers had any problems with that? None seemed to so I said it again, Capt. Harvey is a Marine Officer, he is a serving officer who is stationed at the Center, He undertook a very dangerous mission to get word to me of the goings on in Barstow. He knows the center, and the loyal people he can count on. This will be a dark of the night raid with suppressed weapons which I assume you brought with you at my request? Holmes said yes sir. I used that to bring up the no siring or saluting that we had been fighting as snipers and knew what happened when a nail sticks up.

Capt. Harry held up his foot and said see this? And intentional shot for just over 300 yards when this was all that was exposed, that got the rangers attention.

Harry then added I believe you've seen these three ladies walking around with more gun then Josey Wales? The Rangers nodded, and since they were sitting there near me, he said the sweetie with the light brown hair made the shot about one second after John asked somebody to pin me down since I was with the unit they wiped out without a scratch!

He had them real good until Sandy spoke up and said " Bull Shit ! I ripped a finger nail half off and it hurt! so bite me!" The rest was lost in the loud laughter, but I could see their eyes on Beth who was just smiling her calm smile.

I held up my hand and said so for you Rangers, I know you're tough and as well trained as any troops in the world today, but these civilians sitting around you were just in the fight that killed over 600 enemy with not a scratch, I pointed at Sandy and said Zip it babe! She flipped me off so May followed suit.

Beth being in between them put a hand on each shoulder and they smiled and scooted closer to her. PFM! ( pure fkn magic!) I wish I could bottle it for when Beth isn't near.

I told them the plan to fire bomb LA and got some cheers and then I told them about the 105's that were coming but they already knew that.

One of the Rangers raised a hand and said Sir and stuttered to a stop and said "Uh John, will we be in on the LA gig? I said you sure will and before we leave here I want you to go thru our armory and pick out a good heavy cal. Rifle to use because we won't get closer then 300 yards to any of the trash running for it and while I know the 16's you carry are fine but a real reach out and touch somebody round is pretty nice, I added to the LT that as soon as we break here gather your troops and follow Willy and Joe then we will meet at the range. And just for shits and grins I winked at Capt. Harry who jumped up and bellered out in good Marine Drill Instructor voice

"Attention!" and everybody there snapped to! I was surprised. I laughed and said that is the last time you'll do that! And Dismissed!

The Girls had even snapped to so I asked about it and they ratted Harry out saying he leaked the plan to them so they told everybody, so much for Op-sec (Operation Security), but it was fun to recall the old days.

I noticed LT Holmes and Capt Harvey getting acquainted so I left them to it and headed off to find some chow which I had 10 seconds to enjoy in peace and quiet before "they" bounced in to shatter the eating and noises records. I did notice they kinda set it up so Beth was beside me and they were across the table, so I asked what was going on and they said Beth had been down a bit so they were giving her some extra John time, Beth blushed and shook her head. I thought for a moment and said "Bull Shit" what are you up to that requires you slipping away from both of us? Beth laughed and they just smiled.

May said I told you it wouldn't work? You did not! I did and you said oh sure it will be easy! It went back and forth until they remembered they had food so they stopped. I asked Beth why she was down? She said this would have been her wedding anniversary if her first husband hadn't been killed and she worried about me because I take chances.

I pointed out who was laying beside me in
the rifle pit during the ambush, she did think
about it and smiled and said well yes I guess.


So there, that's settled so now what? The
girls said they wanted to head to the range and
see if the Army could shoot, I said I didn't
care because Beth and I were taking a nap!
They high fived and Beth leaned closer. They
left and we had a real nice nap. I woke up a
few hours later to find them in bed too, a
group power nap.

When they woke up I said I was gonna take
a swim with the soap so they all trailed along,
the only way to get in the water this time of
the year is to just suck it up and jump, I did,
they sniveled and whined until Beth pushed
them in! then dove in and surfaced behind me,
they came up screaming and sputtering
looking for her, I think her long hair gave her
away because we both went under in the
attack, it was fun but the water was a bit cool
for this crap so I started scrubbing off and
they joined in. We have a community shower
with solar heated water but it's a long walk
and the lake is about 30 yards away from our
door.

We got dressed and headed out to check in
with Joe and Willy, the girls had said the
troops had a bit of trouble getting into the

different style of shooting but I knew their training would get them up to speed right away, Willy and Joe both said the same and had planned a few hours a day for the next few helping the ones who had trouble, mostly city boys who didn't grow up hunting. They are among the best in the world but very few people in the military train with bolt guns and long range shooting, not that 300 yards is long range but they may need to hit at 600 + yards.

Three days later the trucks pulling the big guns rolled into the area and they looked awesome!! They had to travel slower then usual because each truck was as full of ammo as it could be. Anti personnel ( frag)  White Phosphorous ( Willy Peter and bad shit!) HE ( High Explosive )they even had some canister shells!! ( think big assed shotgun shooting hundreds of steel balls) hell I never knew they had that for the 105 but I'm old and traded in my Musket for house slippers a long time ago.

So we had a big load of ammo but it was slowing the trucks down, we can fix that, I ordered the guns loaded on lowboys and the ammo load split up with other trucks, that way we can make good time. Lowboys are awesome units and seem to not get used as much as they should be.

I was also thinking about leaving the tracks here because they can be replaced by the

LAV's, Fast and deadly was my motto.

Sandy and May asked if they would fire a few rounds to let us see the power but I reminded them this was Navajo land and blowing up a mountain might offend them.

They got me again because Charley showed up an hour later and asked if him and his scout teams could see the big guns do their thing. I glared, Beth laughed out loud and "they" bumped butts and high fived. Why do I try?
( right buddy boy!) stop it! (And I'm getting looked at again.)

The crew of gun one ( they all have numbers in case you don't know) wheeled into action and asked Charley where he wanted them to put a few rounds, He looked around and finally pointed out a round bald knob sticking out by it's self maybe two miles away. The gun commander said ok since it's so close how about we put one round at the base then walk up in 50 yard increments? Charley just nodded.

The gun crew were doing their magic stuff which as a former grunt I confess I have no clue. We were all watching the bald knob when the gun crew leader came over and said "uh sir we have a problem" I knew without looking. Beth said I'll be right back and took off. She was back shortly with two pissed off wild cats who were arguing over who got in the way and got them kicked off the gun.

In my misspent youth I had occasion to need fire support and usually had a radioman who could call in fire better then anybody I ever saw so in truth I had no idea what kind of PFM it took but when the gun boss yelled "Fire in the hole!" then " Round out!" the crash of the gun scared the shit out of all of us then off in the distance we saw the base of the knob turn to dust and before it cleared another round hit, then another until the last round hit the top of the hill. Then for good measure they lowered the muzzle and fired a canister round at a rock face about 500 yards away and it was just total devastation, it was like shooting a bucket with a 12 ga shotgun at 20 feet. It was scary to think what that round could do to an attacking force.

The gun boss came over to us smiling big and said well that was fun!! Seems he had never fired a canister round! He was attacked by "them" who informed him that someplace down the line he was gonna show them how to shoot the gun, he looked at me and I just shrugged, he could see I was beat so he surrendered without a fight and agreed, they both hugged him then headed for the gun, he looked at me as I smiled and called him a wimp and a pussy for not holding out longer.

He said well if even a third of the things

I've heard about them is true then I'm staying
on their good side! I assured him they were
not only true but he hadn't heard nothing yet.
That got his attention! He looked at Beth who
just smiled and nodded and said "true", then
offered he might try to save his gun from
them, they were looking over the towing
system and I knew what that meant. He took
off and got his crew to cleaning the gun which
interested them as much as shooting it. Some
how some way there will be a 105 sitting on
the ridge and a gun will be missing from the
Texas state Militia. Combat loss will be the
word of the day, I know this like I know the
sun will rise.

Charley wondered over and said I hear your
building a stone fort on the ridge? I asked
why he called it a fort? He pointed at "them"
and said when you have a big stone building
with cannons it's called a fort and you know
that gun will be missing when they head back
to Texas right? Beth laughed out loud and
headed off to gather in the two before they
killed the gun crew and stole the gun.

Charley and I wondered off to a shady spot
in the lee of a cliff and settled down to just be.
After the usual silence he made his polite
cough and when I didn't say anything he said
" are we really going to burn LA?" I said yep
why? He just nodded and said "good" it's a
sewer and was one before the EMP, now it's a

sewer full of rats and it needs to be gone. Well I was surprised at his attitude but I could understand it. The Navajo people love their open spaces and the quiet of it and I guess the filth most big cities hold and the loudness just offends them. He waited a bit and said the Old Woman had told him that there was a very bad sickness growing in the cities and when it got loose it would spread and kill many of the people who had survived so far. He had no clue as to what it might be but he knew if she said it then it was true. She had told him fire was the way to kill it.

I asked if she said "LA" he said no, all the big cities. Damn! How was I supposed to handle that? He didn't know. All I could do was pass that information along to the communications people to pass along to the people everywhere who had commo. They could handle their areas themselves. LA had become personal to me so we would deal with it.

Charley said I'd probably get further if I left out that the information was from an ancient Navajo woman out in the desert. I had to laugh at that, but he was right.

But there are so many big cities that turned into death traps and were filled with bodies that still lay where they fell. Rats and god knows what else were spreading whatever it was to the living. I had an issue with the fact so many innocent people might be caught up in the fire storm that I settled it by telling Ralph to prep his chopper to be transported to the coming battle where he would drop fliers warning the people of the coming battle, they were directed to head toward our lines where they would be cared for, anybody staying behind was in grave danger.

I also wanted a warning to anybody showing up with Gang ink that they would be dealt with in a less gentle manner. It might not do much but I'll sleep better knowing I tried.

We rolled out on a clear and beautiful morning, heading right at Barstow, scouts out, guns up and not in a mood to screw around. Anybody who shot at us was going down hard and left for buzzard food.

Capt. Harry had left two day earlier with his Rangers and our commo people which of course included "talkers" They were driving HV's and trailers with fuel and ammo and were not stopping for anything except a break down.

We headed south until we hit I 40 and there we hit it, pushing as hard and possible without leaving vehicles along the way. And I must admit we made one hell of a picture!! Every vehicle was flying Old Glory! We had Scouts out front, looking for trouble, HV's leading with others in the convoy, we rolled with guns up and gunners watching every thing close to us. We saw people who just stared but most were waving and cheering, why I don't really know except I guess it seemed a sign that America was open for business. Not yet, and I don't know when but it will be!

We rolled thru the day and night switching drivers every four hours, we even had rolling bunk rooms for the drivers to get some good sleep, the rest of us slept where we were. I must admit I came to envy the girls, all three were like cats, they were small enough to curl up any place and sleep like kittens whereas I couldn't do more then sit.

The trip seemed to last forever but it did come to an end. When we were fifty miles out of Barstow we got the word that Capt. Harry and his Rangers had taken the base. No KIA's and five WIA's the fact there was help inside made it very easy. He said the outlaw element had become so complacent that it was a cake walk.

They got all their wounded at the main gate where one of the guards was awake and manning a machine gun and got off a few bursts before being cut down. The rest surrendered.

The former XO pulled his on plug rather then face a rope, General Sweet was in good shape because the people around him had remained loyal to him and their oaths which a lot of them did, but not all, sadly. I hated the thought of Marines turning their backs on their oath and their Corps, they would be dealt with.

Sneaky always works best, I like sneaky, fewer losses of people and equipment. We rolled right up to the gate and found Harry and his troops on parade all they needed was a band playing. I could see pride on all their faces and they earned it.

Harry took me to see General Sweet, I found him looking far better then expected, he had spent his time doing his physical therapy under the eyes of the base Doc and his corpsmen. It's seems there was a bit of deception going on when reports of how bad Sweet was.

I had last seen him on a jungle trail long ago, I was heading off into the bush while he was about to fly out to a much nicer place.

But he had personally made sure my team had everything they wanted for our little adventure and because the supply lines were screwed up with thieves stealing so much stuff to sell on the black market I owed him big time.

We looked at each other for a bit then shook hands, he gestured to a chair so I sat with him and talked about the long ago but mostly the now, he had heard my name on commo traffic and knew it had to be me and from what they were hearing he knew with my help he could rid the area of the traitor who stole his command. So now here we were, I told him where we were going and my plans for LA. He said "The whole place??" Yep I replied, you can't burn a part of the bush to get the snakes out you have to burn it all.

He nodded and smiled and said never half way with you John. After spending a couple of hours with him I headed out to get my people settled.

I found Capt. Harry ahead of me, the troops were settled into barracks and the chow hall turning out food, soon all were showered and fed and sleeping like the dead, it had been a trip.

Harry had put us in the VIP guest house so I headed there to shower and then gather my flock and go eat. I found Beth but the troublesome twosome were gone, I had to ask and wasn't surprised when she said with all this stuff that goes bang and boom you know they are walking off with all they can carry, how well I knew that.

Showering with Beth is fun as it is with all of them, we headed for the mess hall and found the girls eating, surrounded by Marines who had been listening to the tales of their exploits, at the moment they were telling how I burned down Las Vegas.

Beth and I took a seat close by and since they hadn't seen us I figured we could listen to the BS, I should know better, they both turned around and flashed those killer smiles and said " There he is!! With wife number three!! Beth! Beth groaned while I just shook my head, they said goodbye to their audience and headed for us, hugs and kissed for both of us and then they commenced to tell us all the stuff they had "found" and all the stuff they had "borrowed" and could they have a truck? Now I groaned and asked why they needed a thousand hand grenades? They of course said coz we don't have any. I pointed out that there are plenty of them in our demo storage area, but OH NO!! they don't have any of their own! I gave up, then they asked me if I knew anything about Claymores, if my food trey hadn't been in my way I would have pounded my head on the table. But I know better then to not answer them so I admitted I knew about them.

They are so happy. I asked what else they had stolen, they looked around and May whispered, 50 K rounds of 45 ball ammo!! Now I was impressed but I had to ask why so little, Sandy said well we need a bigger truck which brings us back to can we have a truck?

I just looked at them for a moment then said, ok here's the thing, where did you get all this stuff? They said the place was full of it, I asked what kind of base is this? Both said Supply base dummy!

I smiled and said, you steal thousands of rounds of ammo and mines and you can't steal a fkn truck?

They sat there for a minute and looked at each other then played the blame game for a couple of minutes until it dawned on them they were in the candy land of supplies and they were gone with a fast kiss for both of us, I slumped forward while Beth rubbed my neck and said John you're the most wonderful husband three women could ask for and then laughed and said I'm going with them it sounds like fun!! And with a kiss she was gone.

Now I wasn't worried about Beth because she was the more adult one of the bunch but I also knew she was corruptible around those two. They have a way of getting everything they want so I did have a moment of worry about Beth. It was like the door to the vault was thrown open for them. I left to take a nap in peace and quiet.

Napping is good and it lets me escape from the reality of the world around me and the things I've done under the guise of stopping bad people from hurting good people or some such shit. Anyway I like naps, I also like waking up to somebody snuggling close to me. I didn't have to open my eyes to know it was Beth. She just walks into a room and calm flows in with her. Finally I asked where the James Gang were at the moment, she said "well John, they need truck drivers", I mumbled "shit" she said yep their reputation arrives before them and they are taking full advantage of it. Then she laughed and said well I think one truck is all mine. I raised up and looked at her and she blushed and said well girls like new stuff and I'm a girl so... I asked her what kind of stuff, she mumbled something that sounded a great deal like Barrett, so I said ok, you got a Barrett? She said well kinda, I asked how you could kinda have a Barrett, she replied that " A" was maybe a bit short, I sigh as usual, she admitted she now has 5 Barrett sniper systems and more 50 cal ammo then she can ever shoot. I said "You shoot?" Well she said I guess I'll have to share a bit with the girls then she started giggling and said John it really is a candy store out there. She also said there was a truck load of 25mm ammo! That we need!

And ammo for the 40 mm auto grenade launchers on our vehicles, this made me very happy because we had been short of them all along. I did have to ask if they were stealing it and she said no that General Sweet gave the orders to give us whatever we wanted, he also said any of his Marines who wanted to go along to help out could but not so many as to leave the base security weakened.

He was still a good officer, he knew his men were chomping at the bit to be out doing and helping instead of standing guard duty. For this I was grateful but I only wanted the ones who could operate some of the equipment we were getting. I have shooters, I need people who can operate the equipment and keep it running.

Beth and I headed out to see what was going on and to get the latest intel info.

I had also forgotten the main reason for our coming here and that was the leader of the rabble here at the base and shortly found out he had headed south after the last ambush to get more crud for his army, I had to assume he knew by now that the base was lost but he didn't know how or why so he really had no idea we were coming for him.

Capt. Harry has said he changed his name more often then his skivvies so names mean nothing but he was a product of the inner city gang areas even tho he had served in the military and wasn't stupid and also had never trusted Harry but was afraid to try to do anything about for the moment, he figured by sending Harry off to chase me down he would likely get killed so didn't object when Harry offered to go.

This whole mess was more then I really wanted to deal with but it was there and dealing is what a good leader does, I asked Harry to see if the base print shop could run off about a hundred thousand fliers telling people what was coming and to get them out asap. He got right on it. I took time to check on all of our people plus the Rangers and making sure them and the Marines were playing well together.

I figured I'd end up having to break up some problems but not at all! They were working their asses off getting ready to go to war. It was funny that all these trained warriors with the rare exception had less combat time then my civilian army. I might need to make sure they had some of my folks sprinkled thru their ranks.

Now we just had to get the C-130 here and get this show on the road, Harry had gotten the airport cleaned up and lights working so the C-130 was coming in tomorrow morning early. It was time to check that everything was loaded and ready to go.

My staff and I spent the day checking and rechecking that we had everything we could think of plus stuff we hadn't thought of but others had. As soon as the big bird was on the ground the chopper was going to do the flier drop, I was giving them 24 hours notice and then the roof was gonna cave in.


Morning found us at the air port watching a small speck getting bigger by the moment until the 130 seemed to fill the sky, it had been so long since we had seen anything bigger then our small plane in the air that we were just blown away, everybody was yelling and cheering, most of the town had turned out for the event which more then anything seemed to point to better days, some day.

After the pilot shut down the engines and the crew came down the ramp we headed for the plane, the Lt. Col flying the bird looked around before asking where the commanding officer was, I had to smile knowing he and I weren't gonna get along at all.

Sandy of course spoke up with" He's standing in front of you, you stiff necked prick! I swear he puffed up like a toad!

Looked at me and said to his crew "load up we're leaving right now!" Before he could turn away I said Col, you are free to leave anytime you want, but the plane stays, we have people who have more hours in a 130 then you do! ( A lie but fk him!) that stopped him and he marched right at me like he was gonna run me over but he stopped when he saw three 45 muzzles right in his face. Even Beth was ready to splatter this asshole all over the ground. His people were scattering from behind him in case. Well he stood there sputtering until I said Col, really sir, get the stick out of your ass and follow me over to the shade, I was walking away and he hadn't moved so I stopped and quietly said Col. that was not a request. Now move it you pampas ass! Well that got him moving and when we were alone I told him one more out burst and he was walking home so please tell me what his main problem was. Well he went thru the "My plane this and my plane that until I said Col. It's my plane and has been since the people in Texas agreed to it so I think your out of line.

He wouldn't listen to me at all and wouldn't shut up so I made a motion to the Ranger LT and held up three fingers and made the double time arm pump and he pointed out three Rangers and ran to me.

I said LT, the Col is under arrest, please take him to the BOQ and place him under house arrest, if he says one word out of line take him to the brig. After sputtering a bit he said wait can't we talk about this? I said no, I offered to be reasonable and you weren't willing to play so here it is.

He said he would toe the line but I just

smiled and said until your off the ground and heading back to Texas right?

I had him, he turned red as a beet and I told him to never play poker with Marines.

The LT took him away and I returned to the air crew and looked at them then said ok! Who else can fly this pile of beer cans? Well that got some laughs from even the airmen and a Major said " Well sir I spect ahm your huckleberry" with a beautiful drawl. I smiled and said sounds like home. He said yep, raised around East Texas not far from your family compound! I said then you heard of us? He said yep and I tried to tell that asshole but he just won't ever listen so now what?

I asked if he could fly without a co-pilot and he said yea but it was nice to have somebody who knew how to wind up the rubber bands, I was liking this guy! I told him I had a chopper pilot with a lot of fixed windg time but not big stuff.

He said that was fine, just somebody to drive when he went to piss and get a cup of coffee. He said something to one of the air crew who took off at a run back up the ramp and returned with the most beat up dirty Stetson I ever saw, after he put it on he stuck out his hand and said " Major Arnold Minor" sir! While we all smiled at that he said his lady friend back at the base was a Capt. Mary Bumps who had a real nice set and when she made Major she would be "Major Bumps" now we were all laughing our asses off, if this guy could fly half as good as he could talk he was an asset Texas might not get back.

I noticed the girls heading for the ramp and I yelled "NO!! damn it NO! they flipped me off and trotted up the ramp.

I asked Arnie as he said to call him if he had left the keys in the ignition, he laughed and said nope I heard about them two long before I knowed we was comin here. And there ain't a thing in there they can walk off with!

He said Harry had warned him before they left and also told him to be prepared to fly the mission because he figured the Col was heading for a problem. He asked about the girls pulling the pistols and if it was a show, I said your buddy the Col was a ounce of trigger pull from being splattered all over the run way.

He said yep Harry said they was cute as a bug and as deadly as a pit full of rattlers. He was watching Beth heading for the plane, he said Harry had told him about Beth and how she had just joined the family and was already kind of in control of the "rabid badgers" as Harry put it. I said I didn't have the full story yet but I knew enough to know the girls had watched her for a long time and got to know her and really liked her before asking her if she was interested. I said I had little to do with any of it I just went along with it mostly but that I had drawn the line at the three of them. They were happy, so I was happy and I think they had planned to use Beth to keep me distracted while they run rampant but it worked out that Beth was calming them down to a degree and they were dragging her along with them to a degree.

I heard the sounds of the chopper coming back and we watched Ralph coming in pretty fast, the props were still spinning when he bailed out and started running around the bird, we joined him and found him looking at a couple of damn big holes in the left door, the man who went along to kick out the fliers was still white looking, the rounds must had fanned him as they passed. Ralph said the bastards had some fifty cals in there that must have come from the base here and they almost fried his ass except the gunner was untrained and opened up too soon but still got two hits, he said they were at the far end of their loop and had dumped the last of the fliers when it happened. Luck, pure and simple.

Ralph looked at the 130 and said sweet!! I asked if he ever flew one but he laughed and said no but I'd give my left one to try it. I smiled and said well good because you're the co-pilot! I thought he was gonna kiss me! I did the intros between the two and they walked off hands waving and diving and talking a strange language.

Pilots and tankers are very weird ducks but we need em, so… I saw Beth herding the girls down the ramp where they stopped to say hi to Ralph who must have said something about getting shot at because Sandy was yelling at him for getting "Her" Chopper shit to pieces, Ralph looked at me, I shrugged and smiled. He flipped me off, Beth saved him by heading for the chopper where "they" joined her, Sandy was heard to say, That?? That's almost getting shot down?? What a pussy!! God.. One second your damned if you do and the next your damned if ya don't. I've never seen one like her, May might be close but she ain't there yet. Given her way I think Sandy would become a War Lord but on the side of good. ( HA! Already am!) stop it! (Looks again..) I need a nap.

I got my nap and for a while didn't have to share the bed, then all three trooped in and that was the end of sleep, they piled on the bed and turned it into a pajama party. I rolled over on my belly and Beth rubbed my shoulders and back and then I did sleep.

I woke up in a pile, they were sprawled all over me and the bed. Beth was beside me and laying with my arm around her, I went back to sleep, we were gonna need it as we had learned in Vegas.

Morning came and I couldn't move, they were still sleeping so I started easing out of the tangle and made it to the bathroom before I peed the floor then I got in the shower and steamed the place up, Beth joined me then May and shortly Sandy squeezed in, it was crowded but kind of nice. Slippery is good.

I got out followed by Beth giving them more room and bitching about running out of hot water. I got dressed kissed Beth and ran out the door before they could jump me all wet and fussing over cold water. I smiled all the way to the mess hall where I found the entire staff, I should have felt guilty but I didn't. I'm old! I don't have to care.

Everything is done, the 130 is loaded and ready to roll as soon as we call, with nothing left we rolled out within the hour heading south, we circled around on secondary road to the west to avoid the piled up freeways, here it was so different then out in the heart land, millions of cars that just stopped dead in their tracks. And the remains of the beginning of the crazy times following the event, sometimes it looks like people just got out of their vehicles and started killing each other.

It is sad that the people with more then any nation on earth could revert to savagery in the blink of an eye, I'll never understand it.

As loaded down as we were we took two days to get there, stopping for nothing, we bypassed small settlements who's people either ran for cover of stood and cheered us on. I have to admit I was surprised to find these settlements this close to the cities but even murdering assholes need food so killing off the food growers don't make much sense, I expect these folks had to pay a hefty tax to be left alone. Well I hoped this trip would end that shit.

On the evening of the second long day we made it to the sprawling edges of the city and it looked like Dresden after the Air Force fire bombed it, desolate didn't cover it, wasteland may come close to it. With a big wrecker with a plow on the front to move cars and make a road we rolled forward, as we went some people started coming out and they looked like they had been freed from a Nazi death camp, we could become bogged down here so I ordered the troops to start tossing MRE's away from the road, the people fell on them like a pack of wild dogs.

Bottles of water were added to the menu. I was amazed that so many could still be living here and it put a heavy weight on my shoulders. I asked the medical team to pick out a few of them and question them about what was ahead, they took in three men who after eating a bit were able to say they had been further inside the city when the fliers came and they at last took the chance to run for it, they said the main city center was all gangland and that any non gang bangers had either left or died long ago.

After learning all they could the med team left the three with a huge pile of MRE's and water  that I hoped they doled out to others. We couldn't spare the time or people to do it.

I had never really been to LA but had been close enough to know I never wanted to visit. We drove on until we could see the center of the city. I would have liked to spread the guns out over a very wide front but security wouldn't allow it so we did the best we could by spreading their front so one gun was firing into it's own sector,  We had decided Ralph was needed more as a spotter for the fight so we took him and his chopper with us and one of the planes officers flew as co-pilot.

Ralph and a spotter were up in the chopper well above ground fire and worked at fire control center. The gun crews were set up and ready so with nothing to gain by waiting I gave the order to open fire. The crash of the guns sounded like the gates of hell slamming shut. Ralph could see the shell fall of each gun and the idea was to fire and move the next shell fall to the right about 50 yards, we started with Willy Peter and the fires started roaring. Cars with fuel remaining and who knows what but there were explosions in the mess, they fired until the barrels needed cooling down then changed elevation and started again, it went on all day with my people replacing the gun crews where they could, Ralph said it was hell in there, I asked him to land and pick me up which he did but of course I wasn't allowed to go alone, so the four of us go on the chopper after it was refueled and once we were over the city I could see it was an inferno, we went higher and flew over the city and I could see the rats running, cars bikes whatever they could find, on foot if nothing else. They were doing just what we wanted, running right into the coming blast, there were hundreds then thousands, hell they were even fighting each other as they ran, fine with me! We were well ahead of the shells and could see the line of explosions slowly walking at us.

We flew higher and further south and could see the mass of trash piling up as they got bottle necked. I called Big Bird and said "come to Papa" Ralph gave the coordinates and got us out away from the area, we would see the effects of the drop.

About half an hour later Big Bird called to say they were going to make a pass from west to east and make their drop at half mile intervals but I said save the last one for the mass of rats in the bottle neck.

We saw the plane and saw the first package slide out and the chutes open, it was interesting, the plane flew on dropping the load behind, Ralph said it looked like it was taking a dump which got the girls laughing.

The first package was still in the air about 500 yards above the city when it turned into a small sun, the shock wave even shook the chopper causing Ralph to haul ass away from the next one. The went off like they were supposed to and left a raging fire storm behind them. The last load was right over the packed bottle neck of gang members when it went off and when the smoke cleared there was nothing moving, just flattened everything for a long ways, Big Bird flew away for the next load and we headed back to the guns.

I called ahead to tell them to cease fire and we landed in a quiet like we had never heard. It was just silent, the sounds of the guns cooling were the loudest sound.

I got with the leaders and told them what we had seen and offered any of them the chance to go up with Ralph for the next run. Joe and Willy both said they would go but nobody else seemed inclined to and I couldn't blame them.

We moved the guns to a new area and started it all over again, I was already tired of it all but it had to be done. Beth had a sad look on her face so I asked her if she felt bad for them she said hell no I feel bad about all the beautiful museums and the Libraries that will be lost for ever, all the knowledge of the ages lost. I told her we had save as much as we could store and that I hated it too.

I asked her what the best museum was in the city and she told me, I asked Ralph if he could find it, he said sure, I said ok, we will send in shooters for security and see if the assholes left anything to save, she said it was too dangerous but the girls were up for it so I said I was going in the first load with all the shooters we could lift off with and the girls could come in the third load, I stopped the fight before it started and for once they didn't fight. We loaded up and took off and true to his word Ralph flew right to it, He admitted he had been there several times and was glad we were trying to save some of it.

We circled the Natural Museum of History and decided to land on the roof, we bailed out and Ralph was gone, we checked out the area and did over watch for the next load, we had come in really heavy on fire power, plenty of SAW's with everybody slinging a 16 across their back and loaded with Mags. Water and one MRE.

Ralph returned and of course the first ones out were the girls, two smiling and one just shaking her head, Ralph was shaking his also. I figured they would pull this because they went for the third wave stuff to easy. Ralph took off and returned two more times until we had 20 shooters with us, Ralph left the bladed turning and stayed with the chopper with two shooters for security. We started down thru the fire door, we all had gun lights but it reminded me of that movie about Raccoon City and the crap that got loose, it was flat scary and I shit you not I didn't fight too hard when I was pushed back while a pair of Rangers took the point.

We made it to the top floor and I could see this was going to be an impossible task for just a few people but even tho we could see some signs of plain vandalism it wasn't as bad as I expected, we did a fast walk thru ready for most anything that might be there and my imagination was working over time, we moved down another floor and it was the same. All the way down thru the dark we expected to be hit any second by Zombies or god knows what but nothing jumped out. We finally made it to the ground floor and looked out into complete hell, it was a combat zone.

Beth took my arm and said lets go John, nothing here is worth the lives of any of our people. I felt bad but at the same time I knew she was right.

We headed back up and found the security guys and chopper as we left it, I sent the girls out on the first run over their objections but for once they minded me but I knew I was going to have to mend fences later.

We all returned safely and the war went

on, the rats were still running in the thousands
and as soon as we had enough in a bottleneck
we fried them, when we got a bunch in range
we shelled them.

For 50 years the gangs had ruled parts of
the city and now they were getting pay back
for all the hell they caused. I had to close my
mind to the innocents caught in this mess and
made the decision to stop shelling unless we
spotted a large group, as long as they were
heading south we let them run and when they
ganged up in one spot we nailed them. So in a
way we were saving a lot of the city and I had
a thought I'd try to look at as soon as I could.

For three more days we herded the rats
with shell fire and fire bombed them when we
got a big bunch located.

After a week of it we stopped. And quiet
settled over the city, then we mounted up in
our LAV's and armored vehicles and rolled
into the mess, when we got shot at we simple
dropped the hammer on them, they didn't
learn, but just moved ahead of us in small
waves getting larger all the time until Raplh
said to stop then he called in fire on them, the
guns used Willy Peter and it wasn't pretty,
after that cooled down we started again,
spread out over several streets in a crescent
we moved forward taking fire and returning
it 10 times as heavy and they still gathered in

places to wait and Ralph did his thing. They still piled up in the bottle necks leading out of the city and the 130 still fried them. I sent heavy teams of shooters around to watch as many roads as they could and the snipers went to work, it wasn't fun but it was there to be done and we did it. I knew we would never get them all the way we were going and finally stopped again.

In the rear there were people coming out of the rubble, I had them stripped and searched for gang tats, those were taken away. The citizens we took care of, some had settlements amid the ruins, some had armed themselves and using the roof tops of buildings and parks had farmed as best they could, growing enough to stay alive, these were the people we wanted, the fighters, the survivors.

After tents were set up and portable mess halls were feeding and the medical teams were tending them we started asking questions and listening and soon enough the natural leaders showed up, the ones who had organized the rest into groups, the ones who made treaties with their neighbors, the ones who fought back. And these I wanted.

After they were cleaned up I met with them, ten men who were the leaders in the area. I told them we could arm them and leave food and water but it was up to them to clear out the remainder of the gangs.

They were to a man ready to go right then, but their people were in need of time to get back on their feet and food and care was gonna do that. So we planned it out with them while we waited for the people to get their strength back and in the mean time more and more people turned up.

We stayed there for a week watching for more runners and we found them and a few rounds of shell fire with Ralph spotting took care of them.

At the end of the week there was around a thousand people who were cleaned up and able to start cleaning up their area, later they were going to start street by street until the city was clean of the outlaws. I claimed up on a truck bed and addressed them, I told them that we had other places to go and clear out and that they were on their feet and able to fight back and were armed and had been given basic rifle training. I looked right at the leaders and said we will be checking back and if any of you try to become Kings or Warlords we will deal with you just like the gangs. This is your chance to start living. What you do with it is up to you.

One of the people in front said " Why can't

you people stay and fight, your trained, it's your job, We need food and water and power we don't need guns". I looked at him and said, If I was in charge of this place you would be in a vehicle getting your cowardly lazy ass hauled into gang land and left for them to eat. So shut the fuck up and get off your ass and go to work!

With that we rolled out and headed South, we had a date down the road with the gangs who had stopped running thinking they were safe. They weren't and won't be, as they run for the border they will find us on their ass all the way and the border don't mean shit, never mattered to them so it don't mean shit to us, killing these dirt bags is all that matters.

One thing that bothers me is that burning the cities loses so many things we need to help rebuild the nation but I won't risk my people in house to house fighting to save things that may or may not have already be destroyed by the survivors, I find myself blaming the wanton destruction on the bad elements in society when in truth just the act of trying to survive can and does cause so much damage.

Hell look at all the busted in doors and safes Sandy and I are responsible for. Sure we are the good guys but is a busted in door any less busted if it's done by good guys then bad guys? Hell are we the good guys?

I gotta stop smoking this shit whatever it is I must be smoking to be thinking like this. I know we are the good guys, and I know the gangs are bad guys, but if we burn a city to the ground to drive them out are we really any better? I remember back long ago in the land of bad things when some news hack asked some grunt if they really had to burn the village they had just taken, the reply was something like " We had to. To save it" I never actually heard it so hell maybe it was some POS reporter blowing shit.

I need to have a talk with the command group but first I need to talk to Charley. He will explain more in ten words then a committee meeting will in eight hours.

We headed East and a bit South on our way out of LA, the idea was to get ahead of any that made it and hammer them again before they can duck out of sight in some place between here and San Diego on their run for the border. But in truth I'm beginning to think this job is just too big for us and it's not like a city in some rural "red" state where a city might be huge with a hundred K people, here we are talking millions of people who had lived there, where were they? All dead? Hiding out in basements? I was afraid we were going to need to look deeper into this before we did anything else. So, when in doubt, stop, recon, ask questions of whoever we can find.

So this is what we are gonna do. We will get away from any larger type city, maybe stop in a town so to speak and use the time for vehicle maintenance and other prep work.

After setting up near a small settlement of around 200 people who were doing a good job of holding things together we had a meeting with their leaders and found they had fought almost weekly battles with the gangs foraging for food but hadn't had to face the heavy weapons that we had seen. Maybe because they were well off the traveled routes or weren't big enough to make it worth the loses, who knows? They welcomed us and sold us fruit and veggies which were a welcome change from MRE's but outside that they had no information for us, they had worked at holding a low profile and who could blame them?

Ralph was flying daily looking for targets worth  expending ammo on, he was spotting small groups heading south but nothing like we got before.
What we did do was fly out sniper teams well in advance with a mortar team as back up in case they were hit by a large group. They were getting a lot of kills but not enough  to make a difference. I was also worried about this flu bug or whatever it was, we had seen

no signs of it but I believed it was coming and if so there was nothing to do but back off to our nice hot desert and stop all traffic coming into the area.

I've always doubted myself and my abilities but this was a problem way above my pay grade, what to do? We can't just go from city to city shelling and burning, first it's a task too huge for our small group plus we had accomplished most of what we set out to do, which was to deal with the bad guy from LA.

I don't know if he's dead or like the rat he is was able to slip out a back door leaving his flunkies to keep us busy. We would never know unless he popped up again.

I called a commanders meeting and laid out all my thoughts and doubts, I asked for help in deciding what was the right thing to do. And bless them they all came thru with the unanimous vote to go home and await developments.

We were all scared of the thought of a plague spreading across the land and just wanted to get as far away from this place as soon and as fast as we can.

As soon as the meeting was over I passed the word to be ready to roll come first light. I could tell everybody was feeling the urge to hit the ground running. It was a restless night but come the crack of dawn we were on the road and making a beeline for home.

I feel in a lot of ways that we did a lot of good but in many way's I feel it was all just a waste of resources which of course it wasn't, by wiping out all those gang bangers we have save many times that in innocent lives and that alone was well worth the effort, we had accomplished all this with no KIA's on our part, wounded? Yes, but those are better then digging another grave on some lonely hill.

And something I'm not admitting to anybody, I'm tired, tired of fighting and tired of killing and tired of putting other people's lives in danger, sooner or later if this shit goes on it's going to cost me somebody dear to me, god forbid it's one of the girls, Charley, Joe, Willy, on and on, so many chances to lose somebody close and it will break my heart, but for now, I'm just tired and I wanna go home and go up on my no longer secret spot and let the sun bake the tiredness and fear out of me. We stopped for the night and just set up tents and ate MRE's and called it a night.

I laid down in our tent alone and felt all the days thoughts still locked in me and making me feel like I would never know peace again.

And of course along comes my own personal "joint" to relax me with her calm warm touch, Beth, the best addition we could have ever brought into our family. I somehow think she was sent more then found if that makes sense?

She settled in beside me and never said a word just took me in her arms and held me close, and I woke up to the promise of a sunny beautiful day.

The girls were still sleeping so I headed out looking for coffee and found it then headed for a small hill to greet the day and was soon joined by Charley who never intrudes with his presents, we just sat and watched the day together.

When our coffee was done he made the quiet cough he does to signal he's wants to speak, when I didn't say anything he said " Your spirit is better today, you were tormented for several days and I'm glad you made the right decision to abandon the chase and go home. It was time, we need to be there to settle in and prepare for what comes.

When I didn't comment he went on, he said "Old Woman" said it was time to come home because we need to close down access to our home land.

She says the People are coming from all over to be away from the coming troubles. He sat a while and I thought about asking how he had talked to her but maybe I wasn't ready for the answer. I was looking at him when he smiled and I knew who was coming.

Beth arrived with more coffee and the usual effect her presents has on us all. We thanked her and she turned to leave but I stopped her and patted the ground beside me, we sat in the quiet of the new day knowing shortly it would be broken by the arrival of "them" and yes here they come both carrying a lot of stuff, they brought more coffee in a carafe and some home made granola bars that we make in the canyon which are so much better then the old crap we used to buy.

The girls were on their best behavior and were quiet, one leaning on me the other on Beth, is there a better way to face the day?

We made it to the place where the Texas folks would split off to head home in around a week, a few breakdowns, a few flats but no gun fights!

We all said goodbye and waved as The Texas Militia left us, once again driving their trucks pulling their guns along with the Rangers, we watched them roll away and I missed them already.

I wondered how they would explain the two missing guns, I looked at the girls and sighed while they had the good graces to not say a word, I looked at the low boy with two canvas covered loads and crate after crate of 105 rounds all chained down.

Finally, Sandy ( as usual) said, Daddy, they followed us home, can we keep them please? Followed by May adding "can we daddy? Pretty please."

Hell even Charley busted out laughing out

loud, in fact everybody was laughing, they do this shit so well. The icing was Beth tossing in a "Please daddy!! We will be really good and make it worth your while"

I looked at Charley who said " You are so easy even for a white man."

I did the hand whirl and yelled "Forwardddddd" and the Boos and air horns wiped the rest out.

Home, we are almost home.
TJ

I hope this one live up to the series, I got lost in it a bit, I had to stop and think about what it would take to bring control to a city the size of LA and the surrounding area and I believe it would take an entire Marine Division to do the job. And I realized I had set too huge of a task for John and his group and had to weasel out somehow. I don't function in cities and I can't write about functioning in cities. For the last fifty years I've lived in either the desert or the high country, never a lot of people, so I have trouble writing about what it would be like fighting a war in a huge city, hell a small village is bad enough. So please forgive me for bailing out of the chase for the never seen bad guy, but he may well show up again.

I know I get lost in the antics of the girls but that's ok because they are so much fun and I'm glad they brought Beth into the family, we needed an adult in the house.

Take a few minutes to think about a SHTF issue, if it happened right now, what will you do? Have food put away? At least enough to last six months? Remember it don't take an EMP, a tornado can undo your life in a heart beat, the crash of the dollar and our economy can put us all in extreme danger, hungry people with kids to feed will become as bad as the MZBH ( Mutant Zombie Bikers from Hell) of most PAW books.

I've had good friends when asked if they

are prepping say no, we will just come to your
place, and sadly, they meant it.
So think about it, there is so much you can do
to keep your family safe or as safe as it will
be for anybody.

I try to put some of my thoughts in these
books but I think I fail at it. Others can do it
so much better.

TJ

# A long Lonely Road

## A Dish Best Served Cold

### Book nine

## By TJ Reeder

Have you ever had a nightmare so bad you wanted to scream? A nightmare you can't wake from? That won't release it's grip on your heart?

That's where I am, I see flashes of bad things, things that are breaking my heart but I can't escape this fkn nightmare.

I keep seeing the same scene as if on a video loop and it's killing me.

It's a beautiful day and I decided to take a ride since we haven't ridden since Vegas and that was just too long, Buck and his clan were starting to think retirement had come. So I broached the idea to the ladies and it was greeted with squeals of delight and hugs, which are a good thing!

So after breakfast we headed for the box
canyon we used for a corral where we found
Buck, Rab and the "Horse with no name"
waiting as if they knew, hell maybe they did,
who knows, life is a mystery and always has
been and who are we to solve it? Not me, I
don't care enough to care.

After we had them saddled we stopped at the
Cave as I call it and loaded the stuff we took
as we would a BOB. Saddle guns, over night
gear and some food and water. The plan was
to just have a nice day trip but to be prepared
to be out over night, common sense even if
the world wasn't in melt down.

We spent the best part of the day just riding
and looking and feeling the easing of tensions
that being on a horse will bring. Riding is
better then all the Prozac ever made. We
stopped often just to look across the land
which with the rains that came had turned
green for a while, it was beautiful.

We were hading back home and on a trail that
cut off some miles when something spooked
Buck causing him to toss his head and jerk to
the left. The next thing I knew blood was
flying off Bucks head and he was rearing up!
As we went over my last sight was Beth
falling off her horse, her chest covered with
blood. Buck and I hit the ground and

everything went black but I could hear gun
fire as if thru a long dark tunnel then nothing.

This dream was the cause of my breaking
heart, and I couldn't wake up. I thrashed and
thought I was yelling for Beth but she never
came. I called Sandy and May and heard them
from afar, they too were in the long black
tunnel and I couldn't find them.

I make a promise that if I can wake up I'll
never sleep again, silly huh? I felt hands
grabbing at me in the dark and I was filled
with fear.
 I tried to fight but I was being held down, I
couldn't move my arms, I had a lot of bad
dreams after the war but never like this. At
last I felt hands on my face and a wet cloth,
thank god, somebody was trying to help me.
    I heard Sandy and May both saying "Wake
up John!!" like they always do when I nap,
and usually waking up involves bailing them
out of their latest problem.

    I heard a mans voice, one I know, but I
can't place it. He's telling me I need to wake
up, well shit! Really dude? Like I'm stuck in
the fkn black tunnel because I wanna be? I
should wake up so I can slug the silly bastard!

The voice calmly says. John, Beth is fine,
Buck is fine, And John, The Baby is just fine.
I sat up and fell back but my eyes were open,

I could tell I was in a darkened room with just a bit of light.

I looked at the man leaning over me and said "Hey Doc, how's it hanging? I smiled and said what a fucked up nightmare! He smiled back and said John, what did I just say to you? I had to think for a moment and feeling very proud I repeated it to him, then I stopped smiling and said Doc? It wasn't a nightmare was it?

He said no John, you got a very bad concussion when Buck went over on you, lady luck was with all of you.

Then his words hit me, Buck and Beth were ok? That means there weren't ok before they got ok.

Then his other words hit me.
BABY? What baby? We didn't have a baby!
He looked at me and smiled and said well no shit you old fart, but congratulations John, in about six months you will have a baby. I was confused, where was I gonna get a baby? I saw the girls standing behind the Doc and held my arms up and they gently hugged me, not at all like the dog pile I was used to.

I asked where Beth was and they pointed to the bed next to mine and there she was! All smiles and wrapped in bandages around her chest. I tried to jump up but the room got drunk and spun away. When it settled down I

asked for food and water and then said ok,
somebody tell me what the hells going on.

Sandy spoke up first telling me that just as
Buck spooked and turned a bit a rifle bullet
passed thru his ear, missed me and hit Beth! I
looked at her still smiling and reaching her
hand out to me, I reached out and took it. I
asked if she was really ok? She said yes but
she needed a new pistol, I must have looked
lost so Sandy opened a drawer by the bed and
pulled out Beth's STI 10 mm, the slide was
bent and had a bullet sticking part way from
it!. I looked at her and the doc spoke up
saying the wounds were from the metal
splatter from the impact, all shallow cuts that
bled a lot. She has a big bruise but was ok
otherwise.

I asked the girls where we were getting a
baby? They both lit up and made the Ta Da
thing with their hands at Beth. Looking at her
I said where are you getting a baby? She
smiled the most beautiful smile and said
"from the usual place John" I'm slow, even
without a concussion I'm slow and it took a
bit laying there looking at all three of my
wives all radiant and happy looking.

Then it hit me! My mouth fell open and I was
making some kind of sounds that sounded like
Ba BA Ba BA!!! All three nodded and smiled
even bigger.

I still had Beth's hand and looked at her and asked the age old question… A baby? She nodded. You're gonna have a baby? She nodded. How did that happen? They all laughed, even the Doc thought it was funny.

I fell asleep or passed out for a bit, then my eyes popped open and I bellered " A Baby? We are having a baby? When? Who's is it? Beth was still smiling and said well John I guess it's yours since you're the only man I've been with since my husband was killed, so yes love we are having a baby.

Sandy and May were bouncing like balls, they looked like they were having the baby, but then of course in a way they were. I was too shocked to think.

I'm too old to have a baby! How will I support a baby? The girls went to the other side of Beth's bed and pushed it against mine so Beth and I were close together. Dizzy or not I managed to raise up and kiss her then hugged her then the girls who were on the beds with us. Doc was just smiling.

After that I fell asleep for real, and no dreams. I slept for ten hours according to the nurse lady who was there when I woke up, I was hit with several emotions all at once, I knew I was starving, I knew I needed to take a leak really bad, and I looked at Beth who was sleeping with a smile on her face and her hand wrapped tightly in mine.

I just laid there for a long time watching her and wondering how in the world I had managed to make her pregnant? I'm old, really old and tired and hard to live with and …old, too old to be having kids. But it looks like I'm not as old as I thought. But was this the world to bring kids into? Couldn't be any worse then the ones brought into the  middle of a world war.

Whatever, it was what it was so I'd deal with it as always, one step at a time. I watched Beth breathing, looking for any sign that things weren't right. I trust Doc but I believe in trust but verify.

She looked beautiful laying there and her smile was so sweet. I sensed motion behind me and looked in time to see the girls tiptoeing into the room, both stepped out of their shoes and like cats just flowed onto the bed and curled up with me. All of us watching Beth sleep, they were smiling softly and almost purring.

The look on their faces it was like self Congratulations, and I suddenly  wondered if they had set this whole thing in motion? And like clock work both sets of eyes swiveled to meet mine and both smiled like a cat with feathers sticking out of it's mouth.

And I knew right then and there that both of them had conspired to bring a small bundle of joy(??) into our lives and it explained the bigger house. I looked at them and wondered if Beth was in on it or was innocent? And both simply shook their heads "no".

I didn't know if I should beat them or hug them but from the look on Beth's face I knew the answer. Our own warm, kind, sweet spirit of peace and love was going to bring something to our family that was lacking, even if I didn't know it. So I took the chicken way out and hugged them both to me.

 Someplace in there we went to sleep, all four of us together as it should be. When I next woke I was alone in my bed and still holding Beth's hand, she was watching me sleep and smiled when I opened my eyes, then her smile failed and her lips quivered so I dragged myself close to her and just held her close while she softly cried, when she stopped I kissed her tears away and said so you're making me a Dad? She said nope, you're making me a mom! We both laughed and then the Doc came in and said hell I think I'll kick you both out this morning.

He checked my eyes and everything else and pronounced me as ok as I was gonna get then checked Beth and said she was fine. The door opened and the girls came in with clean clothes so Doc left us alone while we got us up and dressed.

In a few minutes walk we were home and I was ready for bed again but just plopped down on the slab bench I call the stump and sat. The girls all went inside and soon were giggling and carrying on like a bunch of teenage girls or at least what I assumed teen girls would sound like.

I looked up and saw Charley walking toward me but he stopped and made a hand motion so I walked to him and we headed for a more private area. After we were seated he asked what I knew about the events after I was knocked out and that was nothing, I was aware that nobody was talking about it and figured they were hiding something. But I figured it could wait a while.

Charley said he had gone over the area with a fine toothed comb along with his best scouts, he read it like this.

The shooters had come into the area from a southerly route, moving at night and laying up during the day. My first question was to ask if we had just been unlucky? He said no, these people were sent in here to kill you. I thought a moment and said how did they find us out there? He said pure dumb luck on their part. They were infiltrating into our area and we rode up on them causing them to jump the gun so to speak.

He said he found where Buck had spooked and that it had been Walker who alerted to the danger and had leaped in front of Buck as he raced to the point of the attack.

When Buck jerked he moved his head into the area in front of mine and I slipped to the right. The bullet intended for my head hit bucks ear spraying me with blood and when we went over backwards I hit the ground and it looked like I was dead.

Beth fell at the same time and the girls had opened up with their 45's so fast they had the shooter and his team ducking, before they could regain the momentum the girls had charged right at them with their rifles and just hosed the shit out of them.
Charley said they killed three of the hit team but two got away, first on foot then onto horses and rode them nearly to death getting out of there. The girls had dropped the chase and headed for Beth and me.

They saw right away that Beth was ok just some splatter cuts but they knew I was in bad trouble so May took off riding for the canyon while Sandy stood guard.
When May got to the canyon Ralph bailed into the chopper and May jumped in with the Doc and they flew out to the scene. After checking both of us Doc got us loaded in the bird and leaving the girls to gather the stock they flew us back to the canyon and Doc's mobile hospital.

Surprising me the girls after stripping the

bodies of anything they had on them they headed back instead of trying to run down the two who got away. They were all five Mexicans and not really very good at their job except for the main shooter who got away with one other.

Charley got word right away and within minutes had people on the way to the scene to start tracking the runners while others scattered out across the country on roads and high points waiting and watching.

I was surprised to find out that I was out for three days! So the bastards had gotten away I said. Charley smiled and said no, they think they have, but we have them spotted and can shut them down whenever you say the word.
He added that he figured I would want to know where they were running to and who they were reporting to. He was right but I think we both knew who was behind it.

We sat quietly for a while until I had a thought, I asked if there was any way we could get ahead of them and get close to the border and wait for them to get there. I knew who sent them and he was a dead man walking. And if I had a chance he wouldn't die real quick, trying for me was fair but Beth? No fucking way, for that he was gonna die slow. Charley knew what I was thinking

and said John, you know Beth got hit with a
bullet meant for you. I agreed but wasn't
gonna back off so he just said ok, lets get with
it if you are ready.

I thought for a bit and said ok, here's the
rub, I don't want any of the girls involved. He
smiled and said good luck. But I was not
letting them get into this one, it was all mine.
After talking it over we decided I'd lay back
for a day or so and when they girls were up on
the ridge beating the building crew to go
faster coz they needed a nursery, I would
simply drive off in the truck and meet up with
Charley who would have one of his lads drive
the truck back and hopefully get away before
being tortured to death for what he knew.

Charley and I would then take his truck and
head
south, me with the old hat on and with my
beard I had growing since we left for the ride.
Charley had everything we would need at his
place and would be loaded when we met up.

Now to clear my mind of the details
because I still believe they can hear me think.
Yea I know, it's crazy but there is no other
explanation for it.
So I was gonna work on only thinking
about the coming addition to the family.
Which I admit is really filling my head. I'm
scared and thrilled and worried because I

remember people saying women past their
30's might not ought to have babies or some
such crap. I guess if Doc and all three of the
ladies weren't worried what was I worrying
about? Fk it, I have the right to worry. It's my
job! And I give great worry.

Charley headed out after we agreed on
when and where, he did remind me that I was
gonna be in really deep shit over this, but I
wasn't gonna let them chance getting hurt.
I'm the head of the family and I'm the one
who's the boss…Well that might be a stretch
but I'll still stand on it.

I got back and had just sat down on the
stump when they came out and dragged me
inside for a nap. I had no complaints. We had
dinner on the bum and made the rounds to all
the cook fires where Beth was the queen of
the canyon and I was sorta tolerated. Well not
really. But I like to take on the mantle of
abused. Now they are laughing at me. I think
real hard about the baby. Beth leaned over
and said John, the baby will be fine, I will be
fine, all's well so stop worrying ok? I smile a
weak smile wondering how she knew?
As always dinner on the bum was
awesome, if it swims in the canyon waters we
eat it, the young hunters are having to work
harder finding the rabbits everybody loves
stewed. we made a rule that all hunting had to
be at least a half mile from any of the living

areas to create a safety area for us and the animals, I enjoy seeing the rabbits ducking from bush to bush as well as the deer slipping down to drink so with a safe area we can enjoy seeing them here and eating the ones from elsewhere. Simple. Well except the fish, they get no safety area.

I'm still amazed at how the clan, tribe, bunch, family? have adapted to this life style, no hurrying off to a jib, no taxes, no keeping up with anybody. We were all healthy from living outside most of the time and more exercise, yet nobody was killing themselves working.

I can imagine how it was for the Indians who lived here a thousand years ago, but they didn't have a doctor with a complete mobile hospital and even a dentist.

No we had the best of all worlds and I truly believe none of us would ever again want to live as we did before. The kids never mention stuff like TV or those games they played on the boob tube. We had kids reading and learning stuff several grades above their age bracket simply because nobody said " You can't" They learn at their own level.

We had some young girls learning medicine from Doc.
Some learning how to rebuild an engine on vehicles they couldn't even drive. Our motto is if you know it, teach it, if you wanna learn it go do it.

Some of the older kids have taken up with the miners and are working on our home, learning how to make square rocks out of round rocks. How to make the concrete that lays between each level. They just want to know how and do it.

Charley has sent some of his scouts over to take the kids who are interested out into the desert to learn to scout and survive. So I guess our school is pretty damn good but I'm sure the National Teachers association wouldn't approve but in the words of my immortal old Gunnery Sgt., Fuck em if they can't take a joke!

I slowly got the gear I wanted to take out of the cave and into the truck, I warned the Mechs that one loose word would cause pain, they said "Shit, them girls gonna kick yer ass so bad you can't hurt nobody" see? no respect! They all three headed up to the ridge and I was ready, before they were on the trail up to the top I was at the truck.

I did leave a note saying I was sorry but I needed to do this and couldn't do it and worry about them and that I loved them and would be back as soon as the job was done.

Now I know the note won't save me and won't buy even a tiny bit of understanding, but I needed to do it.

I fired up the truck and eased out and away and was gone. I also figured I had maybe a few hours before they would miss me. And that was all I needed.

I met up with Charley within the hour and loaded my gear in his truck while one of his scouts climbed into my truck, he was smiling and said you two are so gonna get yer asses kicked when you come home and the entire people will be here to see it. And he was gone.

I looked at Charley who said he's right you know, and I'm a fool for getting involved in this, I pointed out that the old woman would protect him, that got me a head shake and the comment of " No, she like them better then me so as you whites are fond of saying. We are good and well screwed"

I've been in more then a couple of wars, small wars but still a war is a war and I've never had a dread of coming home, now it was there. But I was gonna live with it.

We headed South on highway 491, and keeping in the cover of our role of a couple of old coots from the rez we just putted along at about 55 mph, ever watchful because this was rather strange country to us at least since the troubles hit.

The people we were after had handled their job right, they used horses and stayed off the roads and out of sight but that also implied to us that they had a base camp close to the area simply because it was a long ride from the border to our canyon and I doubted they made that ride.

I heard a garbled voice which caused Charley to reach under his seat and pull out a radio mic and start talking of course I didn't understand a word of it. After putting it away he said the scouts were reporting the two runners had gone to ground in an old ranch house back in the rough country and that they had people there so it wasn't gonna be as easy as we thought.

I didn't care, hard, easy, makes no never mind coz I'm ending this shit before I return home to face the girls. One fight at a time, this one I knew we could win, the one with "them"? not so.

We drove on until late into the night until a light flashed from the side of the road where we pulled over and were surrounded by dark shapes, with the motor off and in the pitch blackness of a moonless night I listened to the scouts starting to report in their native

Charley said English, and the head scout who was just a voice from the dark said "Sorry John" I said it's fine go on.

He said we were about five miles from the old ranch and everything was quiet there after a night of boozing and much laughter and bragging they all passed out, the scouts had gotten close enough to hear the two shooters bragging how they blew my head off and killed one of my "Puta's" that one might take a while to die.

I had been pretty calm and quiet ever since I woke up but deep inside me was a burning fire that was about to rage out of control, I've never been a hater nor one to even think about inflicting pain on another human, kill them? Hell yes but that's war, torture is a different thing but if it gets me what I want I'll personally pull their finger nails off with red hot pliers one at a time. Did I mention I was angry?

We drove the truck slowly over the old washed out path leading to the old ranch house but got only about a mile from the highway before we had to get out and mount up on the horses the scouts had with them. Charley thinks of everything. How the white man ever took their land is beyond me.

Riding in the dark can be interesting in the Mountains where there are tree limbs just waiting for you to forget to keep your head down, out here is was rather beautiful with only the stars to see by but the ride ended soon enough and we were walking in to our positions.

I had brought my 308 with the can plus the Ruger 10-22 with it's can, that and my 45 and knife was it. Charlie's lads were armed for just about anything.

The plan was simple, we would wait until we could see and then ease in and take them out. Or at least the ones we had to, I wanted talkers.

These fools didn't even have sentry's out! Some sleeping by the fire and some in the old house, the barn had fallen in and I doubted any were sleeping there. The scouts had reported only ten people here and with the two we wanted that made twelve and I could see at least six by the fire.

I whispered to Charley asking how he wanted to do it, he took the 10-22 and gave it to one of his lads and whispered something to him, he smiled in a very wolfish way and was gone. I next saw him by the fire shooting the sleepers in the head, I couldn't even hear the bolt rattle on the rifle and knew he was holding it shut when he fired. I watched this young man snuff out six people like it was nothing and I guess to him it wasn't.

They all knew Beth and her getting shot was a matter of grave importance to them because they believed they had some how failed by allowing strangers to infiltrate into their home unseen.

I told Charley I didn't agree but he said it didn't matter what I thought it mattered that they felt it was a matter of honor to end this problem and leave a message to stay out of Navajo country.

I couldn't argue with their logic. I felt like I had taken my family right into an ambush and even Walker had been slow picking up the danger, but he had saved my life when he scared Buck so I owed him big time, shit I might start being nice to him, Charley quietly laughed. Shit now he's reading my mind. He sighed.

After the six by the fire were out of the picture the rest of the scouts just seemed to lift from the earth and like shadows flitting across my vision they were gone. I started to jump up but Charley stopped me and said wait. Shortly a small light flashed from the dark and he said ok lets go and simply walked right in.

The house was really trashed and inside we found six men on their knees with their hands on top of their heads, all looked like they were seeing a dark pit in front of them, I guess in a way they were.

Charley pointed out two of the men and said they are the shooters who got away. Both jerked their heads up and looked at me and I swear they turned white.

One made a moaning sound while the other tried to cross himself and was rewarded with a rifle butt tap to his head. I just stood there looking at them for a bit then said separate them all well away from each other, put blindfolds on them and plug their ears with something and strip them.

This was done in quick order and Charley and I started asking questions, when your naked, kneeling on rocks and have a blindfold over your eyes you have a come to Jesus moment and all these ol boys were finding God pretty fast, every time one tried to make the sign of the cross he was smacked with a rifle butt, no asking for forgiveness in this church.

All I wanted was a name and a location for the mystery man who had evaded me and caused this whole mess. The first man knew nothing and it was obvious, he was just a gun thug along for the food and any loot he could find. Charley said something to his men and they tied the man while one of them fired a rifle shot into the dirt, we left the man shaking and pissing himself but unharmed.

It went that way until we got to the third hired man who gave us a name, El Gato Negro. Of course, The Black Cat, uh huh, gonna be the dead black cat soon enough. But he didn't know where to find the man, he too was "executed" so to speak. The forth man gave the same name and told us the man was hold up near the town of Twin Lakes which is a Navajo town, this surprised me.

But if he was keeping his head down and not hurting anybody I guess the people would leave him alone. After "shooting" this guy we got to the two we had been chasing.

We asked them the same questions and got the same answers but a more precise location for the one I wanted.

After we had pumped them dry I had them stood up and their blind folds removed. Both stood there blinking in the bright sun light. Both were sorry examples of humanity, also one had been clipped with a bullet. I was so proud of my wives, they had charged into an ambush with guns blazing and took out three men and clipped one more and I've no doubt would have killed these two but for worry about Beth and me.

I just looked at them and tried to work up to just shooting them out of hand but I just couldn't, they deserved a nasty end but just shooting them seemed to easy. One of Charles men spoke up and that started a long discussion which I didn't follow but I believed it was more to confuse the prisoners then me.

Charley took me aside and said his man
had a really good idea, we drop them off
naked, alone and with only a canteen of water
each out in an area with no people,
blindfolded until they were tossed out of the
trucks.. If they had their shit together they
might make it.

I said I was fine with it as long as there was
no good folks living within miles of the drop
off point. Plus we could drop them close
enough that they would maybe find each other
and fight over the water. I liked it.

As soon as it was dark we did just that, we
dropped them about half a mile apart in the
dark with one canteen each and then we drove
on into the dark and drove in circles just to
confuse them more. I think Charley felt better
and I know I did. They could survive if they
used their heads, but therein lay the problem
facing them.

Now all we needed to do was locate the Cat
and finish his nine lives. And I wanted that
task for myself. As my old grandpa said
Revenge is a dish best served cold. In other
words don't rush in all heated up, ease in slow
and get the job done.

We gathered back at the old ranch house
and loaded up everything usable to us, we
took their horses and vehicles with us. We left

nothing for them if they made it back here.

Charley had sent a couple of his men into Twin lakes to see what they could find out about strangers in the area. We met up with them several miles from the town which was almost empty because the people were heading into the canyon lands where it was safer with the coming sickness.

But they said some of the younger boys had seen signs of people in a canyon several miles out in the dry country where there was a spring. The didn't go look as it wasn't smart these days but they were willing to show us. Couldn't be better! For us, not so good for the cat.

I was a bit worried that this could be a trap to draw us in since this was Navajo land and not the best place to hide.

We rolled into the small town and were greeted by the few folks left, Charley went to talk to them and returned to say as soon as we were done these people would leave with us for the canyons.

Charley sent five of his scouts with the boys who reported seeing the signs of movement, they would learn what they could and report back. We had nothing to do so we just rested and cleaned weapons and waited. It was dark by the time they returned, three of the scouts stayed behind to observe.

The two that returned reported a camp of around fifty men, all heavily armed with HV's with machine guns mounted. They also said these people weren't slack like the ones we took out, they had people out and weren't making any smoke. Just waiting.

They reported seeing a big Black man who was clearly in charge and was doing a lot of pacing. I had to wonder why he was so restless, the people we took out had no commo gear so he couldn't be expecting to hear that way. It was something to ponder along with how we were gonna handle such a large force. And frankly we were out gunned by a lot.

We talked about it from every side of the picture we could but could find nothing to get our teeth into. We laid out our bed rolls and went to sleep, And in the night I had a dream where my old gunny was talking about how when your looking at your enemy and he's doing something that don't make sense then there is something you're missing so hunker down and wait a bit while looking for the logic of it all.

Time is always on the side of the one who takes his time, well most always.

I woke up fuzzy for a bit and laid there thinking and it came to me that it was a set up, the whole thing, he sent those fools in to draw me out with no thought that they might get lucky and get me. And we did just what he thought we would.

He left the bait out for us at the old ranch and expected us to kill them getting information out of them, Why else would he tell low level people where he would be?

I sure wouldn't, nor would anybody I knew of so it is a trap! And for all I know we might be about to get hit. I whispered to Charley who was also awake and within minutes we had all the others awake and in place to meet a dawn attack. We were in a bad spot. Really bad. We could load up and run for it but if we were right they would have the roads blocked.

We quietly pulled back into the town to the concrete block building the Feds built as a community hall of sorts. We got the people still in town gathered and filling anything they could find with water. We did an inventory of our ammo and weapons, we had gathered all the stuff we took from the bait crew and while it wasn't a lot it beat the hell out of nothing.

Charley got the people gathering anything they could fill with sand to build bunkers inside the hall, the block had concrete and steel in it but a machine gun could just saw thru it if they had the ammo. Better yet there was an inner room that was also reinforced blocks with a heavy door, I asked if they had tornados here in this area, Charley said when the gov did something they used one set of plans for everywhere. We now had a place for the old folks to be safe. Of course all the men were planning to fight and we had the weapons so WTF.

Of course this might all be for nothing but I didn't believe that for a minute. One thing I planned to do was be outside with my 308 and the can on it.

I figured I could do more good there then inside. After thinking about it we decided we would meet them outside and when forced to we could withdraw to the hall. I like this better. So we eased out into the dark and into whatever we could find for cover with our ammo and water.

I found my spot on a small hump that was trying to be a hill but not doing so well at it. We did keep the shooters in pairs so there would be cover fire at a flanking movement. I dug out a small trench and pushed the sand up in front of it with a thick bush right in front of it, the best I could do.

I saw Charley head for the truck and figured he had remembered the extra ammo we had in there. Plus a bag with a dozen grenades from the girls stash, if a thousand grenades is a stash.

I'd kill for one of Beth's 50 cal. Barrett's and a few hundred rounds of ammo, I think I hear my Grandpa whispering in my ear about rushing into things.


Dying here in this place will piss me off to no end, getting Charley or his people killed will wilt my soul, I'm so pissed at myself I could just scream. Not seeing my baby coming into the world will surely rip my very being wherever it goes. Ok so I'm being a bit dramatic, I got my best friend in the world into this shit and I'm pissed.

We were as set up as we could be and could only wait to see if we were right or wrong. I was hoping for wrong but think right will be the answer.

And I can hear the sound of HV's heading this way at speed. Charley eased in beside me for a moment before he would move to my rear. We watched as three HV's roared into the town with guns ripping apart the small thin walled houses. We were not going to return fire until I gave the word and that would be hopefully when I had a shot at the Cat.

The HV's tore thru town and looped back still sawing the houses apart. It was a few minutes before they slowed down and started looking things over, Shortly another HV rolled in and there he was, the big man himself, stepping out of his HV. Only I had no shot, he was tall but he had others taller all around him, smart move!

After looking around they finally spotted the meeting hall and opened up on it, the FMJ bullets were just eating thru the walls and that wasn't gonna work so I shot one of the gunners thru the head , worked the bolt and shot the next one then the third one, when the guns all stopped it took a moment for them to realize they were being shot at, Charley and his people opened up and dropped everyone they could see. I shot out the tires of the HV's including the one the boss man came in. He was hunkered down behind his and the one next to it leaving no clear shot but I kept the cross hairs on the area waiting for a target which didn't take long, he shoved one of the drivers out into the open to draw fire, it did but not from me. I was now listening to Grandpa. Wait and them wait some more.

I could hear more vehicles coming in the distance and figured his ground troops were almost here. I eased back from my hide and with Charley following headed around to the area where the troops would likely unload. I was now wishing I had brought my AR 10 for the greater fire power.

Charles lads were still keeping the enemies heads down which was good but I wish a few were on the side like us, the incoming troops were going to be fish in a barrel for a bit. But

Charley and I would do what we could.

And they were here, four 6x's with at least 20 to the truck. I made the decision to stop them as far out as possible so I shot the driver of the front truck and then the next one, both trucks rolled forward and ended up hitting the edge of the road causing one to flip on it's side and the other on rammed it. The rest of the drivers were slamming on their breaks so I shot them as fast as I could work the bolt.

The Cats troops were here but were a hundred yards or more out in open ground with nothing for cover but the trucks and they were no good to him out there. We had separated the leader from his troops and now we had to try to finish them.

I felt Charley ease away and move to my right using all the cover he could find, I fired at any of the men behind the trucks that showed anything to shoot at. I figured a blown up elbow of foot was as good as a head shot.

I really didn't know what Charley was up to until I saw something fly thru the air and roll under a truck and out the other side and blow up.

God I'm glad the girls stole a ton of them, I only wish I had brought a few hundred of them.

That caused panic to set in and they were running, most throwing down their weapons to run faster. I turned my attention to the leader trapped between the HV's. I watched one of them trying to sneak into the gun turret and shot him as soon as his head was in sight. On that note they took off running for it.

Most weren't making it very far, it wasn't a fight it was more of a gopher hunt. I still hadn't seen their leader running for it and that bothered me. With nothing to back it up I called out to cease fire, it took a minute or two but then it went quiet. Charley rejoined me and asked why I called a cease fire? I didn't know but this had been too easy and it had cost us a lot of our limited supply of ammo.

I yelled out to the few hiding behind the HV's to come out with their hands in the air, it took a minute or so but they started straggling out. Some of the scouts moved in a searched them then marched them away from the HV's.

Charley and I headed for them all the while my mind was elsewhere, something was wrong with this picture and it was driving me crazy.

The leader was still unhurt as were the three men who had come out with him. He was tall and well built but he looked more like a street thug then a leader. I walked right up to him and asked him his name and got nothing.

I jerked his shirt open and saw gang tats, this was not the real leader of the gangs, Capt. Harry had commented on his lack of tats since it was very unusual.

I told him he had one chance to live and that was to answer my questions otherwise I was giving him to the Indians. That got his attention.

I said first question…What is the main bosses name? He said El Gato Negro, I asked for his real name but the man didn't know. Second question… What was the main plan? He said he didn't know except the bossman had said something about fighting fire with fire. Third question… How long was he supposed to hold us here? He said his orders were to pin us in the town but to withdraw at least a mile by noon. Forth question…How did he contact the man? He pointed out his HV with a short antenna on the back. He added that all he was to do was click the mik 5 times when we were pinned down. Last question…when did he click the mik? He said when they rolled in and thought we were pinned in the block hall building. I looked at my watch and it was 10:00 am.

I started to tell Charley to get his men

changing the tire on each HV but they were
almost done, good men! They were also
working on the trucks, In less then 30 minutes
we were rolling out in every vehicle that was
running, we torched the rest to make it look
like the fight was still going on. And we ran
for it, on the road and a few miles away. Then
we scattered off the road, the men doing all
they could to camo the rigs, brush and sand
helped a lot.
We waited and right at 11:00 here came a
large plane, it wasn't a C-130 but it was pretty
good size and it had a drop ramp on the back,
I remember seeing one used by skydivers, so
they could jump massed together. Out the
back slid a strange bundle with a chute, I put
the glasses on it and saw what looked like a
pallet filled with GI jerry cans! Well Ol Cat
Man is innovated for sure!
   But his jump master don't know shit about
dropping loads by chutes, he missed the town
by half a mile and the load was just hitting the
ground when it blew up. Pretty good blast but
no Kewpie Doll.

   I had kept the fake leader with us and
asked if the boss was in the airplane? He said
no way, that the man wasn't one to put
himself in danger if he could avoid it at all. I
also pointed out that the plane had arrived
early meaning he wasn't planning on his
troops to survive the blast. He got that real
fast and started cussing in Spanish, Good he

was pissed and will now talk freely.

I asked where the Real Cat was located and he asked for a map, after looking at it he pointed to Gallup NM, I couldn't believe it! The asshole was only 15 miles away!

Charley asked if the Cat would be pissed that the people in the plane missed the town and we got to listen to the imposter telling us in very colorful language just how crazy he would get and that the plane would be coming back as soon as possible.

Charley told him to get on his radio and make a real big deal about the bomb missing the whole place and that he was pissed about it coming early coz
his people would have been caught in the blast. He needed no prodding to sound angry and did his share of yelling at the man on the other end. Soon another voice came on and screamed at him to stop crying and tell him how far off the bomb had been

Still sounding pissed he laid it on plus added that his people were keeping us pinned inside the meeting hall and we seemed to be low on ammo. The voice said to keep us pinned down and the plane would be back within the hour and shut down with nothing else.

We knew the gang leader only had maybe twenty five shooters with him and without a thought we were going to take it to him. Charles men had changed the tires resulting in all the six-by's but the roll over and all the HV's three of which had guns mounted on them.

With Charles people we had about twenty shooters. The elderly men of the town offered to come along but Charley asked them to drive two of the trucks with all their people and all their food supplies and necessities to Shiprock where they were to wait until we returned.

With that handled we mounted up in the vehicles and were rolling. We needed to be there before the plane took off simply because they would see us coming and radio back to the boss man, and that wasn't in my game plan.

The former Cat said they boss traveled in a big black Suburban like some big shot government man, this wasn't real good news because we had nothing that would go that fast so we needed to have a blocking force on the road south. We had four to an HV so that was twelve shooters, the rest were in one of the trucks. Simple, the truck was the blocking force. It would keep going south and set up a blockade in a low spot with no place to go. The rest of us were going to roll right in with all guns blazing. I was planning to kill the plane but Charley said Ralph might like it. Good idea.

We made the fifteen miles in damn short order and as we came in the reformed gun thug told us if we sent somebody west on the interstate to the next off ramp and they came back on old route 66 while we kept going thru town till we hit 66 and turned west we would have them pinned at the airport, the only way the Catman could run was East into town or West on the one road. So that's what we did, we sent one HV and the truck West on I-40 while we cut thru town and turned onto the old 66.

We slowed until we figured the other team was heading at us and we rolled. We hot the airport and saw the activity near a hanger, the plane was being loaded again, we got within a quarter mile before being spotted and even then nobody moved for several minutes, Then a gunner on an HV opened up but missed us by a lot, our gunner didn't miss, practice makes perfect!

And there went the Black Burb! Hauling ass followed by an HV trying to keep up, we heard the Catman yelling over the radio and the reformed guy said he was ordering the HV to stay and fight us but they chose to turn off the road and head cross country. A burst from the second HV shredded their tires and ended the chase. We kept rolling but were losing ground fast we watched the Burb rollover a hill out of sight and then come flying back over the hill right at us.

Our gunner opened fire and blew the front all to hell and with smoke and steam shooting out everywhere it left the road and rolled. I figured he got the driver. We rolled to a stop and just waited and soon enough the door was pushed open and a small black man wearing camo came out with his hands up, followed by a good looking young lady, and last but not least the boogie man himself.

He was crawling out when I started walking at him and had turned just before I got there and was saying "I want a lawyer" And I hit him with everything I had, with the heel of my right hand with fingers closed, right on his nose which splattered like a ripe tomato. Then I kicked him in the balls as hard as I could and when he hit the ground I treated his jaw like a football. I didn't make the extra point but his jaw shattered, for good measure I stomped his kneecaps as hard as I could. All because he was 30 years younger and 50 pounds heavier then me, never fight fair. Charley rolled him over so he wouldn't choke on his own blood, I woulda let the bastard drown in it.

Just to make sure I asked our reformed

Christian if this was the real cat or another
fake, he said this was the one. I sat down in
the shade of the HV breathing hard and dizzy,
one of the scouts brought me some water and
I poured some over my head then drank the
rest.

On the ground the ghost called The Cat was
gagging and bleeding and still mumbling for a
lawyer. I would hake kicked a rib thru his
lungs but I would had to get up to do it so I
just thought about it.

Finally Charley told his men to pick the
bastard up and cuff him. The one who was
cuffing leaned down and listened for a
moment and said " you want me to call you a
lawyer?" The Cats head went up and down
and they young Navajo said well ok man,
You're a Lawyer, there feel better? I started
laughing so hard I tossed up the water, then
Charley started and soon we were all
laughing, well all but the Cat, hard to laugh
with a shattered jaw.

Right then I heard something coming but
was too tired to move, then it came into sight
and was landing in a cloud of dust. The
engine was shut down and the blades slowed
and out of the dust cloud walked three
women. Armed to the teeth and looking
beautiful. I was so fucked.

They stopped in front of me and just stood

there and finally Sandy said, are you ok? I nodded and said for the moment causing Charles lads to start laughing, May looked at them and said you clowns aren't out of the woods on this by any means, now they weren't even smiling but were looking around for someplace they needed to be. As one they started to move but Beth said freeze right there. And they froze.

I saw Ralph walking at me and I called him an ungrateful bastard to which he smiled real big and said well yes I am but my ass ain't gonna get kicked! I pick my battles.

Sandy said "Shut it Ralph" He still smiling said "yes Sir" and headed for his bird, chicken shit!

Sandy looked at Charley and said something to which he nodded and answered her then nodded at the shithead on the ground.

Sandy walked over to him and asked if he was ok! He mumbled and it sounded like lawyer, Sandy said soon sweetie you'll be taken care of. She walked back to me and said John , really, are you ok? You look bad, I said I had a headache ever since Charley tossed the grenade under the truck, She looked at him and said who had the grenades? The rat pointed at me causing her to say "You blew up a truck with our grenades? And didn't invite us? You're a special kind of dumb ain't ya?

Then she started laughing along with the other two and were on their knees hugging me. They helped me up and let me lean against the HV where I got my first good luck at the chopper, it had been painted with flat colors and sticking out from both doors were M-60 machine guns. Then they told their story. They had been watching all the time, from up high and off a ways, as soon as I drove out they got going on mounting the guns on the bird, and since they could hear the very limited radio chatter between Charley and his people plus the bad guys they knew more then we did! When it was confirmed where we were going they flew out and landed where they could watch from a ways off, they watched the entire thing.

They missed the beat down I gave Mr. El Gato but they saw everything else, and were ready to back us up when and if the time came. Bite off more then you could chew.

I had to ask how they knew and just got that look, so I asked why they didn't try to stop me or at least come along?

Beth stepped up and hugged me close and said because John, we knew you needed to do this, this shithead laying here had become a big booby man in your mind and after the ambush you needed to end him once and for all, so we decided to let you go and do it, But we had no intention of allowing you to get hurt or get in over your head, we have faith in you and Charley, together you are almost unstoppable.

As usual when wrapped in her arms I felt calm and relaxed so I hugged her back and said should you be here with the baby? She just laughed and said John women have been fighting wars and giving birth since the beginning of mans time on earth. Nothings changed.

The shitbird on the ground was mumbling about his lawyer and his rights so Sandy walked over and flipped him over and said " Your rights? You want your rights? OK!

You have the right to remain silent, and she shot him right between the eyes. I never even saw her hand move but between the shoulder holster and her back to me I guess I wouldn't. She can be abrupt.

She turned and looked at me and said This piece of dog shit almost killed my husband and our wife Beth, he got his trial. She then asked Charley to have the trash taken to the desert for the buzzards to eat and then thru him into buzzard shit, fitting end. It was done.

We took a look around and watched Ralph looking over the plane they had been using and talking to the pilot who it turned out was also the owner, He realized what they were planning to do and intentionally flew so the wind would blow the fuel bomb off course. He asked if he could move to the canyon and bring his family who lived in Gallup. We of course said welcome, god knows we need more pilots. He left to get his family.

While he was gone Ralph went into the hanger and yelled for help and soon they were hauling parachutes and sky diving gear out and loading it into the plane. I asked why and Ralph said one of the girls had mentioned how cool it would have been to parachute into the battle and save my ass. I was still saying NO, Not only no but HELL NO!!! when they loaded the last of it and shut the back ramp. Nobody listens to me.

I was informed I was flying home as was Charley and even he didn't argue.

I think we were asleep before the chopper lifted off, I had my head in Beth's lap and a girl on each side holding my hands. I woke up when we dropped into the clearing at Shiprock and waved to Charley who headed off to the café and the Old Woman. We took off again and I went back to sleep and woke up again as we settled onto the landing pad at home. My wives carried my gear and took me home then to the solar shower and washed me like I was a baby, I felt like one.

I woke up sometime later with the Doc standing over me checking my eyes, I was gonna shoot him but they had taken my guns away. Doc laughed and said good luck John they are ahead of you. I laughed and said No shit.

The were all standing around our bed and Doc said I was just tired from adrenalin let down plus not eating much at all and a bit dehydrated. With that he left and I went back to sleep. I woke up in a pile of girls, and I couldn't move a thing so I just laid there and enjoyed the feelings of love and home and happiness. Beth was close against my side and curled up in my arms, May was wrapped around Beth and Sandy was wrapped around my back, I was trapped and it was wonderful. I went back to sleep.
John?...
JOHN!....
What?
We're hungry...
So go kill some small cute little creature and suck the marrow out of it's tiny little bones...Ouch!...

John?....
What?
We're hungry ....
Ok lets get up and I'll find something for us to eat...
John, your being sarcastic!
No.. I'm hungry too.
Well...ok

And they unwrapped, I wasn't sure who was talking but it didn't matter, I either fed them or I might lose a limb.

So I said ok, how about hot cakes and bacon and eggs? Now that got them moving, I knew they would take over because I was a slow cook and when they are ready to "feed" they don't screw around.

We built up the fire outside and got to cooking, pretty soon we had bums hanging out waiting. Life in the canyons. The kids were first as always, we kept cooking and they kept eating, well them and the girls and any adult who came by wanting breakfast. Sometimes it takes a couple of hourse to finish the meal, others came by, one with a huge cowboy pot of coffee, another with real home made butter ( the only kind now days) another brought a big cast iron skillet and a couple dozen eggs. I was soon pushed aside by one of the women and a teen age girl who took over cooking, I sat on my stump and relaxed and watched my wives eating everything that got close. I was worried about feeding them if we ever ran out of food. I smiled thinking about my usual comment about killing some small critter and all three looked at me and shook their forks at me.

Beth was really starting to eat more what with the baby helping out. That made me smile and all of them smiled. Whatever it was

I liked it, most of the time..

After breakfast was done and everybody had wondered off we sat in the sun and made small talk, like what now since things were settling down and hopefully would remain so? I said I wanted to see the house which excited all of them so we walked up onto the ridge and I couldn't believe how much had been done since I was there last.

The walls were all up including the inside walls which were smaller stone, meaning only about 20 inches thick, I knew somebody was thinking bullet proof, I liked it!. The window spaces were perfect, we could see everywhere!

Harv showed up and we talked about what was next, he said he wanted big roof beams, like BIG, whole trees that would be shaped, the place was going to have a open beam ceiling, I said I'd contact Charley to hire some of his young men to do the logging if they wanted the job. Also the high country with the big trees was their land so it was up to them.I guess we could truck them in from Texas, god knows there are Oak trees down there in East TX that are three plus feet in Diameter. That might be the way to go and we could visit the family. I asked the girls and they were all for it so there it was, back to Texas.

I needed to put out the word for a long goose necked flat bed trailer so I got that done and within a mater of hours the call came in from Fort Navajo that they had one located and could bring it up to us.

But the girls decided they wanted to go visit the folks at the Fort and see what goodies they might run off with. So now we were going West and North before we went South and East. Makes perfect sense. Another thing is that we can get logs for the beams closer, but no, not Oak or cedar, why it matters I've no idea except the builder and the wives have decided so there it is.

I'm just the driver. Just driving Miz Sandy and Miz beth and Miz May, could be a movie, maybe I can learn to shuffle along saying "Yazum" missie. Yea, that sounds racist? No, sounds like truth. I loved that movie! But I'm old.

So we loaded the great white Whale with all the stuff a family needs for an extended road trip.

Weapons...check
Ammo...check
More ammo...check
Grenades...check
Food...check
Extra fuel... check
Camping gear...check

I think we had it, our BOB's had clothing and other personal stuff.

But we would be stopping back here before we headed out to pack better for a more extended trip.

Truck loaded, girls high carding for the front seat, Beth wins, I wonder how they stacked the deck to get that done. Sandy and May have become very protective of Beth which is understandable but they carry it too far.

I swear they wanna hold her hand in the bathroom. She just smiles and lets them do as they will, she's the most patient and calm of the three.

We haven't been to the Fort in a while and all want to see what goodies the hunters have rounded up, they send out armed groups of salvagers who gather whatever might be useful and not likely to be produced again for a good while. So much stuff will spoil as time goes by so they just gather it and store it away for later use, even if it's something not needed at the moment.

We made good time and got there before dinner where we found they had killed the fatted calf so to speak and put on a feast in our honor, or at least that's the excuse. All's well in the prison, everything running as it should be, there are now cargo containers neatly laid out and numbered to correspond to a list.

They are doing an outstanding job! I

seldom hear from any of them since they are busy and don't feel the need to make reports, they did at first but I stopped that. Just do what you do and all will be well.

We rolled thru the gate into the court yard, ours was the only vehicle inside the prison, the rest were in a motor pool area behind a tall fence and under the guns of the guard towers which remain manned 24/7 motion sensor lights everywhere outside. Plus a roving patrol with guard dogs. They take their salvaging very serious and don't plan to get salvaged themselves. After we unloaded we were greeted by, well everybody. Hell I didn't know 90 percent of them but they all knew me and the girls knew most of them. After the hand shaking and such we were lead to the chow hall where the cafeteria style serving was laid on. I won't even go into the whole thing, there was plenty of everything.

I grabbed a slab of beef that was charred on the outside and bleeding from the inside, a baked spud with butter and some hot rolls and headed for a table. The girls took some of everything in small servings.

My steak was perfect, except for the forks that kept stabbing bites on my tray. I finally said why? With an entire cow over there aren't you moochs eating your own steaks? Can you by now guess their answer?

"Well, because your's looks so good"

"And you cut it into perfect bites"

"Plus we want you to know we like how you take care of us"
All delivered with sweet smiles…what bullshit.

They aren't even acting embarrassed,, nope just laughing and chattering among themselves. I look up and see one of the cooks heading our way and he's got a large tray with cut up steak on it which he places in front of them. They give him a big smile and dig in, when I reach for a bite one of them growled at me I swear. But then they all laughed and piled a bunch on my trey. God it's like living on a strange planet and not knowing the rules of the native species.

All in all it was a great meal, what I got of mine, desert was pie and cake and god love them real ice cream, I needed to know how they pulled that off. I knew from their reaction that the girls would have the head cook backed into a corner getting all the facts, they do love ice cream. And it is hard to come by.

We settled down and just visited with everybody who came by, all wanted to hear about the chase and end of the so called El Gato, so I told it as it was then the girls got into it telling it from their perspective which sounded way more wild then mine.
They were all thrilled to hear Beth's with

child as they called it, I guess "knocked up" went out of style. I just got glared at by the two she cats who guard the future ruler of all things large and small. They argue over it, May wants a boy, Sandy wants a girl, I just want a healthy baby, Beth just wants us all happy. She smiles at me.

When we told about the ambush and my one point landing on my head and Beth's wounds the women all clucked over her, the guys were agast about the STI being ruined! I laughed at that and got glared at by every female in the room but Beth. She agreed with me!.

Finally we headed off to our bed room which the folks here keep just for us and that's just damn nice but then there are a lot of small bed rooms here. I think they call them studio apartments, the former tenants referred to them as cells.

We passed a very peaceful night, I know I slept like a log. I woke up to Beth and May gone and Sandy laying beside me smiling, I held her close and told her I missed her lately. She said her and May were just giving Beth time to really settle into the strange arrangement. I said I understood that but I didn't like missing my number one wife, that got a really nice response and we almost missed breakfast.

We gotto the mess hall and were greeted with two wives bouncing like balls, I worried about Beth getting too excited but was told to zip it. Beth slid a box to me and I saw the STI logo on it, in the box was a beautiful handgun, An STI Legend in 40 S&W, not a 10mm but close since a 40 is a sawed off 10mm.

The hunters had found a bunch of top dollar weapons in a gun safe in a burned out store but the safe was fine. They heard about Beth's 10mm stopping a bullet and saving her life and of course that the gun was trashed so they had dug thru the piles of gun looking for something to give her, this was at least a $3000.00 gun before the lights went out, now it was a $10,000 gun because when would somebody be making them again?  But then I remembered STI was in Texas!

I figured they might just be in business still. But in the meantime Beth has an almost 10 mm which is cool because it comes with mags that hold from between 15 up to 23 rounds and that's not to be sneezed at. They had a stack of mags to go with it and several thousand rounds of ammo which included everything from FMJ to Flying Ashtrays ( big hollow points) And it fit her shoulder holster just fine, maybe a bit snug but we can wet it down and let it dry around the gun. She was thrilled and asked them if they had any Barretts which got a sad no. She smiled and said you do now!! I swear those ol boys were doing the happy feet dance over a damn gun.

But since Beth had five of them I figured that left one for each of us so god save anybody trying to get at us from across the lake!! Or anywhere else since we could see for miles up there on top of the new house or would be able to when it had the roof on it.

Beth wanted to shoot her new toy so we all headed out to the Fort range where she spent a few minutes sighting it in  and then went to work on the Silhouette targets and was really ripping them up, after the first magazine full she smiled really big and said " I'm faster because of less recoil"! and more accurate.

We all agreed with that. Of course "they" had to get in on it so pretty soon they were all piling up the empty brass but the range boss said not to worry because they were set up with the best of Dillon's wonder machines. Also they said before we left they would put some ammo in the truck for the 40. I figured we probably had more then they did but they were gifting Beth so why say anything.

Even the girls can get tired of shooting, it takes a while but they managed to realize they were starving, I reminded them we ate just before coming to the range, the reply in triplicate was " And your point would be???" We went to eat.

When we were done we took a tour of the "Vaults" Meaning the isolation cells, where the good stuff was piled. I still get a laugh walking past cells stacked with gold then silver and on and on, doors not locked and nobody gives a shit. There are cells filled with works of art, books by the many thousands, these are in some order and you could find what your looking for but it might be in a box under five more boxes.

There was a cell just for dvd's loaded with all mans knowledge or at least a great deal of it, as well as machines to use to study them, all checked out and working. Nothing frivolous down here, this was the stuff that would be of the most use in rebuilding if and when we started. If and when somebody really wanted to. Right now it would be damned hard to find anybody in our area interested in going back to the "good old days".

After the tour of as sandy calls it " king Sillymons mines" we headed up and out to the sunshine. We met with the head "accountant" he who knows where all the skeletons are stashed. He knew we wanted to use a large gooseneck trailer, when he asked what we were doing I explained about the big house and the builders wanting beams so the trip to Texas to get big Oak or Cedar logs.

With the happy smile of a man who loves his work he clapped his hands and headed for his log books and after swishing pages and pages he let out a loud " AH HA!! And follow me!!

We headed out to a golf cart and piled into

two of them, Sandy and May of course
fighting over who got to drive, Beth and I got
in with Mr. Inventory as I think of him and
off we went, it wasn't long before the other
cart passed us with May driving and both
laughing manically, I swear they had
repressed childhoods, Beth was kind of
squirming so I asked Mr. Inventory to toot his
horn which got their attention, we pulled up
and I said ok baby there ya go, and with a
laugh Beth was gone over to the dark side, I
yelled "BABY!!" and got a one finger wave
from two of them and a smile from one.

Wilber the gate keeper which sounds better
then Mr. Inventory said " my they sure are
frisky" I had to laugh at the understatement of
the century. Being a book worm he didn't
really know much of what we were doing out
in the world and I think didn't want to.

He did ask if it was true that we took a
walk thru the Museum of Natural History
before we blew it up? Hmm did I detect
something testy in that?

So I told him all about the whole thing and
he was relieved that we didn't blow it up. I
asked where he heard that, he said two of the
ladies with me were talking about it at
breakfast, I shook my head.

Sandy and May torturing the poor geek, I
would have a talk with them later, wasted air
but one has to try to reel in ones rowdy
children, shit what did I need a baby for? I
can't keep two small ladies under control, at

least they were almost house broke. Maybe the baby would bring them to heel ( laughter??)

We finally got to the container with the right number on the door ( all at 2 mph I might add, lucky girls) ( Sucker I hear in my head) sigh.

When it was opened there was a shiny new something , it looked very complicated and heavy, I said ok, very nice!! What is it. Mr. whipple said well it's supposed to be a portable saw mill! Now I took a big interest and crawled in and over and sure as shit there was a big saw blade thingie, I crawled out and said "I want it!!" How do we move it?

The girls come sliding up in a cloud of dust and they were covered with it and laughing like crazy, how anybody could get a golf cart to move fast enough to raise dust is beyond me, after it cleared I see Mrs. Delicate mommy to be is driving and grinning biggest. Mr. Whipple was saying "Oh my, Oh my over and over and wringing his hands.

They saw bright shiny colors and were all over the saw for a few minutes until they realized it wasn't something to shoot or blow shit up with and came out asking why we needed it, I said well how would you square 20 foot trees into beams? That got some

interest but not as much as if it would blow
the trees down. I went wrong with them
someplace. How can I raise a baby when I
can't raise my wives? They all hugged me
and said it's ok daddy we will be good.
Bullshit.

Mr. Whipple said we could load the whole
container on the trailer and haul it that way,
cool, how do we pick it up? He did his " AH
HA!!" thing and said come along and we
made a slow trip to the main storage center
where he found two guys and said we needed
the big gooseneck trailer and container
number something on it, they said "yes sir!!
We will jump right on it!!
    Mr. Whipple said he needed to get back to
his office and since we seemed to have our
own cart he would leave us to our business, as
he rolled away I looked at the two and said "
yes sir? Right away sir?"

They laughed and said he's really a lost
person, he was a bean counter for a Forbes
500 company and was never suited to survive,
but we found him in one of the places we
were mining and brought him home, he
needed a job so he undertook handling
inventory of all this shit and really had done a
great job, so we just give him a moral boost
every chance we get, now we all laughed but I
was glad we had these kind of people in our
huge extended family.

They said they could mount a gooseneck ball in the truck and load the container and we could leave tomorrow if we wanted to. But in the meantime we were welcome to look around and see what else we might need or want. So I gave them the Dodge keys then remembered Walker who was tied up so Sandy took off with the cart and returned with the mutt…oh yes, the mutt that saved our lives.

So I scratched his ears which worried him since I was being good to him but he decided I was his newest bestest friend who needed a lick in in the face, gonna be a short friendship at this rate.

The girls poked me and said be good he loves you!! I pointed out that they loved me but didn't lick my face. Wrong thing to say when sitting in a golf cart.

When they got done I was all slobbers. And they were laughing their asses off.

We took off on an unguided tour of the place and I swear they had at least 10 of everything ever built! I guess once they got into hauling stuff off they couldn't stop. There was a vehicle parking area that looked like a giant car dealership.

All diesels it looked like but buried in the mess was a Jeep, a forest green Jeep, now that was strange so I said stop and after almost being tossed thru the non windshield I got out and walked over to it and saw it was new but what was it doing here?

I popped the hood and low and behold there was a diesel engine! Now I never seen a Jeep with a diesel, I know they had made them but they didn't seem to go over or something. At any rate here was one and it said Turbo on it. I think it may have been a special order, complete with roll cage and racing harness and was looking wild, I want it! I looked to see if the keys were in it and they were, I checked the fluids, all good and hit the starter but of course it didn't start, I looked and saw the battery was disconnected.

We headed back to the place where we found the two guys and they were already at work on the truck, I asked about the jeep and they only knew it was brought in about a month ago and parked, I said I wanted it and who did I need to talk to? They said shit John, you're the boss, the General, take it. I said oh bullshit, I'm one of the working stiffs, they both laughed and said if you say so boss. The girls laughed.

I asked for some jumpers and headed back to get it running and it fired up right away, after it ran for a bit I backed the golf cart out of the way and watched my new toy heading off with three wild cats in it screaming like kids.

I drove the cart back to the two guys who

laughed and said shit John didn't you see that coming? I had to admit I didn't and should have. One of the men said they would be along shortly because the jeep only had a couple of gallons of fuel in it and sure nuff here they come like bats out of hell with my pregnant wife number three in the damn thing, and of course guess who was driving?.. shit.

But I had to smile they are so much fun and I had such high hopes in Beth to be a shining example of lady hood. But I think she's having fun now because in a short while she will be forced to slow down a lot. I guess we will all be slowing down ( I hear laughter)

Beth scooted over when May got in back with Sandy so I could drive. And wouldn't you know it, the damn seat won't go back anymore and my knees are in danger of bashing the dash, but it is fun to drive! And I hear from the rear two low talking voices planning on how to mount a machinegun on the roll bar. I know I should have tried harder to raise them right, but I failed someplace.

By the time I got back to the shop I knew one thing for sure, the girls had a new toy. And from the back I hear high fives and giggles, beat again. They all leaned over and hugged me and said thank you daddy for the new shiny!!..

To make things worse one of the ol boys said, well did you find out why you seen soccer moms driving these things? Big men don't fit well huh? I flipped them off to loud laughter.

The girls wanted fuel so one of the guys filled the tank and then told them to be damn sure to have the seat belts on because these things will roll if your not careful. They roared off in a cloud of dust but I did thank him for his words. He smiled and said john them girls ain't gonna screw up, they just love jerking your chain and everybody knows it but you. Well I know it damn it but...... shit!

The ball is mounted and we went over to hook it to the trailer which was also brand new and looked as long as a freight trailer, I asked about the cargo container and was told it was a 20 footer and after it was loaded there was room for the jeep if the girls didn't kill it before then, all we could see was dust where they had been.

One of the men got a big fork lift while we took the truck and trailer to the container which we loaded almost before I could get out of the dodge. They had it dogged down with chains and binders and were waiting for the girls to show up which took a good while, so we drove back to the office and one of them went in and brought out three very cold beers,

I had died and gone to heaven!

We had two more before the girls showed up covered in dust and the jeep looked like it was ten years old but it was purring, then I noticed Walker was in there with them, all seat belted in and grinning like a fool.

I just looked at them and laughed, they were as wild as wolves, ten times more dangerous and as funny as a room full of kittens.

They bounced out and grabbed my beer and passed it around, beth took a small sip to wash the dust down, Willard went in to get more and brought out an ice cold Dr pepper for Beth who smiled and said thank you, the outlaws were too busy choking down their whole beer to do more then nod, both finished and belched like a couple of red neck truckers. Wilson the other dude went in and brought out a bucket of beers in ice, that settled them down and I grabbed one before they took the whole bucket.

They sat down on the ground and Beth leaned on me and whispered "thank you"! for what says I? The jeep she said, they love it and they just know you set it up for them. I laughed at that but I wondered if I did. I've never been a jeep fan, they are too small and the last one I drove was the old CJ5 and it was dangerous as a bed roll full of rattlers. The last fatal I worked as a Deputy Sheriff involved one and I never forgot it.

These new ones had longer and wider wheel bases so were much safer, IF the drivers don't get crazy. If they already crazy then ...I don't know. Beth said, they will settle down because the baby means as much to them as anybody else and they aren't gonna risk missing out on the arrival. I hoped she was right, they were so competitive that I worried. But I wouldn't change them for anything.

We headed for the Fort after thanking Willard and Wilson for their hard work and the cold beer. I was in need of food so we headed for the chow hall. The menu for the night consisted of Prime Rib and all the usual stuff that goes with it. The head cook said he wished pigs were as available as cows, I agreed, I loves me some pork roast and ribs. I guess we need to think about raising our own but I'm not sure they will do well out here in the desert, he also said they needed more chickens because they don't have enough eggs. Now that is something we can help with, we are over loaded with chickens and eggs, the boys with their 22's keep the local varmints at bay so except for the Hawks and Owls we really don't lose many and we have a lot of broody hens, I told him we could help him out on that issue, he was thrilled. And on second thought I know Texas is flat over run with wild hogs and we might be able to help out there. Catch them young and raise them

up and they tame right down what with free
food.

We had other things to look for in Texas so
it's not just a trip to better us personally, I
worry bout that stuff,

Between the beer and the long day I was beat
and said I was gonna take a shower and
headed for the room, Shortly joined by all
here of the girls, the shower was plenty big
enough for all of us but the insisted on
crowding in on one shower head, I sigh, they
laugh.

Bed was wonderful, I think I was out like a
light as were the girls, I woke up to one warm
body next to me and it was May, I laughed
and said your turn? She smiled and said naa,
we flipped a coin, I lost! Ha-Ha-H.... funny...
We rejoined the crew in the chow hall and
feasted on the usual, Hot cakes and bacon and
eggs, I figured and was right that Sandy and
Beth had cooked it.

The head cook came over and offered to
buy them but he figured he couldn't afford to
feed them. I told him I got that a lot. We
laughed, they didn't, May asked if he was
implying they were fat? He said OH Hell
no!!, yawlz fine, then he turned red and beat
feet for the kitchen, they have a way of doing
that.

Sandy asked if there was still room for more stuff, I said not if it goes bang, we have enough of that stuff. She said no she had asked and found there was a supply of windows in containers and wanted to look at them, I hugged her and said baby anything you want!! She said cool coz they have a lot of 45 ammo! I was beat. They laughed all the way to the truck to go window shopping.

Willard and Wilson were already and took us right to the containers that held windows. It took two hours but the found what they wanted, tall double hung windows, they explained that with the double hung they could lower the top glass and let the hit air out.

I acted impressed, but I knew that before they were born, I'm old, and wore out, and tired and did I say old? And about to become a daddy...jeeze.. The windows were loaded before I could blink and Willard asked if we had power in the canyon, I said we did and he said pull down three more containers, next thing in the container was the biggest refrigerator I've ever seen, then they said stop at their office where we loaded about a hundred cases of beer.

I was thinking the canyon ladies were gonna steal this thing long before it ever got a beer in it but I never said anything to the

guys. But then I had a brain flash and asked if
they had ever found any reefer vans out on the
roads, they had and brought them in. Now I
was thinking. I asked if they knew anybody
who could drive a tractor with one and they of
course said they would be happy to do it.
They said the reefers ran on propane and they
had been salvaging propane tanks by the
dozen as well as trucks with 5000 gal tanks on
them. They said to head home and they would
be over in a day or two. I love these two ol
boys.

We headed home, slow and steady and
pulled in right at dark. We just parked and
headed for bed. Morning brought getting the
container unloaded and I was right, the ladies
started in about the big fridge, I told them to
hold off a day or two and there would be one
a hundred times bigger coming in, I think they
didn't trust me but Beth said it was so and
they was good enough.

Harv and his guys came to see what I had
and were going bat shit over the saw mill as I
figured they would, I could see it was gonna
get a lot of use. I told them my idea for the
reefer trailer and they were up for that.

I also planned to ask Willard and Wilson to
bring another one for Harv's family area as
well as one for The Bremmers who had
settled in a canyon on down from Harv's
bunch, I figured we could make this reefer
idea work just fine and that would help a great

deal and make life a bit easier for the ladies.

And I could keep my beer cold! And my nice big fridge was gonna go in the new house, we was gonna get half assed civilized. Yea I know, but I'm old and tired and I like cold beer and did I mention I'm old?

I'm still torn over the trip to Texas for big Oak and cedar logs or to the much closer pine tree country. Harvey said in his opinion using Oak was very much preferable, I said ok. I'm easy and I wanted to see Mom and Miz Sheri who was gonna shit over a third wife plus a baby coming. I might not be able to pull Beth away from her. So we were going to Texas, cool.

Only one issue in my mind, was it right to expend fuel just to haul logs back to make our new home even more over the top then it was? I worry about this kind of shit. But when I mentioned it I was surprised to hear the women talking about us bringing back some Hickory because they wanted to try smoking some meat. None of them thought I should be worried about it.

I'm continually blown away at hos peoples personalities have changed in just a few years, things they would have started a bloody feud are now not worth even thinking about. We live in a communal life style and share everything, If somebody came up right now and said hey I want a house on a ridge, everybody would say go find your location and we will help. No time clocks, no rush, wanna stop and take a nap or make love? Go do it, nobody's gonna care unless your endangering the group like walking away from guard duty but that's like maybe four hours every few days so nobody is worried about that, in fact we have people who due to age or an injury can't do much and they are thrilled to have guard duty to be of use. Lecture over for the day, we have packing to do.

Unloading the container wasn't as easy as loading it without the big forklift but we got it done right where it could be of use. The truck was fussed over by the under worked mechanics and it was ready to roll.

The back loaded with the things we needed and all the stuff the girls were taking as gifts from the Fort for our Texas families.

We rolled out early and made good time to Shiprock where we found Charley waiting for us as usual, I will go to my death still wondering how he knows. I know the Canyon Commo people aren't telling him or so they say. I know his young men are all over the place just watching but they don't have hand sets.

I file it under PFM and hear giggling in my head, I ignore it. We stopped for just a few minutes to say hi and for the girls to fill up on Old Woman wisdom or maybe to gather up a supply of powdered bat wings ( You're gonna regret that one buddy boy! In my head ) Shit ( stop cussing!) sigh.

Charley smiled and said John you will never learn will you? I guess not was my reply. He warned us to avoid strangers because the sickness was still far away but people were moving around a lot more.

His men were stopping strangers from entering Navajo country which I had not heard, but if figures. Better early then late.

The girls bounded out and said lets roll buttercup! Which got a laugh from Charley, I think they do that crap just to get to me, Charley said "No shit Sherlock " Now I'm laughing. I also noticed the girls didn't tell him to stop cussing. Rank really does have it's privileges unless it's me. I sigh again, Beth leaned over and kissed my cheek, May leaned forward and wrapped her arms around me and Sandy ruffled my hair, what there is of it. We rolled out.

I dropped the peddle to the metal as they used to say so we could make it to the Texas state line before dark, which we did and found Bear and Harry waiting for us all smiles and big hugs for Beth. Sandy tapped him on the

chest and said if you squeeze too hard I'll hurt
you! He laughed his loud beller and wrapped
Beth up in his huge arms and lifted her off the
ground, she was laughing while Sandy was
kicking him in the shin. He set her down and
was laughing at Sandy when Mrs. Bear
arrived and smacked his head which was a
reach and reminded him she was in a family
way. He never blinked and just kept smiling. I
swear everybody in the whole country must
know Beth is pregnant!

Mrs, Bear herded the girls away from bad
influences and met up with Mrs. Harry who
was hurrying along glaring at Bear who
ignored it all and smiled big.
      I swear, the woman just recently roared
into a fight in a chopper manning a M-60 with
blood in her eyes now she's a marshmallow? I
don't get it. Bear and Harry led me to the
mess hall and the cold beer, life is easy in
Texas, the world goes to hell but by god their
beer stayed cold. I love their priorities!
Protect the women and kids and keep the beer
cold. What's not to love.

      I told them the full story of the ambush and
the chase and the ambush and the chase
leading up to capturing Mr. El Gato Negro. I
brushed over the things I did to him and Bear
asked if Sandy had really just shot the
shithead while he was demanding a lawyer.
      I said yep but you know Sandy, never one

to pass up a chance to shoot assholes, Bear laughed long and loud, Harry was quiet so I asked why, he said he wondered what kind of information we could have gotten out of him.

I had not thought about that but doubted it was worth keeping him alive wasting good air and said as much. Harry sighed and agreed, I love Harry, never stops thinking, Bear? Well he's like a 300 pound almost 7 foot version of Sandy.

Shoot it, if it moves shoot it some more. Both are right.

We talked about the LA war and the coming plague if that was what it really was. They had pretty well closed down Texas as much as possible, the entire Texas national Guard was activated and helping seal the road ways from the big cities where there might be outbreaks, it wasn't gonna be easy but they had plans laid on to have fall back road blocks and if need be would shoot if they had to. It was a crappy thing but necessary to protect the whole. I was so happy we didn't have that issue in the canyons. And with few roads it was easier to close down access.

We spent the night and all had breakfast together and we rolled out early. It was so different in East Texas from our home, the trees were green and of course it was humid which kills me but it was good to be back even if only for a while.

We rolled up to the gate before dark and were met by two strangers pointing rifles at us, this I didn't like. I opened the door and stepped out only to hear one say get back in the truck and head on out of here. I didn't do that I walked right at the fool and asked who he was, he replied by asking who in the hell I thought I was. I said well son, I don't "Think", I know who I am because I knew who my daddy was ( yes I was tired and getting pissed ) which of course pissed off the one talking.

The other looked at me then the truck and then at the very pissed off Red Head who had gotten out of the truck and had taken her light jacket off, revealing the shoulder holster. And said Luke you best back off that's John Walker and the woman is the one they call Wyatt.

Now Luke was possibly inbred or just stupid cause he wasn't gonna back down, so I repeated what the second guy said, my name and that we lived here part of the time.

From out of the dark I heard a voice I knew! Good ol Fred who said Luke you stupid bastard your about the get yer ass killed, point that gun at the ground right now! Luke didn't like it at all and watching his eyes I could see he was gonna be a problem, if not now the later, But for now he did lower the muzzle but just had to add that he would see me later. Sandy walked closer and said "

Well look real close shit head because your later is gonna be real short if you keep the shit up. Before he could raise the muzzle again fred hit him with a hard right to the jaw hinge and we all heard it snap and Luke dropped like a used condom.

I was watching his partner but he told Fred that he would not work with luke again ever and wasn't gonna have anything to do with him ever again coz the stupid bastard was gonna get himself and maybe others killed. I asked the man his name which was Duke and we shook hands while he tried to apologize but I waved it away and told him he wasn't responsible for Lukes stupidity.

Fred told Duke he would send another guard team to relieve him and somebody to take care of the idiot, we dragged him out of the way and drove on in to find Miz Sheri standing by our tent home with her soft smile of welcome. Hugging Sheri is like hugging Beth but even better if possible. She puts her whole being into every hug and you know you're home when she does it.

Sandy and May got their hugs and Sheri looked at Beth, then me and smiled and reached out for her and really hugged her and whispered in her ear, Beth smiled and got teary eyed and just held on to Sheri.

At last they let go and Sheri looked at her

closely and got a big smile and asked when the baby was due, How do they know? Well actually Miz Sheri is kind of a Witch, a good Witch, well Witch is a strong word but she just knows stuff, She hears things others don't. I can't explain it but she's a lot like Beth or Beth is like her.

I headed over to see mom, she still looks got for her age but she's really lost a lot of short term memory, She thought I had been here all along so I just went along with it.

I think growing old is vastly over rated and I think I'll opt out of it.

The tent was opened up and had been airing out for a while, all the spiders had been evicted as well as anything else that had moved in. And it was just as comfy as when we left, Beth loved the earth oven and the fire place. But it had been a long day so we headed for the solar shower house and got cleaned up and found food waiting for us. A lot of the folks were there and had to hear all about our wars and adventures.

One ol guy asked if we really burned Vegas to the ground, Sandy said damn skippy we did! He said good! Seems he had lost a lot of money plus got rolled by a hooker back in his youth which got a good laugh. It was funny how nobody seemed to miss the modern day Vegas. I always said it was a much cleaner and safer place when the mob run it, At least they kept the street crime down.


Being tired we called time out for now but promised we would answer everybody's questions in the days to follow and on that note we went to bed and slept hard.


I woke up to wonderful smells, bread baking in the earth oven, compliments of Sheri, the girls making breakfast over the camp fire, lets see, can I guess?

Hot cakes, smoked ham steaks and eggs and coffee! When they cook breakfast that's what they cook, fine with me! I like it all. And it reminds me about taking hogs back to the canyon.

We sat on the ground and stuffed ourselves, and I have to say I love eating this way, tables and chairs ore ok in their place but nothing beats sitting around the cook fire. It's hard to find anything better.


Breakfast over the girls took Beth around to show her off and introduce her to everybody and show her their range, I was thinking an after breakfast nap was in order but Rick showed up and joined me, he don't drink coffee and never has but he had his never ending can of Pepsi. I swear he must have a ton of it stashed someplace.

He said his family was all well and I

needed to stop over to see Chris which I was sure to, I love her almost as much as miz Sheri, she's a very hard working lady who always looks wonderful and smells good.

Rick said he had been busy getting my logs gathered, I was kinda surprised by that, he said Charley had passed the word up the line on the radio that we needed logs for beams in our new home and Rick being Rick already knew where all the forest giant were that had died in the last year of so, meaning they had dried standing.

He had even located some big cedars as well as the Oak. I mentioned I had a request from the ladies in the canyon for some hickory to smoke meat with. He of course had that too. If a tree dies in the forest Rick hears it.

I said we could start tomorrow on cutting them down, he laughed and said they are down and stacked off the ground, just pull the trailer over when you're ready.

I've never known anybody like Rick. He don't move real fast but he never has to cut twice if you know what I mean. He wondered off to do something and Fred showed up, we sat in the shade and talked about the young fool at the gate, Fred said he had come in with somebody's kin and had been a problem from day one. He wouldn't work and argued about everything, I asked why he was still here and Fred said well he's only been here a few weeks, we were giving him a chance but he's out of chances and will be gone by dark to day.

I knew one thing as sure as the sun rising and that was we weren't seeing the last of Ol Luke, he was a man looking to fill a grave one way or the other and somebody would oblige him. I just didn't want an innocent person being his victim.

I asked Fred if he could be hauled to the state line and dumped out but that was gonna take more effort then it was worth. I knew one thing for sure if he hung around and wasn't careful Wyatt would stop his clock.

Maybe I need to deal with him myself before it got to that point. So Fred and I went to where he was living to tell him to pack up.

He could only mumble around the wired up jaw and was filled with anger to the point I thought he was gonna go for a gun but Fred stepped in and stopped him.

The folks he came in with said good riddance as far as they cared, he had just latched onto them and wasn't kin at all.

So we packed him up and hauled him out of there. He mumbled he had no where to go but that was his problem. We dropped him in town where he could either work or they too would run him out. I had misgivings about dropping him in town but couldn't see any other option.

A week later we heard about s shooting and robbery just out side of town and sure nuff it was luke, The wounded man testified about the attack and that he survived by playing dead. The trial was the next day and they hung him that evening. Justice was served and fast these days.

I asked Fred to go with me to the old mans place who was robbed and shot so we could apologize for our part in the deal.
He was good about it and said trash was trash and nobody was at fault cept for Luke's folks for not drowning him at birth. Another good ol boy who understands how thing work best. He said he didn't even go watch the hanging because he needed to water his garden, priorities ya know.

Well we had been home a week and while we didn't shoot anybody we were kind of in part responsible for a hanging. Well maybe not.
I'm starting to feel like the little guy in the old Lil Abner funny's, can't remember his name but he wore all black with a big hat and a black rain cloud over his head all the time.
Seems like doom and gloom follow us everywhere we go, but then I think of the Girls and Beth and the coming baby and I see the lie to those thoughts.
We don't cause evil but we sure do help eradicate it a lot! Some folks are just born to

die by a bullet or a noose and me and mine
have nothing to do with it.

Fred and I stopped in at Miz Sally's for pie
and coffee and before we got it the door
opened and my brood rolled in laughing and
in general breaking the quiet laws.

Sally ran out of the kitchen and hugged
Beth who she had never met but the baby
rumor mill was in good form, she dragged
them all into the kitchen leaving me and Fred
waiting for our coffee and pie.

Sally came out with pie, it was peach, I
reminded her I ordered apple, Fred ordered
Cheery but she said she was out of everything
but Peach. I got up and walked over to the
kitchen batwings and peeked in and watched
my wives eating all the Apple and Cherry pie
in sight, they all looked up and smiled real
big.

Sally was waiting for me with a smile and
said John, shut up and eat your peach pie, I
did. Fred did. I got to pay for their pie too. I
sigh, Fred laughed and said I sigh more then
anybody he ever met, I told him about a
Navajo out in the canyon lands who sighs
more then me, all at me.

Finally "they" were done eating Sally out
of business and joined us. I just shook my
head and sighed again. They laughed. No
respect.

We headed back to the homestead, Fred said the town folks had come out and begged him to take his badge back.

His wife said she would shoot him herself if he did, besides he enjoyed herding cats for a living so they stayed on the homestead. I was proud of him, it's hard to take off a badge, been there done that.

We went to look at the logs Rick had found for us and I was doubting the Dodge could budge the trailer after it was loaded but was wrong.

They were so big that Harv and crew could get several beams out of each one and all were dried pretty good so the weight wasn't as bad as it looked. There was even room for a couple cords of Hickory for the ladies back home so all in all it was a good trip.

I talked to the guys who do the hog trapping and they had a bunch of young sows and a couple of young boars we could have but how to get them back with us? The trailer is full as is the back of the truck but after the girls passed out all their presents to the family's on the homestead it wasn't as bad.

We put out the word for a roof top cargo rack and had one in two days, Sandy traded some 45 ammo for it. We put it on the truck cab roof for all the remaining gear leaving room for a cage made from angle iron and sheep panels which we anchored to the top of the logs and looking like the "Real McCoys" we were ready to roll. We would have to stop and water the pigs but that was fine.

We made our goodbyes and I spent a while with Miz Sheri just talking about life. Her family is doing ok, She misses me as I do her but maybe next time around. A hug and kiss goodbye and we were gone again.

The trip home was pretty boring, well as boring as it can be with Sandy and May popping off rounds at jack rabbits running along the road way. I threatened to cut off their ammo supply but remembered they stole a truck load in Barstow.

I was thinking it was good there wasn't any of those shoulder mounted tank killer rocket launchers on the base when Sandy said " I wish they had some of those rocket thingies at Barstow.

I told her to stop it and got the poor lil innocent me crap with the other two siding with her, so no it's never boring with them and in fact when they get quiet I really worry unless they are sleeping and even then I worry.

Once again we make it to the state line and are greeted by Bear and Harry, Bear was admiring the pigs and talking BBQ when Sandy told him to go catch his own. He asked for her permit to transport Texas live stock out of the Republic, she told him to go do an impossibility. Mrs. bear came up and twisted his ear then took the girls away. Sandy said bear I can hear you!! Best be good!

Bear asked again as always, How does she do that? And once again I said " beats the shit outta me" one of lifes mysteries.

We sat in the mess hall and had a cold beer and talked about the goings on, I had to tell them the Luke story, both agreed it was a wasted life but at least he failed in killing somebody else.

The admired the logs especially since the biggest tree here was a mesquite bush, They both thought about going over to the homestead and getting a bunch of pigs to raise since they didn't have many of the 5 million or so in Texas. I had to explain about the hickory which also got them interested, everybody loved the Hickory smoked meat for their BBQ's.

Morning found us on the road just at dawn since we needed to try to get home without the pigs having heat stroke, I wasn't sure how this was gonna work but besides knowing rock work the West Virginia hillbillies knew hogs so I expected they would have an idea. In fact I could just see a huge rock smoke house doing it's thing, I can see me hauling trailer loads of Hickory back here often. But for hickory smoked ham and bacon I'd do it!

Dark found us rolling into Shiprock where Charley and Old Woman were sitting on the porch waiting for us. As soon as we pulled in she headed inside to set the table I'm sure, the girls headed that way after making their respects to Charley.

We sit on the porch and talked, He just shook his head over the Luke affair. He was happy Bear and Harry and their bunch were all well. I asked if he might take a ride next time we went that way, he allowed as how he might. I could imagine him in the dense woods of East Texas.

A desert Indian and all. I'd bet he would do just fine there, he's that kind of man.

Dinner was good, different but good, I didn't ask what it was. I love the so called "Indian fry bread" dunk it in the stew and chow down, awesome. I asked the girls why they never fix it at home and got that Oh shit duh look and three sets of shoulder shrugs, never thought of it, bet they would get to it since they love it too!

We headed home early in the am and got there in good order, the pigs were greeted with cheers, not if the Hill Billy's can keep them alive all's well. The logs were a big hit since Harv and his crew were aching to get that saw mill going. Since it was all set up we dragged the logs off and worked one onto the log deck or whatever it's called. Harv fired up the gas powered motor and after adjusting thing cut a long thin sliver off the log, that went well so he figured out how much had to come off to get the first beam right then went to work, it was real cool!

That thing was like a hot knife thru butter, As soon as he had the first side trimmed down he flipped it and did it again, When he had it all square with the world he made four beams out of the one log. He figured it out and there was plenty for extra beams so that's good, there was also a couple of good sized Cedar logs that he cut into three inch slabs and as wide as he could make them, he had an idea for a door and shutters he wanted to try.

The girls headed off to see what was happening in the canyon and I stayed to watch. It was fascinating watching the saw mill working. I could see we were going to get a lot of use out of it but the logs needed to come from closer then East Texas!

Before he shut it down all the logs were now thick long beams and stacked on thin spacers to air dry even more which wouldn't take long here in the canyon. We talked about getting some big pine logs from up in the Arizona mountain area if we couldn't get any from around here.

I next went to talk to the Mechanics about a
project I had thought of just today. I found
them playing cards in the shade of a tree/bush.
I told them I had a idea, one asked it it hurt,
one asked it that was the burning rubber
smell, and one asked what I had in mind, I
chose to answer him. Asshats I said smiling,
sometimes it seems only the smart asses
survived the troubles.

I asked him to explain the reefer cooler
system. He chewed on his cigar for a bit and
then took it out and spit a stream of brown
juice and said " Well, when it's running it
keeps shit cold and when it ain't it don't. I
asked him if I called the girls over could he
answer better, he said NO SIR John! and
launched into a technical speech that I lost in
10 seconds, then one of the others interrupted
and got an argument going, the third wiseass
asked what I had in mine.

I said my new place was almost finished
and when it was I was gonna ask harv and his
guys to enlarge our cave, a lot and I wanted to
know if the cooling unit on a reefer trailer
could be removed and hooked up to turn the
cave into a huge walk-in cold storage place.
All three said Hell yes! But why? I
mentioned the hundred or so cases of beer I
had brought back in the container.

They said to get the miners digging and

they would plan it out and when was the trailer gonna be here. Seems that even wiseasses like cold beer. Lifes rough in the new world.

I asked if we really needed the trailer here or could we just go unhook the unit, they said it was important that the trailer was here, I asked why, stupid question, they wanted it for a machine shop, fine, works for me. I headed for the commo shack and called the Fort and said get the trailer headed this was and fill it with any machining tools they may have found that they didn't need plus more beer!

The commo lady on the other end was laughing when she hit the send button but said right away General! I was gonna correct her but she brok it down before I could.

I looked at our commo lady who was not smiling, I asked her why, she said cold beer was not a joking matter! We agreed! I could see morale was gonna improve vastly!

It was several days before I bothered to go up on the ridge since I had been told to go away while I had my toes, So I headed up there where I was surprised to find the beams set with the wall ends anchored between the top row of huge rocks and coming to a peak in the center where they were pinning them to one of the big cedars that had been set aside for the center support. It had been peeled and some finishing work started. They had built a steel ring with a lip to set the ends of the beams on and were putting large bolts thru the beam and thru the lip of heavy steel where they were bolted into place. It was awesome and almost medieval. Harv called out to me and waved me over to where he was, there I found him and two of his boys building a door out of the cedar planking, each plank was two inches thick and on closer look it was two layers thick with something between the layers, I got close and saw it was ½ inch steel plate! I looked at Harvey and asked if it was gonna pull the house over. He showed me the hing pins it was gonna hang on and they were huge! I asked where they got the steel? He said Charley told him where there was some left from some forgotten government plan that never got done. He cut the piece for the door and used a grinder to smooth the edges and now they were drilling flat steel metal that had been cast into 3/8 inch by 3 inch 10 foot lengths, they had laid the flat iron in a Z pattern a were drilling all the way thru for long ½ inch bolts. With a corresponding Z on the other side this thing was gonna weigh a ton! I asked why? He said well it's a castle and it needs a castle door plus shutters made the same way. I didn't know what to say. I had no words, he just slapped me on the shoulder and said John you give your all for everybody you come across and you've fought and bled for us here so this little project is nothing plus your kid needs a secure home. We both laughed at that as if this canyon wasn't secure enough.

Mostly he said it was something he always wanted to do but never had time, now he could do whatever he wanted and was loving it, I asked if the girls had anything to do with it, he laughed and said Sandy wanted to know how to stop bullets with a door, he said this door would stop anything but maybe a .50 But he wasn't gonna let them try a .50 on it. I was very impressed but I need to ask about the reefer room so I explained the idea and he was loving it and asked if there was any extra cold units? I said lots and a truck with a huge full propane tank on it. He left his boys working on the drilling and we headed down to look at the cave. It was just like all of the ones we had, his bunch had built bigger. He said this could be enlarged a lot but he would want big beams to shore up the roof for safeties sake.

I ask him if they could get on it as soon as we moved out, he said sooner if y'all don't mind living in your camper trailer a while. I said I'd check with them and get back. He finally asked just what I had in mind, I said cold beer, he said we can start tomorrow!! We walked away laughing and ran right into them, May said ok, what you two doing and why are you doing it?
So I explained, Sandy said all that trouble

for a cold beer? And shook her head. Then busted out laughing and ask Harv when he could start? A barrel of laughs a minute.

Next morning we moved out and into the camper, Harvey and three of his people showed up and after moving their drilling stuff off the ridge where they were done working stone they hit it on the cave.

I told the girls I'd be back later and walked away, they asked where I was going and I said to see Charley

They passed me like I was standing still, Beth took my arm and walked with me, I asked her if she was ok, she said yes just tired out easy, but no morning sickness thank got, she was getting a bit of a baby bump and when we were all in bed for the night we all put our hands on it and just seemed to gat something from it, Beth laughed at us but liked it.

We got there to find them sitting in the jeep which I had forgotten about, it was all clean and shiny, they had been busy, I told both of them I was not riding in the cramped up this unless I was driving, first they got mad, then tried the pout thing then promised to be very careful but neither of them will ever be poker players. I took the keys and said where are the weapons, they looked funny and took off and came back with our rifles and extra ammo, I took the bib Bob from the dodge and we were off.

It wasn't the dodge but with only the bikini top on it was nice and breezy. We rolled along at about sixth MPH which was a good speed and the whole area looked different without the sides mostly blocked.

We pulled in and for once we fooled Charley, he didn't know the Jeep but greeted us as we unloaded. The girls all went to him and held his hand a moment, Beth the longest, he smiled a beautiful smile and said Good!! Very good!

They headed in while Charley and I sat in the shade, we talked about everything, the house, the jeep, the reefer cave which I could see interested him so I went into it even more. I said if he wanted the set up I would take care of it. He said he needed to talk to Old Woman but would let me know.

I told him we needed some big logs for shoring up the reefer room and if we could get them closer it would be good. He said no problem we could take them off the land a big rancher claimed. I asked who we needed to talk to, he said him, the big rancher was flying when the EMP happened. We both laughed because he had been a prick to the people whom his grand father has screwed out of the land. What goes around comes around.

He said lets steal the jeep and go look for logs! Which we did. It was only about twenty miles to the gate and another five or so the ranch house where several of the people had moved in, these were some who moved back to the land ahead of the sickness that still hadn't showed up.

We drove on after Charley greeted them and explained what we were about. We climbed higher until we hit timber line and there we found some huge Pine trees,perfect fpor the beams. We headed back and was back sitting in the shade when Beth came out to get us to eat, they didn't even know we had gone or so I thought. May said well will the pine trees work? Sandy laughed and Beth shook her head and said why do you try John? Caught again.

After eating lunch we headed home to line up the logging crew, these logs were gonna be heavy because they were green, I talked to Harvey about it and his idea was to go up and fall them and buck then into the lengths we needed and leave them to dry until needed.

It wasn't much but it was better then nothing so the next day I headed back up with Harv and two of his boys or somebody's boys, they all bred true so it was hard to say.

They had a pair of chain saws and once we were there it was even easier then I hoped, these were huge trees and it only took four to bake all the beams we needed for now.

When they were bucked up they cut the limbs into firewood lengths for Charles people to burn. We filled the truck with the fire wood and headed down to the house where we unloaded it with help from the men. They nodded as did we and we headed home.

Harv had some of the older boys doing the drilling while he and his clansmen were up on the ridge, They had the roof on which was a surprise, they had used tongue and groove Knotty pine 2x6 and it was ready for the roofing metal, I asked Harv where this stuff came from, he said the Fort guys were bringing it over in the reefer trailers,.

What Reefer trailers I asked? He said the ones parked at our place, with a smile, he said it was a surprise they had cooked up, he also said the Fort folks were the worlds greatest scavengers! He said they had more crap squirreled away then could be believed and were hauling in more every week since it was at least that long for them to go out and get back since they had cleaned out everything for many miles around.

The roofing metal was colored in a shade I remembered as Sage which blended in very well and with the stone work the whole thing was hard to see except against the sky where the form stood out. It was beautiful. And I was feeling guilty again, Harv knew me well enough to know what I was thinking, he said to stop it because if it wasn't for me most of these folks would be dead they knew it. I still felt guilty but was gonna have to live with it.

Harv said ya know John if push ever comes to shove this place will shelter everybody here from an attack and nobody will get up here if you don't want them to. I hadn't thought about that aspect of it and could see where he was coming from and knowing the girls they 105's would be here flanking their own LAV. Yea this place would be a tough nut to crack. So I felt better about it.

By the end of the week the boys had drilled everywhere Harv had laid out and Harvs brother James laid the charges and we all cleared the area.
All we got was a thump felt more then heard and dust blowing out the door opening, when that stopped we went in and I couldn't believe it, the small room was a huge room! The canyon boys got into hauling out the rubble and found their "moms" waiting to show them where to put the rocks as they had plans for them. We all pitched in and before days end the room was cleared.

Some shelving and rood supports and it was ready for the cooler unit. We headed up the next day with the trailer to load the logs which wasn't as easy as it sounds, we had ramps to roll them up and since they were all

ten footers we let them hang over on each
side.

We got it done with some scrapes and one
mashed thumb nail already turning black.
Harv took a bic lighter and heated his knife
point red hot and set it on the nail where it
melted right thru and blood shot out and
almost instantly the pain was gone compared
to the way it was. I'd seen it done with a
paper clip and it is the best way to go with a
black nail, let the blood out and relieve the
pressure.

We decided to let the logs dry more so the
beams wouldn't warp and twist which was
fine with me. The girls had been very quiet
and out of sight a lot lately and I was starting
to worry but that evening I found out why.
They told me to go shower and we would eat
after I got back. Fine, so I did. After I was
dressed they kept me waiting forever while
they debated what to wear, being smart I kept
my mouth shit and after an hour or more they
were dressed and I might say looking very
nice, I asked why the dress up, they said it
was just a girl thing and lead me out of the
trailer where I found a crowd of everybody
from the area, all three canyons worth! And
all yelled
"HAPPY BIRTHDAY JOHN!!!!" And
proceeded to sing it, I was happy and grateful
and embarrassed all at the same time.

I looked at the girls and Beth held up my

drivers lic. And said damn John I thought you were younger then this!

All to a huge laugh, I smiled a gotcha smile and patted her tummy and said well I'm not too old I guess! The crowd went wild! We then trooped to the community cooking area for a feast! There was everything one could want, I asked how in hell they had got all this done without me seeing it. And I looked at Harv and said you fart! Getting another big laugh, he had run my ass all over the whole countryside keeping me out of the way.

There was an entire roasted calf from the Bremmers, they had cooked it at home and brought it over while I was being delayed.

I said there best not be a roasted hog and got more laughs. I heard the sound of vehicles and wondered, then the motors stopped and here come the Navajo Nation followed by Bear and Harry and their ladies!! I was blown away.

After everybody settled down with drinks before eating I asked why my birthday was so important and one of the ladies said John, you brought us all here to this wonderful place, you in a sense led us to the promised land, You have fought and put your life on line more then any of us, all because you see it as a duty and that's enough. We all love you John and we love these wild cats they are keeping you young and Beth for bringing you a child, so this is why we are honoring you and this day from now on will be John's day and a feast day.

Well I was humbled to sat the least and I had no words just a lump in my throat too big to swallow. So I raised my glass and said to the good people of Navajo country for allowing us to live here in their heart land!

I had never seen Old Woman anyplace besides her kitchen yet here she was walking up to me and holding out a silver and turquoise necklace and smiling real big she said " Thank you John for your kindness to my people and for your help in fighting our enemies, and for being a role model for our young men. All in perfect English. I was flat out blown out of my boots. Even the girls had open mouths, She finished by saying thank you for bringing these delightful wives of yours to us.

The yelling and laughing went on for a long while, I reached for the necklace but she stopped me and said turn around and stoop down, I did and she put it on me then turned me around and smiled and said you may now hug me! And I did, gently and for a long time and I had tears running down my cheeks, she wiped them away and said
" What's a lady got to do to get a drink around here??" and that brought the house down!

I swear the party, was still going on when the sun came up, there was native drumming and a big fire that lit the canyon as it did eons ago when these people celebrated whatever they found worthy.

Old Woman was the center of the women who were all listening to her like she was a teacher which I found out later from Charley she was! His mom was one of the first Navajo women to graduate from college with a teaching degree. I would never have guessed. What a wonderful woman. I also found out "Old Woman" was more of a title and since she was called that for so many years it just stuck, I didn't find out her name.

Most of us slept where we dropped and woke up to bad heads and a thirst that wouldn't quite. I got up and walked to the waters edge and peeled off my clothes and jumped in and had a heart attack, well not really but close, I came up gasping. Fkn desert water shouldn't be this cold! I floated for a while and watched others coming down to fall in, the best hangover cure, now for some coffee.

The girls refused to get wet and of course Beth wasn't drinking and the girls don't much anyway, they had spent the evening being astounded by the Old Woman who spent the evening telling them all about her life. So the coffee was ready for us when we staggered out of the water. I wrapped up in a blanket and shivered while trying to cool the boiling coffee. In time there was breakfast made up from leftover's heated and stuff like eggs and hot cakes too. After we ate we laid down and slept again, it was a birthday to remember.

Most of the guests headed home the next day, The Texas crew stayed several days looking things over and asking questions. Their wives spent most of their time with the women just watching and asking questions.

Finally one evening as we set by the water I asked Harry and Bear what they had in mind. Both sat a moment and looked at each other and shrugged, Bear made a you first gesture to Harry. He thought a moment more and said Well John, we are thinking about making a move and we all decided if we liked it here and if you'll have us we would like to move here.

I won't say I was surprised, Both men were showing restless signs and being pinned down sitting on the "Border" of the New Republic of Texas had to be tiring.

Bear added that he and his wife wanted to get their kids to move also because they too believed things were getting ready to really go into the crapper. Harry and his wife didn't have kids but both had family that they wanted to move too but it was looking like none of them wanted to.

I told them both they were welcome as were their families, but I added that when we shut down entry it would apply to everybody, family or not, we couldn't and would not rish the whole area because somebody wanted to wait until the end was upon them.

Both men said they understood that and if need be they would stand at the dead line with rifles to turn back even their own kin. Hard but good men, no bullshit with them.

Bear smiled and said besides John you're having way too much fun running around out here dealing with scumbags and speaking for myself I wanna get some! I laughed and said bring a note from Mrs. Bear first, he stopped smiling. Harry and I laughed.

That night the girls and I had piled into the ever smaller camper and they told me that Harry and Bears ladies wanted to move, mostly the same story I had gotten but Sandy said Mrs Bear had said Bear was going crazy to get out and cowboy around with the other boys and if she let him go I had to promise to sit on him so he didn't get killed. I laughed and said good luck with sitting on that big shit! Sandy said yea I know so I promised her I would control him. Now that I agreed with, if anybody could control that big bastard it was little Sandy.

The next morning while the girls were cooking breakfast in the trailer I rounded up the refugees and brought them to eat. While eating I said we wanted them to come join us and welcome! Relatives included as long as they fit in with our life style, if not they could move on further down the lake.

All agreed with that and Harry asked if it wouldn't bebetter if they did as the others and moved into a close canyon of their own like Bremmers and Harv's clan had.

I said that would work since we were all close in case of trouble so we headed out on the Pontoon boat looking for a home for them, and we found a nice place up lake from us they wouldn't have a creek but they had a whole lake to get water from and since the boat traffic had ended it was cleaning up really well. They could use Berkey water filtering units for drinking water as we do.

All in all they would have maybe at the outside twenty five people counting them. They were leaving right away to get things moving. I told them to call Charles commo to give us a heads up when they were on the way.

We needed a commo tower to get better radio service here, that was a problem that needed fixing.

I had taken Harry aside and asked him to try to contact the Homestead and see if they might want to move too. I was worried about them but I also knew Rick and Sheri were not gonna leave their homes and all the work they had done. Plus they were pretty well set up and could defend themselves till hell freezes over.

The work on the reefer cave was going very well, the boys were squaring up the walls and as soon as the beams were ready they would be ready to put them in.

Harv checked the logs and said "lets make beams!" So they fired up the saw and got with it. I'm not sure Pine is the right kind of wood for support beams but these were gonna be some big beams, they were gonna average out at 12" beams, that should hold since there really wasn't a lot of over burden on top, maybe 6 to 8 feet. But we wouldn't want to have a cave in that crushes the beer.

Three days later the reefer cave had not only beams it had ¾ inch plywood above the support timbers and shelving from the excess logs. This sawmill was gonna be worth it's weight in gold! Hell more so because at the moment gold was pretty far down the list. I figured Harv was gonna be training some of their older boys in the fine art of saw milling lumber.

After the cold cave was done on the inside the gear heads took over and started their part which was installing the cooling unit, I stayed out of the way because I know jack shit about it and they said they would charge double if I watched. It took longer to get the cooling stuff working then it did to cut the logs, haul them home, dry them, make timbers out of them and finish the inside.

But the day came when they said ok and threw the power switch on the Propane unit and it started doing it's thing. I won't go into the whole thing but I guess there is a generator that fires the compressor or some such. I'm a shooter, I don't under shit that don't go bang or boom. All I want is cold beer!

We put a few cases inside and shut the insulated door they built and waited two hours and went in and found exploded cans from freezing, back to the drawing board.

They finally decided to turn the thermostat all the way up and start there, two hours later the beer was almost too cold to drink, almost being the operative wording. But we couldn't stay in there and drink it or we would become peoplecicles, we may have to figure out a way to warm things a bit.

One of the gear heads said maybe with more volume in the cave it would change things??? Nobody knows. But we can experiment and see what we get. Mean time anybody can wait a couple of minutes for the beer to warm up to a good drinking temp.

Life's good in the canyons!

It suddenly dawned on me the girls had been very absent since we got up this morning so I set out looking for them and after an hour I had checked every where I could think of except the "airport" as we referred to the place Ralph parked his birds.

I asked him if he had seen the girls and he started fidgeting which was a dead giveaway so I asked again with more statement then question. He licked his lips and his eyes twitched but he finally admitted that while he had helped them hee had also told them it wasn't a good idea.

I was working at not losing my temper when way off in the distance I heard a sound that once heard is never forgotten, I stared at him until he confessed they had talked him into helping mount an M-60 on the Jeep roll bar and they were out in the canyons playing " Rat patrol" which he admitted was his fault because he told them about the old TV show by the same name where the Army was fighting the Germans in the desert and used jeeps with machine guns mounted on steel poles and ran around flying thru the air over sand dunes spraying the area with bullets.

I was still listening to the gun roaring away and figured they would have to come back to reload on ammo pretty soon. While I was at it I walked over to look at the chopper since I barely remember flying home in it but I sure remember seeing two guns mounted in the doors, the guns were gone but the rigging was there, not a bad set up in fact, Ralph used heavy bungie cords to hang the gun on and had rigged up a harness system for the gunner to keep them from falling out during hard banks.

Ralph had come over to the bird with me and explained the set up, I was impressed, I also told him I wasn't mad about the jeep gun it was just that they took every thing in life and made a toy out of it then played with it until they broke it and only pure luck so far had prevented them from breaking themselves. He agreed but said they were really hard to say no to. How well I know that.

I asked if Beth went along with it? He sighed and said Beth was driving. I swear I'm gonna super glue their feet to the floor of the new house.

The distant gun fore had stopped and here they come flying uo the road and the jeep leaving the ground on every little hump in the road. Beth was driving and with her long hair blowing out behind her and the huge smile on her face and the same for the main two delinquents I had to smile, they are hard to say no to and harder to be mad at.

Beth locked the breaks up and cut the wheel and slid to a stop in front of us. She

bailed out and arms around my neck jumped up and wrapped her legs around me and said " I've been bad daddy you need to spank me and laughed so hard she needed a pat on the back, they other two were standing there one on each side of the gun leaning on the roll bar with  dirty faces and big smiles.
God knows they are wild and crazy and may kill themselves at any moment but they will die laughing and trying to out do each other. I sat Beth down and said ok bail out you witches I wanna try it! Ralph was handing them belts of ammo when I climbed in. Beth got behind the wheel and after I was in the makeshift harness off we went, Sandy sitting with Beth in front and May standing by me to feed the belts.

We roared down a dry wash and May pointed out the rocks that were pockmarked from their other runs, I opened fore and went wild! Before I knew it I was out of ammo, three full belts worth, May was a damn good ammo man, she linked the belts together while maintaining her balance and feeding the belt.

We rolled back to the hanger which is a brush arbor and parked in time to be greeted by Harv with a bucked of cold beer, even the girls had one, Beth took some of mine then snagged a drink from her " Sisters" or "co-wives" whatever. Sandy said get your own but Beth said this way I'm not really drinking I'm just sipping, Sandy smiled and said well shit have another sip!

God they are a riot, tomorrow the jeep would be today's toy and they would be getting into something else.

I told them about the frozen busted beer and how that project was going, May, ever the engineer said well stack the beer close to the door and up on a shelf where the temp will be higher, I could only shake my head, so simple it takes a PHD to figure it out in 1.02 nano seconds.

I could see I was gonna steal the information and look really good when I figured out the solution to the problem. But I forgot Harv was standing there, another good chance shot in the ass.

I told them after they cleaned the gun and put it away and turned the brass and links over to the two old armory farts they could come have another beer, they said since I shot it last I could clean it, I reminded them I was the Elder and the Husband and the General! And got pelted with empth and not so empty beer cans. No respect. I helped them with the gun since none of them knew shit about it except load and shoot, that part they had down pat.

It was bum at the fires night so off we went, our donation was buckets full of very cold beer, we were greeted with cheers. Life is good in the canyons, have I mentioned that?

That evening before dark we walked up to the castle in the ridge and walked thru it. To say it's beautiful would be an unforgivable mistake, it's beyond that mere word. And it's just a few days from being ready to move into, there are things like water but they have a plan, also furniture but they have another plan, and some lighting of some kind and they don't have a plan for that. They say I need to contribute something to the place so lights is my thing. Sigh.

We headed down to the camper and got our shower stuff since we were covered with dust from Rat Patrolling and off we went.

Showering in a big shower room with several different heads is nice except they all have to crowd under the same one, but it makes showering very interesting.

We used the propane stove in the trailer to make coffee and settled down for the night. Walker was crushing something in his jaws, Since the boys have been restricted from hunting within half a mile it opened up prime hunting for Walker, he don't comprehend the term "Half Mile Safety Zone". I went to sleep with my coffee on my chest and felt the cup being removed from my hand and that's all I knew until daybreak.

I woke up with one warm body in my arms,

it's fun to keep my eyes closed and to figure out who it is. Later Sandy and I joined the girls at the communal fires for breakfast. Oat meal with butter and brown sugar and a hand full of raisins for me, Beth and May will sometimes put raisins in their oat meal but Sandy will cut off her thumbs before she will eat one, she says they are decayed grapes which makes me laugh and the other people wanna stone her. Good breakfast talk!

There is so much we need to start growing or trying to grow, grapes is one, and raspberry's hell anything berry and fruit trees

I guess we need a road that don't involve killing people and burning down cities. A trip to gather things to grow, create life instead of taking it. I decide to have a talk with our resident green thumb, a lady named Mable. She's black as the inside of a chunk of coal and has the greenest eyes I've ever seen, like a panther I guess, We got her away from slavers and she stepped right into the life style.

She had many suitors but seemed to be waiting for Mr. right, she said she had a couple of Mr. wrongs and wasn't going down that road again. She can grow anything so I'm gonna ask her, Beth came along with me but I told the girls they could jeep all they want but no more running thru 10,000 rounds of ammo.

They fooled me, they were heading to the reloading dump to help reload their recovered brass. I reminded them that powder and primers and bullets aren't being made these days.

It's a waste of time because they got an entire truck load from Barstow. I'm not sure what all they have since they are pretty close mouthed about it. "Their Trucks" are parked and covered and the mech crew in fear of their lives haven't allowed anybody near them.

Beth and I found Mable in her garden, talking to her plants, she also sings to them. We all love our Mable. She could make a rock smile.

She took a break in the shade of a tree she waters every day and it looks like it's happy as a clam at high tide. I explain what I'm thinking and she shakes a finger at me and says "Ain't nothing like a good man finding out he gonna be a daddy to make him start paying attention to real life." Beth laughed and I said "Oh shit Mable knock off the Aunt Jemima routine" which cracks her up but she settles down and then talks like the very well educated lady she is.

She did say again that she was glad I was thinking with the big brain for a change, I sighed. Then we got down to it, she already had a list she had been planning to talk to me about between city burnings ( ha ha ha still being funny) She went for the list and showed me and I handed it to Beth who looked it over real close and asked a lot of questions about "Will this grow here?" or wow it would be great to have these growing!!

My two bits worth was ok, lets go find this stuff, Mable said have you bothered to ask that bunch of land pirates hanging out in that prison? Head slap and a quiet under the breath "shit" ( stop cussing!!) Shut up!! ( giggles).

Mable said them girls gonna drive you crazy if you don't clean up your act John! I looked funny I guess and she said John everybody here know they in your head, My god boy when you gonna smarten up? Beth laughed and I sighed. I don't understand it I said. Mable said well no shit John, nobody else do either but it don't change a thing. I said uh your slipping back into the Auntie J routine again. She laughed and said sorry John but I love jerking your chaine too.

So I was gonna get on the radio and see if we had any seed and other garden stuff. Mable said come on I'll go along coz sure as god done made dem lil green apples you gonna screw it up, I swear white folks is sumptin else.

Beth was laughing so hard she had tears, I was worried about her tummy jiggling too much for the baby. She patted my hand and said chill out white boy then her and Mable were off laughing again.

Well once again I'm proving I'm not a leader. Not only is there like a ton of seeds at the fort, they have every fruit tree they can find planted and growing, I asked about winter and they said " Uh green houses duh? I said we would be there tomorrow and signed off. I was feeling pretty stupid but Mable said John you have life and death problems facing you almost daily, how are you gonna think of everything?

With those words ringing in my head I put out the word to all the people in all canyons to come to a feed and a meeting, then informed the ladies we were hosting a meal this evening. I think a few years ago they would have killed me, now they just wondered off talking about who was gonna do what. I really can't believe the change in all of us.

By late afternoon everybody was drifting in on boats of every type even those amusement park paddle boats where you sit and peddle like a bike. We find fun where we can.

After we had eaten I stood up and explained how the day went with the gardening thing and how Mable had wanted to do this but didn't mention it and I wanted to avoid this in the future, I explained that no one person can be in charge of everything and we needed a central place for people to bring their wants and needs or ideas so we could get to it.

Beth spoke up and said since she was going to be moving slower pretty soon she would be the central fixer and that all they had to do was write it out and "FAK" it. That got their attention. She smiled and said " Write it out and " Find a Kid!" send it to me and I'll get to working on it. Everybody was laughing and talking about "FAKing" but it made sense, the kids were all over the place so one could run or boat a message easy. And just like that another problem solved. By Mable and Beth.

We sat around and shared some cold beers and talked until it was just light enough for folks to get home before dark, goodbyes and they were off.

The girls were excited about learning to load ammo but they said they get it on wasting it after a day of working the presses.

The girls headed for the camper and I sat with Joe and Willy for a while talking about nothing, Willy is worried about the plague, Joe's wife told him today she's gonna have a baby! Her and Beth about the same time, I asked why he was just telling us and he said they just wanted to have it to themselves a while. Me and Willy laughed at him but we both shook his hand. I swear he was red in the face.

I guess I would have been but I was out for

three days and got the news as a jilt to wake
me up. But I knew how he felt, so I said Joe
don't worry, the world went to hell but we are
rebuilding it and can you think of a better
place to bring a baby into the world then right
here? He agreed and did look relieved.

I headed to the camper and wondered
where I was gonna sleep since they were
sprawled all over the bed but they did let me
squeeze in. I waited a bit and said " Joes
gonna be a daddy. It was quiet for a moment
and all three sat right up and turned on the 12
volt light and started pounding on me asking
why I hadn't said anything, I said coz I found
out five minutes ago! Jeeze.
   Now sleep was set aside for plans for a "
baby coming party" I went to sleep, and woke
up alone, I mean really alone, and feeling a bit
hurt about it, then the door flew open and they
all jumped on the bed and talking at once
never noticed I was there. I thought of those
old kings who had a hundred wives and five
hundred concubines and wondered how they
did it, They lived else where that's how!

We had to get moving because we were
going garden shopping today so while I
hooked up the gooseneck they went after
Mable and then I realized we needed more
room so Sandy and May said they would
drive the jeep! Mable said she wanted to ride
in the jeep so off we went, I made them stay

in front of us so I could keep an eye on them.
But they fooled me coz I saw May stand up
and reach over the seat and raise up the M-60
and place it on the roll bar while Beth
laughed, I said they had this planned didn't
they? She said yep and she was sworn to
secrecy. I sighed.

As I watched Mable stood up and placed
the harness around her waist and swung the
gun back and forth but I could see there was
no ammo in it but I'd bet there was a mile of
belted 308's in the Jeep. My sweet little
loving wives were ahead of me as usual. Beth
said they just wanted to show it off to the Fort
people, that I could understand, what's the
sense of women getting shiny's if they can't
show them off?

But a fkn m-60 on a jeep? Why not a ring
or some other girly bling? Beth scooted over
and leaned against me and said John they are
just living the life they never could have had
the lights not gone out. I knew and I often
wondered how with so much death and
misery all over the world from our stand point
it was an improved world? That seemed so
wrong in so many ways.

I used to say that when any species over
bred it's habitat that Mother Nature would
solve the problem and that mankind was there

and Mother Nature was gonna shake us off one day. But we did it to ourselves. And this plague might be the icing on the cake. Time would tell.

We got to the Fort and were greeted as usual like we hadn't just been there a while back, the girls headed off looking for the storage crew to show them the jeep while Beth and Mable got with Mr' wipple as I can only think of him. He took his papers and off they went in the golf cart with me following along.

Suffice to say we made a haul, we had every fruit and nut tree known to man with burlap covered root balls and a ton of garden tools and a ton of seeds of every kind on the frigging planet.

Mable was smiling from ear to ear. We even got a couple of big roto tillers and the promise of a new John Deere tractor if we wanted it with all the tools for working land. This was turning into a lot of farm work and as I know I pointed out I'm not a farmer.

Beth patted my arm and whispered calm down love, Mable is the farmer, let her run free! And run free she did! One one of her trips she threw her arms around me and said OH John!! Thank you thank you!!! I didn't know what to say so I just hugged her back. And she was gone again.

The girls came back grinning and I got worried but they were just proud that they had the idea of getting a towing hitch put on the jeep and had found a 12 foot trailer to help haul stuff, I swear they are growing up! ( HA!! Watch it buddy!) shit ( stop cussing!) sigh.

We settled in for the day and had a great meal. Mable had toured the entire place and glanced at the piles of gold and other stuff but spent hours going thru the green houses and gardens, I could see the wheels turning and before I could say a word Sandy said Mable guess what!!!??? Mable just shook her head and May said tomorrow the storage guys will be bringing your green houses over and will help set them up! I swear Mable almost cried. It's good to make people happy and Mable loved her gardening but knew she needed more and now she had it! I smile!

Next morning at breakfast Mable said well that's the first time I slept in a prison next to a gajillion dollars worth of gold! Sandy said OH? Did you miss all the silver and diamonds and other stuff too? Mable just shook her head and went back to eating.

We rolled out followed by the storage guys

driving a big diesel truck pulling a big trailer. When we got home they asked Mable where she wanted her garden shed? She asked what shed? That one pointing at the 40 ft box trailer, They said they were gonna take the wheels off and drop it onto some beams they had, leaving her a super shed! They worked it out and with everybody helping out we got it done before dark. We did have to unload it first and stack things out of the way. When we got the green houses out there stood a small garden tractor with all the goodies to work small truck gardens. It was a Kubota with a diesel eng. Gardening had just gotten easier!

Standing aside I whispered to Beth that I thought there might be some romance going on as one of the guys was really taking an interest in Mable as well as her garden. Beth said yep she had seen that too.

I knew Willard was married but Wilson wasn't, so maybe. After they were done Mable invited them to her fire for supper and Wilson jumped at the offer while Wilber said he was going to visit a friend so we took off and left them alone.

I for one hoped the smoke had a tiny bit of fire under it, the girls said they knew Mable would make the right decision and it was her business, I said ok, I'll shut up getting me smiles.

To make a long story short, Wilson stayed to help get the tractor set up and working then to get the green houses set up and never left. Well he did go back to get his personal stuff but Mable went with him and they brought back a lot of things to make their plans go better.

Everybody was happy for them and two weeks later there was a wedding Canyon style and a feast. Life is pretty good here in the canyons in case I never mentioned that.

Oh, a word on canyon style weddings, the happy couple simply stand and pledge to love and honor each other until they can't or they die. We all know nothing is permanent anymore and people can either live with each other or not, but nobody wants to remain in a relationship if they are unhappy and here it's not necessary. Yet with the easy out things seem to last, I think because the only "issues" are maybe getting killed in a fire fight, everything else is pretty well nothing. Plus there isn't the push to be successful, just remaining alive is success enough.

Plus we are surrounded with people who are true friends and who are where they want to be. I guess or at least that's what I think.

The mechanics had worked on the cooling system and found a way to turn the temp up some so now the beer was cold and nothing was freezing.

Now we could hang a beef or deer and just use it as we needed it, one of the guys had some abilities as a meat cutter so he would cut up the meat in the proper manner and put it in pans on the shelves, the cooks just went in and got what they wanted. It works so it's good.

We pitched in and helped Harvey's clan and the Bremmers with building their cold storage and now everybody has cold beer! Well and meat kept fresh until it was eaten.

Harvey's building crew decided to build entry ways into the cold rooms so you can go in and shut one door then open another thus keeping the cold in and the heat out, great idea. I was thinking a room off the cold room maybe a cool room with comfy chairs would be nice, a great place to drink beer and nap.

That got shot down by "them". Sometimes I feel like I'm being controlled! ( laughter) Shit! ( Stop cussing! The baby can hear you!) WHAT???... sigh.

Well it's been a busy few months, we tracked down the Bad guy and he's now the former bad guy. We have a new home to move into and the whole area is getting organized to the point I hope it stops. To much organization leads to problems we don't need. We have pleant of time to play or read or study, nobody is killing themselves unless they just want to. Mable has found her a wonderful man who is at her side every minute of the day working right with her, Those two are going to feed the whole damn area and are so happy doing it. I hate farming.

I did find time to remember poor Bucks ear and went to see him, he seems to think we are bonded brothers since we both have parts of our ears shot off. Promised to take a ride later, he said no shooting!! I love old Buck! Rab and the Horse with no name are crowding in for attention and I notice them looking over my head and know I have company.

They come marching up and ask when Beth gets her own horse? I said I guess when she says she wants one and should she be riding? I was informed riding is good exercise for a woman who's PG.

Now I didn't come in on the last banana boat and I know when I'm being played and this is more about a trip to Charles then a horse for Beth. But I say 'Well I guess we need to bring Charley in on this so we get a really good one. First they frown then after deciding I'm not being a smart ass they smile.

So off we go to see Charley and Old Woman which is what they really wanted in the first place, I wonder why they don't just say what they really want? ( because it's fun to beat you up?) Shit ( stop cussing the baby can hear you!)

To my readers, I kind of cut this one short because it wanted to end here? I have no idea why it just did.

So if it feels short it is, by about a thousand or so words. I hope nobody feels cheated.

TJ

Made in the USA
Lexington, KY
30 October 2014